Cause and Affection

Praise for the works of Sheryl Wright

Don't Let Go

Georgie and Tyler are wonderful characters and the way their relationship changes from purely professional to a romance is lovely, with good pacing. This is a clever book on many levels, and it really kept me on my toes, intellectually speaking. It was both challenging and heart-warming in equal measures, and I absolutely loved it.

- *Rainbow Book Reviews*

Nothing is quite so refreshing as something completely different to the norm. *Don't Let Go* is a traditional romance, set in the corporate world and with a twist of a corporate intrigue to add to the action. What makes it unusual is that the main character in both the romance and the corporation is a Vet who has suffered a traumatic brain injury and is suffering from a range of seemingly catastrophic aftereffects.

- *Lesbian Reading Room*

Queen of Hearts

...is a sweet romance about finding love when you don't expect it and recognizing that everyone deserves a happily ever after. I was impressed with how Wright was able to give such a large cast of characters their own distinctive personalities and prevent so many female characters from blending together. This is a robust cast of side characters who bring humor and drama to the story. *Queen of Hearts* is an entertaining romance. It was such a quick read for me because the scenario is so appealing. A reality TV show full of interesting and beautiful lesbians looking to find true love is something that I would clear my schedule for. This book is a lovely break from the daily grind and if you're looking for something light and fun, check it out.

- *Lesbian Review*

CHAPTER ONE

"Why are we sitting in business class?" Joanne Bryson-Wexler asked, uncomfortably fussing with the seatbelt and expecting a challenge to their presence at any moment. "It's against company policy!"

"We're flying business class because this stupid airline doesn't have a first class section," her sister grumbled, eyes fixed on the world outside the jetliner's convex portal.

"Since when?"

"I don't know. I don't own the airline."

Joanne huffed, "That's not what I mean, and you know it, brat! Answer me!"

Kara Wexler's attention was fixed on the layers of morning cloud the airliner blew through as it climbed out of Toronto's Pearson airport. "Fine. Since I decided I wasn't going to listen to Dad's bullshit anymore."

"Wait!" Joanne asked, panicking, "This isn't coming out of my events budget, because if it—"

"Will you relax, I paid for the upgrade out of my own money. I do have some you know."

Joanne just nodded, waiting while a trim flight attendant took their drink order. Once he delivered their premium booze, and in real glasses, he turned his attention to the other passengers. "Thanks, sis. Sorry, I guess I'm just tired of having to justify every cent my department spends. It gets old fast. Sometimes I just want to tell Dougie…"

"Our brother is not responsible for the nickel-and-diming going on, and you know it. Geez, Jo, why can't you just admit the old man's the problem?"

Joanne grumbled under her breath, taking her time to try her drink before commenting, "It's really all our fault…"

"Stop," Kara begged. "Please, let's not have this argument again."

"No! I want to have my say. You get to have all your politically correct stuff. Why can't I say I just want us to get along?"

Staring out the cabin window, Kara didn't immediately reply. When she finally turned to her sister, her constant exhaustion was as present as were the tears in her eyes. "Jo, is wanting to be treated the same as the next person being politically correct? Is treating strangers with respect being politically correct?"

"Why do you do that? That's not what I meant. You keep taking things all wrong!"

Kara was struggling emotionally. The turmoil of the last few years had started with the American electoral victory of hate. Now Canadians were jumping on the bandwagon too. Suddenly their baby-panda hugging political leader wasn't as fashionable, and some were pushing for the old ways. The country seemed evenly divided into those who were too scared or ignorant to move forward and those too tired and depressed from having always to be the face of a fairer future. "You keep talking about newcomers not respecting our beliefs. What you're actually saying is they don't look like us, and that's wrong—because? Don't answer that. Think about it this way. What did the indigenous people do when Cartier landed?"

"They…they spent all winter nursing him and the crew back to life and curing their scurvy with natural medicine." It was a line every Canadian school kid could recite.

"And did they insist Cartier and his men change their style of clothing and hair, adopt their spiritual beliefs, or adapt to their matrilineal laws or politics?"

"Well, no, but that was their mistake. Besides, it's different, they are a defeated people and have to adapt to our ways."

Kara groaned to hear this common misconception. "Defeated by whom? The only enemies we've fought on our land are the French—if you take the English standpoint. The English, if you take the French standpoint, and the Americans from everyone's standpoint. It's the Americans you should be worried about, not a handful of well-educated displaced middle-class professionals who just happen to be Muslim."

"That's not the point! They come here and just take over. It's not right."

"Why? Because it's what Dad says, or do you really think that a guy who's lost everything isn't entitled to come here, work at a crappy job, and care for his family who've already suffered through hell just to get here? How does that hurt you? Come on, tell me how it affects you or your family?" Not waiting for her answer, she raised her glass, signaling the flight attendant for a second drink. On the headrest monitor in front of her, the air map showed they were barely a quarter of the way to Las Vegas. There was a time she would have relished this conversation, looking forward to schooling her baby sister on opportunities of fairness and equality. She couldn't help but feel that those days were gone. It wasn't that she didn't care, but caring hadn't helped her life or made it any easier to deliver a vision of a fairer world to her family or company. There was a time when she loved the challenge and lived for a heated debate. Now, not so much. She'd given up on intellectual sparring when the champions became those who shouted the loudest. Her sister could be like that. Regurgitating every piece of crap that fell from their father's mouth. "Why am I here?" Kara asked, more a rhetorical question than evidentiary.

"It's the annual sales convention, silly. Everyone will be here this year."

"Except you keep forgetting I have no desire to attend." At her sister's gaping look she added, "Jo, I handed Dougie my resignation on Friday. I'm only here because he begged me to deliver the pivot-or-sprint analysis."

"If you quit, why do you care?"

Kara finally turned to look at her sister. Even in the poor cabin lighting, it was easy to see the sadness in her eyes. "I'm not quitting because I don't care. Jo, I've just had enough of Dad's bullshit. Stop, I see it in your eyes, I know you don't really understand. After all is said and done, he's your daddy, but for me, he's just the bastard who spent every moment we had together telling me why I don't deserve his attention or support. That, of course, was on the few occasions he bothered to recognize my presence at all."

For the first time in a long time, Joanne was uncharacteristically quiet. Finally, she broke the silence between them. "Dougie told me about the resignation letter. He said you promised not to tell anyone until after the convention. Will you keep your promise?"

"Will I keep…I'm not the one making promises all over the place, promises he'll never keep. I swear Dad's more overboard this year with his ridiculous campaign to get Dougie in the top job. I would think announcing my resignation is just what he needs to get the board to roll over."

"He won't do that."

"Jo, really? I know you still have faith in Dad. So do I. I have every faith that he will announce my resignation to the board but he'll be sneaky. No need to give anyone time to look elsewhere. Instead, he'll wait until the meeting on Saturday. He'll pull out my resignation as he makes the motion to recognize Doug as the next CEO."

"He won't do that," she repeated.

Kara's look was a mix of disappointment and doubt.

"He won't do that because I hid your resignation in my office safe. He hasn't seen it, and Dougie promised he wasn't going to tell him."

"What the... Why? Why would you two do that?" When her sister didn't answer, Kara covered her ears with her hands, rubbing small circles above her brows and along her temples. Eventually, her fingers steepled together and she lifted her head. "I appreciate what you're trying to do, you and Doug, but Jo please, I'm burnt out, and there's just no coming back from this."

"Of course there is! I know you're hurting. And I know you've been walking away from things, not just work things but friends too."

At Kara's questioning look, she explained, "Leslie called me. She was worried. She said she hasn't seen you this down since you and trailer trash broke up. It took you all of three weeks to get over her. This is different. You've been sliding away for a few years now, but this last year has been the worst. I don't understand why. Please, Kara, let me help?"

* * *

"Take it," Franco insisted, pushing the envelope forward. "I don't even want my commission. It's all yours."

"I...I can't, you know..."

"Hey! It's not like that. I checked these guys out. They're legit. It's all according to the script. You just get her back to the room, give her a nice kiss and off you go."

"Off I go, letting this woman—I will remind you I'm straight—a woman no less, who I'm supposed to make fall in love with me then send her off with a quick peck on the cheek? Come on Franco, I—"

"Hey, they say they studied her and everything before they created this scenario. Evidently, she just wants the girlfriend experience, you know, hand-holding and that kinda shit. You can handle it. It's all about showing her around and helping her let loose. They need her on the ball Saturday and ready for some big boardroom smack down. All you gotta do is lay on the charm, get her pumped for battle, and send her off feeling she's got some mojo going on."

She grumbled under her breath, reading through the dog-eared script. It was all of nineteen pages long and mostly contained entries like where to take this woman and what to say when they got there. And they specified the mood she was to create. Yes, it did sound like she just wanted an escort to attend stuff. That wouldn't be too bad, and the venues and restaurants were all the best Vegas had to offer. She tapped her fingers on highlighted text on page four. "I've never been backstage at Cirque du Soleil, how the hell do you expect me to give her a backstage tour?"

"It's all arranged." He opened the large envelope she had been ignoring, retrieving a smartphone. It was new and a big improvement over what she was using. "You get to keep this, after. It's got all the contacts, the times, even your tickets. There's a credit card too." He handed the gold plastic to her.

She was expecting a prepaid card, but this one had her name on it. "What the hell?"

"It's in the script. Saturday morning, when you walk through Caesar's Palace, you'll buy her something to give her confidence. If you need to spend more than ten grand, send me a text, and I'll make sure her people are expecting it."

"Her people—won't she think it's weird that I'm buying something for her with her own money? I mean…"

"That's the thing, it's all a surprise."

"What? You said she wanted the girlfriend experience, now you're saying 'her people', whatever the hell that means…"

"Maddie baby, give it a rest! It's just how this experience thing goes. These rich people pay for the whole thing to happen sometime in the future. Hell, for all we know this chick may do this every place she visits. They say she travels a lot and expects to meet people and have adventures. Maybe it's just her thing! Come on, you know how weird rich people are."

It wasn't like she could say no. After ten years in Vegas, she was sure she'd seen everything. Of course, she was sure her career and her life had hit rock bottom too. Maybe the only way to test that hypothesis was to take on this stupid pantomime. Besides, she owed Franco. Her new and overstuffed Grand Cherokee in the parking lot was his. He had won it in a backroom high stakes poker game and had handed her the keys sight unseen. "What do I need with another Jeep? You keep it. This way I know you'll make it home. I couldn't forgive myself if I sent you home on the bus."

She was staring at the bulging manila envelope which she knew contained the opening payment of ten thousand dollars. Successful completion of the scripted weeklong romance promised an additional ten grand. One thing for sure, this might be rock bottom, but she wouldn't be leaving Vegas beat down and broke like all the rest. She wouldn't be going home a star like she promised her family, but she could return to Minneapolis with some pride for having tried. Couldn't she?

CHAPTER TWO

Kara followed her sister through the casino to the elevators. After arriving and checking in, Jo had dragged her out to the Strip to some theme restaurant for lunch. A six-hour flight and fast food had left her feeling even more lethargic and uninterested than normal. Still, she followed her sister to the offices of the catering manager.

Joanne, the youngest of the Wexler children, was their father's daughter in every way. She held the job of company event manager, was a social butterfly and had been since the first day her daddy brought her to work. It was different for Kara and Dougie. As the oldest, Kara had been tested at every turn. As Doug became an adult, he too started at the bottom, but unlike his sister who excelled, his constant failures were swept under the carpet. Everyone knew the old man wanted Dougie to take his place one day. The board also knew Doug neither wanted the job nor could handle it. They needed Kara, and Doug and Joanne had joined with several others to make that happen. If only Jo could get Kara interested in the board meeting—or anything, for that matter.

In the foyer to the catering offices, they were asked to wait just a few minutes while the catering manager finished his appointment with a VIP guest. The receptionist, a stunning blonde with a badge reading Lucy from Australia, tried to interest them in a beverage while they waited. Joanne was pleased to accept and sit patiently. Kara paced the open space, taking no notice of the stunning young beauty from Down Under.

Joanne surreptitiously watched her sister with her fingers crossed. Kara was in her own world and had been for far too long. Long since tired of trying to connect with her big sis, Joanne quietly drank her coffee. When Dougie and Zack had come to her and Samantha with this plan, she was sure they'd made the whole thing up, but once they looked through the website and had a conference call with the guy from Ultimate Experience, she was in. Her sister needed some nice girl to keep her company. Maybe this actress escort lady wasn't the kind of girl she would have picked for Kara, but these women knew how to talk to people. Wasn't that what they did, got these guys or gals talking and having fun? She wasn't sure that having a girl on Kara's arm would solve anything but her sister had been alone a long time, and this was much easier than trying to find her a date. God knows that had never worked out.

The moment the door to the catering manager's office opened, Joanne was on her feet, hooking and dragging Kara by the arm. "I'm Joanne Bryson-Wexler, and this is my sister Kara Wexler."

The introduction caught everyone off guard including the hotel guest just shaking his hand and saying, "Thank you again for finding a way to fit me in. I can't tell you how much I appreciate it. It does appear I've been monopolizing your time," the guest added with a nod to Joanne and a wink for Kara.

Kara, caught off guard by Joanne's hasty behavior, stood with mouth agape, staring at the woman before her.

Joanne didn't seem to notice, launching into a nervous conversation with the catering manager and the other VIP guest. Finally, the guest excused herself, and Kara seemed in a trance as she watched her leave.

"I wish they still had a football team here."

This was the first thing out of Kara's mouth? *She meets a pretty woman, and all she wants to do is to see a football game?* "Football, really?" Joanne challenged her sister. "Back in the day, you would have never let a woman like that out of the room without getting her phone number!"

"What, wait…" Kara asked, still not really in the moment. "Do you know her?"

For a moment Joanne knew she looked like she did know her, then she blanked it out. Back when she was a toddler and got caught stealing Kara's Legos, she would do the same thing. Kara seemed to suspect something was brewing but Joanne brushed it off, offering a sweet smile. "Of course not. I'm just making a point."

"I'm here to witness my father take our company back in time and obliterate any chance we have of joining the twenty-first century, not find a date!"

"We have a week," she whined at her sister, adding feebly, "You might as well have some fun."

* * *

As the script directed, Madeleine Jessepp returned to her hotel suite after her first encounter with her assignment. Now, stuck in a makeup chair, she listened as the director argued over the phone. When he finally hung up, he turned an expectant eye on her. "It wasn't perfect, but it wasn't a strikeout either. Now, let's see…" He turned his attention to the racks of clothing. "In the next act, you will encounter each other across the poker table. Your costume…" He wandered into the bedroom—now dressing room—carefully combing the wardrobe for her performance. Script, Wardrobe, Performance. Everything they said made this sound like it was a stage act. *Then why didn't my supposed stage girlfriend take an interest in me?* "Maybe she prefers dykes or something like that?" she asked the director. "I don't exactly look like a lesbian."

He hushed her impatiently, ordering the makeup woman to strip her face. "Just a little eye shadow and a touch of lipstick.

I want you to be au naturale!" He carried a pair of well-worn jeans, a bottle green, deep V-neck sweater, and boots. Something that looked suitable for an Australian cattlewoman, not a Vegas showgirl.

Madeleine just sighed, unsure of her situation and the role to come. "Am I supposed to beat her at poker or let her win?"

"Oh my dear, just play it like the script says. Play the table as the hands come, but don't bet against her. You can bet with her and against everyone else but not her."

"Don't you think she'll figure that out?"

He just giggled as he fussed. "That, my dear, is the point."

* * *

"Why are you dragging me to the poker tables?" Kara asked with ire.

"Because you love poker and because I will not let you spend this whole week hiding in your room. We have a lot of work to do. A lot of goodwill to repair and we can't do that if you're acting like a big grouch-pot! Now go play. I'll come back and fetch you in time to meet the West Coast reps for dinner."

The idea of wasting a few hours playing cards didn't sound so bad. This whole week would be a waste of time as far as she was concerned. Her resignation was already written, signed, and delivered. She had intended to hand it to her father before Vegas. The truth was, she'd had no intention of making this trip at all. It was all Joanne's doing. She'd convinced Kara to spend the week helping her cover the conference events and talk with the freelancers who fed work up to Wexler-Ogelthorpe, along with a hundred or so account reps. "Come with me. Spend a week playing nice with the regional reps and goofing off on the company dime. It'll be fun. You'll get some desperately needed down time, and when we get back, you can still kill our father with your resignation."

"Oh for God's sake, Jo. I'm not trying to kill the old man. I'm just trying to prevent him and this damned job from killing *me*!"

"Look." Joanne nodded to the pit boss, "A chair just opened. Take it. I'll come find you, *later*," she emphasized, pushing her sister toward the poker tables.

* * *

Madeleine almost panicked when she saw the small line for the poker room. That was a problem. Taking a quick inventory, she could see there weren't enough people to open another table. She knew poker players were the serious type and rarely gave up their seats, at least not until they went broke. From where she was standing, she could just see the Kara woman at the 20/40 table. Before she could decide what to do, she felt a hand on her elbow. "Ms. Jessepp, how lovely to have you back. I believe your regular seat has just opened up."

Surprised by the attention, she was momentarily stunned then remembered, this is all scripted. "It's a pleasure. Tell me, is the table warming?" she asked as the pit boss led her to the same table as Kara. An elderly man had vacated a seat at just the right moment. The other people in line waiting to play poker grumbled but this was Vegas. And everyone dreamed of hitting it big one day and becoming a VIP, so they let it slide.

"I'm sure things will heat up now that you're here." As she took her seat, he gave her the spread, the table limit, and set a tray of ten and twenty dollar chips in front of her, before wishing her luck.

A waitress appeared out of nowhere, wearing one of those skimpy costumes all women servers hate. Madeleine always tipped well and tried to be extra kind to the female servers. During her decade in Sin City, she had waited her share of tables too. She knew just how bad it could be.

"Welcome back, Ms. Jessepp." She delivered an unordered drink announcing, "One dead bastard with brandy and bourbon. As usual."

Madeleine thanked her then remembered the script called for her to be gregarious and generous. She didn't know what a dead bastard was, but it probably deserved a good tip. It was a good thing players at tables drank for free, but she'd have to be careful if she was going to pull this off. She was sure her new employers wouldn't be pleased if she got drunk during her "performance." As she reached out to sample her cocktail, she noted a subtle warning look from her server. A good thing too. With her mouth and face all set for some premium booze, the refreshing taste of unadorned ginger ale was a shock. She kept her face neutral, now understanding the warning. They wanted her to look like she was enjoying herself, just not actually have any fun. She plastered a satisfied look on her face and beamed at her tablemates. Most were playing stoic, and trying to pretend they could actually be high rollers. She stifled a laugh, taking another healthy gulp of her fake drink to hide her amusement as she waited for the dealer button to pass. Most of the players, she'd cast as pensioners and near-retirement baby boomers playing make believe. If any were really interested in hauling in a rake, the 20/40 table wasn't it. She chucked in her twenty for the small blind and watched across the table as the Kara woman knocked out her signal to check. She had to remind herself to stop referring to her as "the Kara woman." She was also hyperaware she was beginning to see her as a mark. She immediately checked her concern. She wasn't trying to con this woman. As the director had stated repeatedly, this was an interactive performance. Something the woman had signed up for. *Who does that?*

* * *

Kara had just lost her second hand and was seriously considering cashing in and looking for a place to hide for the afternoon. But now the woman from the catering manager's office was joining the table. *God, she's an attractive woman!* Tall and lean, with the look of a dancer. What the power suit she was wearing earlier hid, the deep V-neck sweater and the formfitting jeans accentuated. But it wasn't like the sweater showed off her bosom. The woman was not so endowed, and for a moment Kara caught herself smiling, thinking how perfect she was.

She'd always left the big-breasted ladies for her brother to chase. Judging by Dougie's pick for a wife, he liked them well-endowed and softly curved. Not her. As her brother loved to tell their friends, "Kara always goes for the tall skinny chicks." And he was right. Back in the day she wouldn't have wasted a second before charming this woman up or asking her out. Had this lifelong battle with her father taken that much out of her? She had no intention of wasting time on the question. *I'm here now, and that woman is smiling at me!*

The betting round had finished, and she watched the woman intently, as intently as everyone else watched the dealer lay down the flop. Watching the dealer was a mistake, Kara believed; this was a game of wills. There was a certain amount of luck involved, not to mention math, but that was all secondary. This game needed to be played in the mind, the mind of your opponents. Across the table and sitting beside the woman from the catering manager's office was someone Kara would categorize as the table bully. Aficionados might call him a classic aggressive poker player, but Kara knew better. If this guy really knew what he was doing, he'd be playing at a no-limit table, not sitting here. Still, he was a pain in the ass, going to the limit on every round, even before the flop. She hated guys like this. They made the game too aggressive for most of the other players who would probably be content to spend half the day losing their money. No one wanted to go bust inside their first half-hour. She was planning on taking him on with this hand, but the new woman followed his bet. Instead of calling, Kara carefully checked her cards, counted her chips for the table to see then shook her head, and folded. She planned to repeat that little fake tell over the course of the afternoon. Experienced players never fell for such subterfuge, but she was sure Mr. Poker would. Right now her number one concern was for the woman in the V-neck. She sat back to watch the action unfold, hoping the new player had caught his number too.

Kara had heard the pit boss call her Ms. Jessepp. Jessepp with an E, not a U. Scandinavian in origin, but changed somehow, modernized? Was that why it was Jessepp, not Jesseppsson or Jesseppsdóttir. Americanized? Yes. Midwest? Definitely Midwest. At least originally... She watched in awe as Ms. Jessepp took a hand from Mr. Poker. He seemed as surprised as the rest of the table. As the dealer dealt out the next hand, she remained focused on Mr. Poker, watching as he checked his cards. Interesting. Judging by his flaccid expression, Kara was sure he had one face card, but that was it. Most players would limp in with a hand like that and wait to see what the flop looked like. She expected the weaker his cards, the more aggressive Mr. Poker would be. Sure enough, when the betting round reached him, he called the blind and raised to the maximum. Sitting left of him and last before the buck, Kara called his raise. She was surprised to see everyone call the bet except the new woman. She smiled at Kara as she folded her hand. *Interesting.*

Focusing her attention back on the table and the remaining players, Kara watched Mr. Poker as the dealer delivered the turn. There was no reaction from him, and it was all she needed to see. When the betting reached her, she maxed out, again. She sat back to watch Mr. Poker's reaction and almost fell off her chair to realize that Ms. Jessepp was watching her. She nodded some sort of approval before turning her attention back to the game. As the river card was turned, she let a satisfied look escape before pulling her poker face. Mr. Poker was watching her keenly as were the other two players still in. It was her turn to bet, and she went to the max again. Mr. Poker wavered, and it was all the other two needed to stay in. She had no idea what they were holding, and she didn't care. Her sole aim was to bust his ass off her table. *My table!* She laughed at her internal language, watching him struggle to match the bet. Kara could only guess he wasn't used to having to play the cards he'd been dealt. She was experienced enough to know it wasn't the cards but what you did with them. It didn't matter if she was playing poker or fighting for a new account, she always believed her first step in controlling the game was to align herself with another player. Just one. That looked to be settled and by Ms. Jessepp herself. She liked that, and she liked that name. Next order of business, kick the bullies out. Mr. Poker took one more look at his cards then met the bet. She knew he would. At this point, he would see himself as pot committed. Kara turned over her cards. While she didn't take the pot, she was pleased to see Mr. Poker lose too. He sat back in a grump then began raking the room for the waitress. She could only hope he was ordering a drink to drown his sorrows. If he ordered a meal, well, that would not be a good sign.

The player beside her asked to cash out and took his winnings to the poker room cage. According to poker etiquette, the last player to join the game was entitled to the new seat before it was offered to a new player. Kara was delighted and frightened as all get out when Ms. Jessepp nodded to the pit boss and made her way to the empty seat beside her. The waitress returned at light speed, further irking Mr. Poker by taking first Ms. Jessepp's drink order then Kara's before checking on the rest of the table and accepting his.

They were halfway into the next hand when the waitress returned. This time she acknowledged both women. "Here you are Ms. Jessepp, one dirty bastard. And for you, Ms. Wexler, one Labrador Tea."

Kara grabbed a ten-dollar chip from her stack but hesitated. Ten seemed like too much to tip even if the woman knew her name. Then she watched the woman next to her slip the waitress a twenty. Deciding to err on the high side, she grabbed a second ten and handed them to the waitress as she made her way around the table. It was obvious she'd left Mr. Poker for last. He huffed when she slapped down his beer and walked away.

"I have to ask," the woman, Ms. Jessepp, said, leaning in and saying in a conspiring tone, "I thought a Labrador Tea was made with gin. That thing looks positively like…" She blushed.

Kara raised her glass, inspecting it with her. "I like to call this hue 'first pee of the mornin' yellow'."

That got her laughing, and she offered her hand. "I'm Madeleine, and yes, that does look like a sample you might leave in the doctor's office. I'm assuming it tastes better than it looks?"

Kara smiled, folding her hand on the flop and sitting back to enjoy the company. "It's gin. It's just distilled with flora regional to Labrador. I think it's the wild rose hips that give it the color. What about you? What's in a dirty bastard?"

"Hey, don't I get a name or should I just call you Miss Labrador Tea?" She smiled before turning her attention back to the game. She took note of the turn card, then added two twenty-dollar chips to her bet. She turned her eyes back on Kara who was stuck somewhere between watching the hand play out and listing to this stunning woman speak.

"I...um... Sorry. It's Kara, Kara Wexler. Pleased to meet you, Madeleine?"

"I know," she offered in sympathy. "Madeleine is a handful, not to mention very old-fashioned."

"I don't know. Madeleine suits you. I think I would've been disappointed if your name was Debbie or Sue. You must hate it when people call you Maddie?"

"How... Okay, now it's your turn to explain." She raked in her winnings then turned back to Kara while the dealer cleared the table and shuffled the cards.

"It's how you introduced yourself. It was second nature, no hint of a more common version. Do you let anyone call you Maddie?"

The woman seemed torn between answering her and just plain walking away. As the opening betting round continued, she pushed out two twenty-dollar chips to call the bet then answered with less enthusiasm, "You must be a student of human behavior."

"Sorry, professional observation, that's all. I didn't mean to be a dick."

Madeleine laughed, eyes on the table as the dealer turned over the flop. "I hate to ask but what kind of work do you do? Oh God, you're not some sort of detective, are you?"

That question had Kara grinning, "Close. I do spend an inordinate amount of time nosing around but not on people. I investigate trends." She watched Madeleine chuck her cards while Mr. Poker was max betting again. Clearly, his fresh beer was fueling this latest push. Kara smiled at the woman beside her and called his bet. Both women watched while the betting round preceded. Once complete, their chips were added to the pot. The dealer burned the top card before flipping over the turn card. Mr. Poker was first up and maxed out the bet. Kara listened as a few of the old boys grumbled. How very interesting to be sitting beside a beautiful woman and surrounded by grumpy old men. She had been paying more attention to Madeleine than the other players and had missed Mr. Poker's reaction to his cards. Judging by his non-reaction to the turn card and his continued aggressive betting she was sure he was bluffing, again. She met his bet even though she had yet to check her cards. *Too late now.*

Beside her, Madeleine intently followed the hand, sipping from her cocktail and quietly humming to herself. Others might have found that bothersome but Kara was enjoying the sound and the woman when Mr. Poker shoved his last chips forward in a move that signaled he was all in. His commitment was meant to scare others, and she was surprised to see two players immediately fold. That left just her, Mr. Poker, and two old boys at the end of the table. It would be a good hand to win. Even though she had no clue what she was holding she smiled the most condescending smile she could muster before pushing two hundred dollars in chips forward. "Call."

The dealer signaled for them all to turn their cards over. The old boys were sitting on respectable hands. Mr. Poker had fisted his cards waiting for Kara to reveal her hand first. She kept the condescending look on her face knowing the dealer would make him present first. It took a minute for him to realize they were waiting for him. He complained but finally tossed his cards over, then huffed back in his seat looking very much like he wanted to spit in Kara's face. He'd tried to run the table with a three and a seven. Kara turned her cards over, seeing her hand for the first time. She took the pot with a full house.

As she raked in her chips, she felt the woman beside her give a subtle shoulder bump. "Nice."

"Thank you, grown-up Madeleine, never little Maddie." Kara could feel the woman's eyes on her and chanced to look. She assumed she'd be pissed or at least annoyed. Her amused smile was the last thing she was expecting. She returned the smile while something inside clicked into place. They spent the next few hands in relative silence. That was all it took before their allied play busted Mr. Poker. Kara almost cried to see him pull five one-hundred-dollar bills from his wallet and buy back in. That was the downfall of playing an open table as opposed to tournament play. If he'd gone broke in a tournament match, that would be it, but as long as he had money, he could sit and play.

Kara marveled to watch Madeleine take him on. It was remarkable how intuitive they were with one another. They had become an unofficial tag team, taking turns to take out Mr. Poker while never betting against one another. It wasn't like they were cheating. They would both check their cards and more often than not, pay to see the flop. By the time the second betting round was complete, one or the other would fold, and it looked like they each intuitively guessed who had the best hand or the greatest chance of besting the table and Mr. Poker.

"Thank you."

That stopped Kara. She smiled before checking her cards and calling. "You're welcome. I don't know what you're thanking me for, but you're most welcome."

"You're Canadian, aren't you?"

She looked around before answering. "Guilty. What gave it away? Was it my hypothetical accent, my sense of humor, or was I too polite?"

As the betting came around, Madeleine checked her cards again, seeming to look hesitant, maybe even confused before increasing the bet. Her bet was marginal but perfect, too. Kara always considered the limping players a pain, except when the player used it as a tactic against a bully. It was a perfect move. Kara, next in order to place a bet, made like the cards were bad and chucked her hand. She made sure to inch back in her chair. She wanted to watch Madeleine take him on but didn't want to risk him noticing her mirth. It was also a perfect angle to watch Madeleine in profile. In the advertising world, the profile was the beauty shot. Kara had noticed her hair before, but under the lights of the business office, she had registered a darker tone, maybe Avenger Auburn but down here under the house lights, she had to admit the perfect glossy waves were Riddler Red. She should know. She'd been stuck naming sixty-four shades for a hair coloring campaign just last year. Although considering it more carefully now, she would have called Madeleine's natural hair shade Bad Ass Red Brass. Of course that name had been rejected long before it was even suggested to the client. It was still her favorite. As if hearing everything she was thinking, Madeleine turned to face her, a smile so radiant her eyes were alight. Green, light mossy green…

"Order me another drink?" she asked, delivering a wicked grin with her request.

Her attention was back on the table, the game, and mostly Mr. Poker whose head was beginning to resemble a great big sugar beet. His stack of new chips had dwindled fast, and it looked like he would have to call Madeleine's bet or try to limp his way through one more hand. Of course he could always buy more chips, but she had a feeling either his pride or his bride had set his limit. It would be interesting to calculate all his options or lack thereof.

Madeleine's poker face smiled ever so slightly at the river card. Kara knew it was more for the effect than anything and noted the steam rising from Mr. Poker's ears. Would his head blow right here? With just forty dollars in chips left, he made the classic mistake of following the pot. He was all in. That didn't mean he wouldn't buy more chips. As the betting round continued, Kara focused on him and his aggravated mood. He was tapping nervously on his cards and mumbling under his breath. He was also fixated on Madeleine's hand. Not the player, just the cards, and it hit her. This guy was so sure a woman couldn't be beating him at poker, she had to be what…cheating? It was all she could do not to laugh out loud. Where did guys like this come from? Did they have a special school or something?

Cards were turned over, and Mr. Poker freaked out. He threw his cards across the table. An infraction in poker that had you removed. He stood, knocking his chair over. The stunt with the cards had already caught the attention of the pit boss. Now the chair thing invited security into the mix. Kara was a little shocked at how fast two hulking gentlemen in suits appeared, both latching onto the flailing arm of the irate player being evicted from the game.

"Fucking dykes!" he hissed as he disappeared into the main casino floor.

The pit boss said, "Ms. Jessepp, Ms. Wexler, gentlemen, please accept my apology. I'm happy to provide complimentary dinner passes for everyone."

Again, Madeleine turned a brilliant smile on her, eyes alight with mischief. "I'm more in the mood for a quiet drink somewhere. How about you?"

Kara found herself lost in the brilliance of her eyes and had to replay the moment in her mind, "A drink? Yes," she answered with a decisive smile. A drink with a beautiful and genuine woman was something far and away too absent in her life these last few years. "Absolutely. Yes."

CHAPTER THREE

Lily's Bar wasn't far from the poker room and provided the best view of the casino floor and a perfect place to enjoy a quiet conversation. "That was amazing!" Madeleine said, leading Kara past the velvet rope barrier to a seating area marked reserved.

Kara was surprised to watch her plop down on the couch next to her instead of one of the nearby seats. Madeleine immediately angled herself to face her, her actions open and inviting. As she moved and spoke, her hands moved with her patter, while her knee kept lightly brushing the edge of Kara's thigh. Was that just a coincidence or was it intentional? Before she could decide or move, the waitress delivered a round of drinks, then hurried away.

Kara joked, "I thought Mr. Poker's head was going to explode." Both women laughed before trying their drinks. *That smile. That warmth and natural beauty…I could put her on the cover of any ad campaign and not be surprised when sales spike.*

She sat transfixed as Madeleine watched her knowingly, all the while raising her cocktail glass to her lips, practically caressing the tumbler as she took another sip. Never letting her eyes break contact, she asked suggestively, "Are you always the ruthless opponent at the poker table, Ms. Wexler? If so, remind me to stay on your good side." This she added with a wink.

"Don't pin that one on me. It was all you." She couldn't help but laugh, really laugh again. Was Madeleine's excitement rubbing off on her? "Besides, I'm not the one who laid the final blow."

"To teamwork then," Madeleine said, holding up her glass for a toast.

Talk about passion and an incredibly creative problem solver. Did she do that for me? No way she could know how much I hate guys like that. Incredible! She raised her glass to meet Madeleine's. "To teamwork." She let the taste of premium gin warm her throat while the hot woman next to her took care of the rest. She was losing track of how long she'd been staring, staring and listening, when a couple of guys invited themselves to join in. They were drunk and obnoxious, and she was surprised when the hostess quickly rushed in to move them off to another area, promising them a better view of the action. As far as she was concerned, she had the best view in town.

"Back when I was a kid," Madeleine began, "I hated bullies like that. They think the world owes them something just because their family has a bit of money."

Kara listened, noticing a momentary flinch in Madeleine's eyes. The way she veered from professional to personal like that, she was definitely not shy about her point of view. If she wanted to learn more about Madeleine, a few questions should be enough to pinpoint her buyer persona. *Stop it! Get out of work mode and just enjoy yourself.*

When her sister had dragged her to the airport that morning, Kara never would have imagined sitting here twelve hours later with such a beautiful and charming woman. She might be among the best at what she did professionally, but attracting pretty women was not on the list. She had long since given up on the idea that anyone could find her attractive. Especially after her last relationship. She had come to believe she just wasn't relationship material. Worse, she had learned to be suspicious of women who pretended to be attracted to her. Short in stature, and considering herself plain, she was sure all the rowing and lacrosse she did added little appeal. If anything, her adherence to an unconventional fitness routine and obscure sports just made her seem weirder to most women. These facts hadn't abated her attractions, but the dismal results of her love life had never been worth the trouble.

Ever since she'd joined the family business, her love life had suffered. Of course, she never lacked for company, but one night stands and casual dating didn't mean much in the grand scheme of things. Most women were simply out for her money and ran for the hills the moment they found out she wasn't as liberal with her wallet as she was with her affection.

When she met Chrystal, she'd hoped she was different. She had her own career and seemed to be thriving, and the woman's looks and charm did the rest. Chrystal's supposed success had been the key to Kara lowering her guard. It wasn't long before she found herself on Chrystal time. Kara could wait hours for Chrystal, considered an A-lister among Toronto's arts and film industry elite, to prep herself for each outing. Kara could admit she enjoyed having a lovely woman on her arm. As their relationship grew, so did Kara's trust. The two women were well-known and well liked on the red carpet and often found their relationship held up as an example of a great celebrity couple: Kara, the iconic publicity mogul, and her partner, Chrystal, the gallery owner.

Except Chrystal had lied about owning shares in her gallery, she just worked there. By the time Kara learned that little detail, Chrystal was fully fused into her life. They were happy together, the money issue seemed inconsequential. It looked as if all was going charmingly until Kara's workload got the best of her. That and her father's constant interference and emotional battering. Her successful relationship became one more fact driving his disdain. And while his personal and professional attacks escalated, she told those who cared that she was forced to focus her diminishing energy on business, no longer able or

she wanted the extra money. She knew she couldn't throw her success in her parents' faces, but she wouldn't be returning broke and busted either. She may not have made it to the big time, but it would seem like it to those she knew back home in Minneapolis. *Ten years in Vegas and this is my biggest job yet.* The thought depressed her.

As she thumbed through Kara's personal and professional achievements, she made a note of several details she could use as talking points. But how was she supposed to bring up her rowing club in conversation? *Oh, Kara! What strong, lovely arms you have! You must row a lot!* She laughed to herself. She did actually have a great build. And she did like the look of her hair, thick and dark. Kara was shorter than her, but it was hard enough finding men taller than her much less women. Madeleine continued down the bio and looked for something she could actually use. She noted one of Kara's side projects, partnering with a developer to turn several historic old warehouses into lofts. *This woman has more money than she knows what to do with. When does she ever sleep?* At least this was something she could use. Her own father had been in construction her whole life; she had grown up around blueprints and drywall. She was also very aware of how particular rich clients could be about the smallest of details. Her dad would often come home worn down from dealing with their daily demands. Her more than ten years in Vegas, her childhood experiences and impressions of people with money—it all had left a sour taste in her mouth.

Reading further she saw a paragraph extensively outlining Kara's current emotional state. Apparently, the woman's father had greatly impacted her both personally and professionally. Kara's confidence had been worn down over the course of her work for the family company. If she was going to get Kara's mojo going by Saturday, she had to get her head in the game, and for that she needed a game plan. Picking up the script again she made a note of the when and where of the plans for the following days.

How in the world was she supposed to get this woman where she needed to be? There was nothing in the script that said "sleep with the woman," yet Madeleine got the impression that it was somehow implied. *Great. I'm a fucking whore now.* She pushed the thought away and thumbed through the script again looking for a better way to accomplish her goal in time. It was pointless. She was going to have to get somewhat intimate with the woman, or it would never work. It was easy to see that Kara was attracted to her. So why hadn't she acted on it? Had Kara been waiting for her to make the first move? Maybe it was just how lesbians were?

She was going to need to step up her game. Tonight she planned on having a real cocktail or two to soothe her nerves. Maybe a stroke to the arm or pushing her hair behind her ear would do the trick. It was exactly the same as flirting with a guy. Besides, it wasn't as if Kara was unattractive. Actually, she was quite beautiful in a boyish sense. She was certainly charming. She tossed the script and the fact sheet onto the desk and smiled to herself.

Just then Franco popped into the suite, announcing, "Show time!"

With a deep sigh, Madeleine adjusted her dress and headed out the door prepared to give the performance of a lifetime.

En route to the hotel bar, Madeleine sealed a plan in her head. She wanted to wear down the reserved Kara and returning to the same bar sounded like a safe way to start the evening. She was pleased to see that the same table was still reserved for them, especially considering how busy the place was, and Kara was already seated.

They stayed where they were and ended up talking for hours. But afterward Madeleine conceded that she hadn't been able to crack Kara's public persona enough to get a feel for the real woman. She was kind and open, and interestingly enough, spoke with enthusiasm about ideas, beliefs, even regionalization of culture and language, but she never spoke of her father or family and skirted any mention of the topic. She never talked about the substance of her business career, except to make a joke or tell a funny story about an advertising account and the way many companies simply rebranded outdated products for a new market.

Madeleine was good at improvisation and people and decided the fastest way to get Kara to open up and have fun was an evening stroll down the Strip. Kara admitted she hadn't seen Las Vegas Boulevard in years and would enjoy a little adventure. "Come on, let's walk. We can talk and check out each of the casino's entry displays. I have a feeling you're a fan of the pirates?" she said, gesturing down the street toward Treasure Island.

"Who doesn't enjoy a little swashbuckling now and then?" In the bright lights of the Vegas Strip, Kara apologized for her mood. "I'm sorry if I seem a bit secretive. The truth is, this isn't just my fourteenth Wexler-Ogelthorpe sales conference. It's my last. On Friday I plan to deliver what we call 'the long game analysis.' It's something we do every year to help us make decisions about the direction of the company. The interns call it pivot-or-sprint plan. My father is CEO, and he's a classic sprinter." At Madeleine's concerned look, she explained, "Sprinting is a metaphor. If a company is deemed to be on the right path, the strategy is to run faster than the competition. Lead the field so to speak."

"And you're not a fan of business as usual so you what, plan to tell them it's time to pivot, head in another direction?"

Kara spoke sharply. "I plan to break the S.O.B. with twenty years of data on the growth and maturity of the Internet, online sales statistics that prove once you remove boomers from the stats, which he insists is still the consumer base, we find every campaign we have run in the last four years failed with Gen X, millennials, and whatever it is we're calling the new kids, ah, Gen Zed."

"Zed? Oh right. Zee. Okay, I get that you're a bit edgy on this and sometimes shock is the best way to get people to consider options they never knew existed, but what about your family. Won't this hurt them?"

"Every minute he wastes taking them deeper down the rabbit hole is a day closer to complete failure."

Madeleine was bothered by the terminology and found she couldn't look at Kara. Walking with eyes cast down, she finally asked, "You say 'them', not 'us' when you're talking about your family. Why do you distance yourself if you're planning on making changes?"

"Making changes…no, I'm done with trying to make changes. I'm going to deliver the painful reality of the situation to the national account reps. They deserve to know their future is headed for the toilet."

"You haven't told them yet? How were you supposed to get them to make changes if they didn't know?" Madeleine was getting riled and for some reason couldn't pull back the attitude. This was as bad as trying to converse with her folks. For some reason they always expected her to know things they had never shared and berated her when she didn't.

"I told the board, I advised the board, I even went as far as to send them monthly updates on my analysis and the change announcements coming from our industry. Everything I say or do is shouted down by 'he who knows best.'" This she added with ridiculous air quotes.

From Madeleine's perspective, it sounded like Kara's research couldn't have been very compelling. Still, torpedoing the management team seemed underhanded, even mean somehow. "And the board. Are you meeting with them?"

"That's on Saturday, and yes, I'll give them the numbers again and then my ultimatum. He goes, or I do."

"What?" Her tone was incredulous. She stopped dead on the Strip forcing the swarm of pedestrians to swim around them like a street performer that tourists just ignored. "This is your father we're talking about, right?" Madeleine couldn't control the rush of words that sprang up from some deep sense of propriety. "What's wrong with you? Why don't you talk to him, or your sister? She seemed very nice and you said your brother would be here tomorrow. I hear your frustration but taking him down in a public ultimatum…who does that?" The blame game cut too close to Madeleine to take at face value. Suddenly she was off script and challenging this woman's behavior. She didn't care. It was too much to handle. What Kara was doing to her family hit way too close to home.

"Madeleine, you don't know anything about me or my situation." Her fists rested on her hips in defense mode, the superhero pose attractive in a strange way. Shaking her head, she warned, "Don't do this. Don't judge me until you know the whole story."

"Kara..." she said, seeing nothing but angry sparks in her eyes and recognizing that her plan was rapidly spinning out of control. *Shit. Franco's gonna kill me!* She had to get her strategy back on track but wasn't sure she wanted to. She did her best to put her own emotions in check and took Kara's hand in her own. For a second she thought it might work when Kara's soft fingers began to interlace with hers. But Kara quickly yanked them away. "I can't do this," she said, stepping into the street. She held her arm high, immediately flagging down a cab.

"Come on. Let's just drop it," Madeleine pleaded. She'd wanted her to open up but certainly not like this. She'd pushed way too hard on a sensitive situation.

Kara was now giving the taxi driver instructions, her face still angry. "I'm leaving," she told her and slammed the car door.

"But we're supposed to be heading the other way," she said, pointing toward Fremont and leaning in the cab's window.

"I'm going back."

"But I made plans for us. You don't know what I had to pull to get these tickets on such short notice," she said in a huff.

Kara gave her a backward look to say she didn't care as the taxi pulled away from the curb. Her only concession was a nod and a mouthed, "Sorry."

Shit. Shit. Shit! Madeleine was left standing on the curb, all dressed up with nowhere to go. She didn't know what to feel beyond anger at the stupid woman who'd hired her in the first place; anger at Franco for getting her into this mess; and anger at herself for opening her big fat mouth.

With no idea what to do next, she turned to walk back to the hotel and the production suite made available to her. She needed time to think about how she was going to fix this. She couldn't bring herself to call Franco and admit she'd blown it. Of course he'd have a backup plan, wouldn't he? He'd probably already gotten some other woman to play the lucky whore to the poor little rich girl. She sighed and walked on.

CHAPTER FOUR

"I knew it!" Joanne challenged as she entered the suite. "You're supposed to be out with that pretty lady, not sulking… What happened?"

"I hate women!"

Joanne rolled her eyes. "Oh boy. What did she do?"

"Nothing, okay? Just leave me alone."

"No, I can't! You're my sister, and besides, some of the guys want to hit the clubs and I need a tail man."

"Wingman," Kara corrected, tossing a cushion at her. "And you're nuts if you think I'm going to sit around getting drunk and watching a bunch of middle-aged account execs getting drunk and drooling over my baby sister and women half their age."

Taking a seat on the big couch and taking her hand, Joanne asked with tenderness, "What happened on your date?"

It took a few minutes for Joanne to break through the lone wolf façade.

When Kara finally opened up about the walk and the talk, she realized she'd overreacted even before Joanne's confirmation. The voice of reason was not what she expected from her baby sister and it helped to dissipate her mood.

"Your lady friend may be feeling a little embarrassed, too."

Kara hadn't thought of that. But she hadn't thought of much else except Madeleine. She couldn't get the woman out of her head.

With a knowing smile, Joanne turned the subject back to the account reps and her need for a wingman. "It's not the old guys who want to go out and party. Well, they do, but they know better than to let us know where they're going. It's the West Coast boys. They want to hit something called the Fruit Loop."

"You do know it's not called that anymore."

"What isn't?"

"Fruit… I might have said yes, just to watch you squirm all night in a gay bar."

"There you go! Always a silver lining and why don't you call your lady friend and ask her to join us?"

"You know she's not my lady…hmm, why the hell not," she said sarcastically. "I can make an even bigger jerk of myself. Make it a complete bust from the get-go."

"That's enough from your lesser self, sis. Now, since you're not going out with your friend, go get your jammies on. You can help me check off all the items for tomorrow's reception by the pool, which you will be attending."

"The pool? Shit! Now I have to shave my legs."

* * *

Madeleine entered the VIP pool area as scripted, wearing a skimpy but elegant one-piece, a somewhat see-through wrap, floppy sun hat, and oversized designer sunglasses. She looked every inch the vacationing starlet. She took a quick survey of the reserved cabanas, choosing to stretch out on a partially shaded lounger where she could keep surreptitious watch over the Wexler-Ogelthorpe reception. Today would be her second shot.

Last night she had returned to the hotel expecting to be fired. Instead, to her astonishment, the director and her manager Franco told her they thought the evening was a success. Kara, they explained, needed to feel she was meeting the real woman and the argument and sudden departure would work for them. It made her feel a little queasy wondering how upsetting this kind woman, much less deceiving her, could possibly work in their favor. What did that even mean?

"Hey," Franco explained, "this chick needs to feel like the hero. You know, riding to the rescue of the damsel in distress. She also likes them feisty. You showed her the feisty side last night; now you get to be saved by her."

"Saved?" She questioned the idiocy of the setup. She was supposed to accidentally bump into Kara and her group at the pool. Then at some predetermined time, some creep was supposed to get all handsy with her, giving Kara a chance to play the protector. She didn't like the scheme. It was out of character for her to need a protector and she was sure Kara already knew that. All this would do was drive her suspicion and distaste into a higher gear. Still, she hadn't written this stupid fantasy thing, and she wasn't paying for it, so who was she to say? She was the actor who was about to abandon her character's principles, along with her own, to play this thing out. *I can't wait to leave this town!*

From her shaded corner, she watched as Kara and her sister made their way to their cabanas in the VIP area which were separated by raised planters and potted palms. It looked like the Wexler group had reserved all of the cabanas except for the one being used by her. Kara and Joanne, she noted, were not alone. A striking, curvy blonde walked beside them, joking and carrying on some discussion that clearly made fun of one of the men in tow behind them. She could guess which man was Kara and Joanne's brother. He could easily pass for Kara's twin, except he was six inches taller. The second guy was shorter and more wiry. He wore a vintage beach swimsuit with matching terry cloth jacket and towel. It looked great on him; she had to admit she hadn't seen one years. And that's when it hit her. He must be Zack, Joanne's husband. She was carrying the same matching towel and beach bag. Even her suit was in a complementary color. She held back the overwhelming need to snort and laugh as she sipped her morning glory. She now realized that the other woman, the gorgeous blonde, was most likely Kara's sister-in-law, Samantha. She was dressed similarly to Madeleine herself, in a floppy hat and vintage one-piece. In contrast, Kara was hatless, with aviator shades concealing her eyes. She wore the cutest boy shorts that showed off her muscled legs. The matching tank top covered most of her trunk, leaving a gap at the waist that hinted at well defined abs. Whatever she did to keep in shape was definitely working for her. Madeleine quickly buried the thought of gently pulling that tank a little higher to get a better look at those sculpted abs.

She kept her seat while the Wexlers inspected the area and made sure their company signage and branding were positioned properly. Joanne's husband was the first to the bar and wasted no time getting himself a morning beer. Madeleine was nursing her morning glory, intent on switching to something non-alcoholic. After all, it was barely after eight o'clock in the morning. And even if this was Vegas, it was way too early for her to tie one on. Judging by Joanne's reaction, she felt the same way about her husband. It looked like she would have it out with her hubby, but resigned herself to decorum as others began to arrive. While Joanne and Doug began welcoming guests, Kara took a seat on the edge of the pool, her legs dangling in the crystal clear water.

Yesterday, sitting at the bar and talking, Kara had joked about this regular pool reception. "I do not see the appeal of standing around a pool watching a bunch of sales guys in golf shirts and big baggy shorts all boozing in the hot sun and drooling over my sister-in-law or making inappropriate comments about my baby sis. Either way, the whole thing leaves a bad taste in my mouth."

Sure enough, the guys were arriving in groups. They always seemed to travel in packs on holiday or when attending conventions. She wasn't sure which was more dangerous for a single woman, the unscrupulous pack, or the lone predator wolf. No wonder Kara didn't enjoy these functions.

She knew Kara hadn't seen her. So she put up with the overt glances from the newly arrived attendees wondering if Kara would intervene before she was forced to confront them herself. The minute she came close to finishing her drink, the offers for a refill and to join her started pouring in. She was about to escape to the pool and hopefully Kara's consciousness when a pack took the opportunity to approach Samantha where she lay on a lounge. She was polite, but her body language made it clear she was not interested in their company or conversation. Oblivious to her discomfort, they stood surrounding her, a drink in one hand, the other in pockets, expecting to be entertained. She understood Samantha's predicament. These guys were mostly young and clearly stupid. Instead of wandering off, they just stood there uncomfortably. When they failed to offer any scrap of conversation that drew her in, their civility began to slip. Soon enough, one of the guys made an inappropriate comment about her tan lines before another asked for proof.

Without thinking, Madeleine was on her feet, pushing her way into the pack. She offered her hand. "I almost forgot," she explained insistently, "but we have to do that thing for Joanne."

Samantha locked eyes with her. You could count the beats of her heart as she considered this rescue attempt from a stranger. "Oh my God. I completely forgot. Thank you," she said getting to her feet and grabbing her sun wrap. "Sorry guys," she said, hooking her arm through Madeleine's. "Duty calls."

They walked together from the pool area toward the public washrooms. Clear of the VIP section, Samantha dropped her arm and thanked her sincerely. "They never get it, do they?" She was bristling as they walked into the ladies' washroom. "They crowd around you like some rape gang. I never know who to be madder at, them for their behavior, my husband for not stepping up to save me, or me for just putting up with it. I wouldn't do it, put up with those assholes, if they didn't work for the company."

"Hey, don't sweat it. I swear most of it is just this town. You have to be dumber than a box of rocks to believe that 'what happens in Vegas stays in Vegas' crap."

"Oh God, I know!" Samantha agreed, offering her hand. "I'm Samantha Wexler. Pleased to meet you and thank you for being my savior today."

"You're welcome, Samantha. I'm Madeleine." The moment she said her name she saw both recognition and surprise on the woman's face. "Yes, that Madeleine," she said simply. She knew from Joanne that Samantha was aware of her existence and that she was involved with the fantasy experience, but she didn't know exactly how much she was privy to, so thought it best to not say more.

Quiet for the longest time, Samantha finally smiled. "Smart and feisty," she said with a crooked grin. "No wonder Kara's so bent out of shape. You are just the kind of woman…"

They were interrupted by Joanne's hasty arrival. "What the heck!" The woman seemed frantic as she grabbed them both quickly, then made sure they had the place to themselves. "What are you two doing? They were supposed to be chatting with Madeleine, not you!"

"Joanne, for God's sake relax," Samantha said. "I don't know what division those creeps are from, but Madeleine rescued me seconds before I went ballistic and took them out myself. You should be thanking her for coming to the rescue, and me for not causing a scene!"

Joanne's protest died on her lips as she watched her sister storm into the public restroom. Kara stopped to look them over, her surprise and confusion evident. "Samantha. You're all right?" When she nodded, Kara let out a breath of relief. "I don't know who the hell those assholes were. They don't work for us. I kicked them out. Actually, security's showing them out of the hotel, so it's safe to rejoin the group."

"Thanks, Kara. I'm all right. Madeleine here intervened just in time."

Kara looked at her and nodded, remaining silent. Turning to her younger sister, she said plainly, "Pretty much everything is back to normal, except your husband. He seems to have forgotten last year's case of alcohol-induced sunstroke."

Joanne just groaned, shaking her head. "Why did I ever get married? I gave birth to two children, but for some reason, I have to care for three!" This she said while stomping from the washroom.

Kara stood silent, looking over the other two. Finally she asked, "Are you both okay?" They both nodded, then explained what had transpired. "I'm so sorry. I was sitting on the pool edge, in my own world. I should have picked up on those assholes."

"No you shouldn't have," Samantha said bluntly. "Kara, as much as everyone likes to pretend you're responsible for the world, you really aren't. What happened here had nothing to do with you. Actually, if I wanted to be mad at someone, it would be my husband."

"He's waiting outside. Samantha," she cautioned, "he's beside himself."

Now it was her turn to groan. "Don't worry, I'll assuage his manly worry."

"At least he's not threatened that you were saved by a woman."

Samantha thanked Madeleine, asking her to stay. "It doesn't get a whole lot better but the food is to die for, and the rest of the guys are tolerable, at least when Kara's holding the whip."

That picture made Madeleine smile. Turning to Kara, she said, "I have a feeling your services as Sheriff of the Pool will be in high demand."

Kara shrugged, accepting a brush-by hug from the departing Samantha before suggesting, "I could always use a good deputy. Listen, I…"

"It's okay. I was out of line last night," Madeleine offered. She looked around the washroom, and the teens making their way in. "I have a cabana. It's right next to the ones your group has. You could come join me for a quiet talk and still be able to keep an eye on your pack." She didn't know which made Kara smile more, the description of the Wexler-Ogelthorpe employees as a pack or the invitation for a quiet discussion. "You were right to challenge me. I really don't know you or your situation, but I'd like to."

Kara nodded, signaling for Madeleine to lead the way. "I'm sorry too. I didn't realize just how raw I was. This whole thing has taken such a toll but it's no reason to be a jerk, especially to you. Please forgive me?"

They had just reached the VIP Pool when she stopped to look at Kara. She wanted her to see her face, to know she meant what she said. "Will you tell me about it? I want to understand but more than that I want to be a friend, and as your friend, I think you need to get this stuff off your chest. Kara, carrying all this emotional baggage must be killing you. I can't pretend to understand your work or your family, but I can listen." She watched as Kara considered her request. God, she was a frustrating and fascinating woman.

Kara finally smiled, then offered her arm. It wasn't a necessity as much as a statement. Madeleine accepted, holding her head high as they walked through the throng of account reps and senior staffers milling around the pool. They moved through the group like they were parting the Red Sea. Madeleine couldn't tell if the reaction was a show of respect, especially after the ejection of the party creeps, or fear. Did the guys respect Kara or fear her? Deep down she knew only time would tell.

CHAPTER FIVE

Madeleine looked over her costume for the night. The designer little black dress was a far nicer cut and fabric than anything she owned. She could admit she pulled it off too. "Shouldn't I be wearing pants or a suit? Something more—I don't know—lesbianish?"

The director laughed at her assumption. "Trust me, with that dress, every lesbian in town will be after you."

That did little to settle her nerves. Running out of excuses, she pointed to the three-inch heels. "I'm already taller than her. Shouldn't I be wearing flats?"

"Oh goodness me, could it be stage fright? I do believe the lesbian doth protest too much." He stood with one arm crossed over his chest, a hand supporting an elbow, the other hand bracing his chin in a dramatically gay pose. He seemed miles away as he hemmed and hawed, finally saying, "My dear. I appreciate your whole 'I'm straight and don't know what lesbians want' shtick so allow me to interpret. One, lesbians are not like men. They do not need to be taller than you to feel secure. If anything, your subject has a preference for taller ladies. Now I know this seems counterintuitive from the straight male standard but lesbians, especially this one, prefer women to be authentic. Yes, she will be wearing pants, maybe even a suit. That's just her, and yes, she will appreciate the dress with the heels because you look stunning. You wear it better than your own skin. That's what she'll notice and what lesbians want. Now, that is also the last time I will play the cultural interpreter. From now on just ask yourself, 'as a woman, what do I want?'"

* * *

Joanne sent Kara on ahead to collect the West Coast boys from the bar and meet her at the limo. Kara hated it when Jo called them that. Yes, they were account executives for the US West Coast, but her father used that term in a derogatory manner. It was the most offensive he could be about two gay men without risking them quitting. Michael and Mark were good at what they did, leading one of the few truly profitable divisions in the company. Her father might get away with calling her names, but he couldn't abuse the guys without consequence.

In the bar, the guys, enthusiastic and ever cheerful, were insisting they needed a little liquid courage before taking straight-laced Joanne for a walk on the wild side. Kara couldn't argue and found herself laughing at their inane jokes and less concerned with the schedule. Anyway, Joanne said she needed time to fix her stockings. Did women still wear stockings? Did they even make stockings anymore? Maybe she was talking about pantyhose. Even she, a lesbian, knew that women didn't wear pantyhose in ninety-degree weather. Or did they? Whatever. They finished their drinks, finally making their way to the casino entrance and the line of waiting limos. She listened in good humor as the guys debated the etiquette of entering and exiting a limousine. She had just decided she would bypass their pantomime when they spotted Joanne. Michael let out a wolf-whistle which Mark stifled with an elbow to his ribs.

Kara expected to see Jo and her flowery summer dress, and she smiled spotting her making her way to join them. Then she saw someone else. Someone completely unexpected. Mark, standing behind her, leaned in whispering, "I wish I had a sister who could conjure a vision like that."

Kara smiled but colored. What else could she do? As much as she wanted to run and hide, Madeleine, in her little black dress, was a vision. And it wasn't like this was a date. Madeleine must have run into Joanne on her way out. Maybe she was on her way to her own…

Stepping up to the group Madeleine offered Kara a gorgeous smile. To the guys, she said, "I'm Madeleine. Please forgive me but I ran into Joanne, and she convinced me I wouldn't be a fifth wheel. You all don't mind?"

Michael stepped forward, all grins. "Welcome to the party."

"Actually," Kara added, "the guys were just explaining the etiquette of entering and exiting a limousine. They're all for the last in, first out theory. What do you say?"

"Far be it for me to correct the gentlemen but last in, first out works for a team bus but if we were to follow Emily Post, we would exit by social order." This she delivered with a grin.

"Well that puts me at the end of the line," Jo announced.

Mark, always the gentleman, corrected her. "As the only married lady in the group, it puts you squarely at the top of Emily's food chain."

"Really!" Jo chortled in delight.

It didn't take long to reach the first gay bar on the boys' list. Kara had been there before as had the guys. They knew the layout and a few of the staff. Even Madeleine had been there more than once. It was one of the few places in Vegas where a woman could have a drink and not be hit on.

It was always hard to find a place in a gay bar where you could talk. Lucky for them it was too early for the DJ. Instead, a canned dance mix belted from the speakers on the empty dance floor but was somewhat muted elsewhere. Joanne found them a place to sit, and it wasn't long until they had drinks in hand and the conversation flowing. The noise levels forced a certain intimacy in conversation. Joanne, Kara noticed, was snuggled in between Mark and Michael and was laughing uproariously at something they were sharing. She looked the picture of the popular girl surrounded by handsome admirers, a la Scarlett O'Hara.

"Kara, please don't be mad. When I ran into your sister, she filled in a few more details. I'm so sorry."

Kara said, "I know it sounds like I'm a complete asshole over this but that's not my intent." Madeleine, leaned in closer, raptly listening. The movement, the scent of her hair, her close proximity, her lips just inches from her ear drove everything from Kara's brain. Instead of debating or discussing, she asked simply, "Tell me what you would do."

Madeleine danced with everyone, the guys, Jo, and even Kara but it wasn't until the last bar, Sin City's most famous gay dance club, that she turned her attention solely on Kara. At first, she'd convinced herself she was just playing out the scripted scene but had to admit it was easier than imagined. She'd convinced herself she wouldn't like this socializing and dancing part of the evening but talking had come easily for them and close physical contact easier. All evening, they had been forced into each other's personal space to converse. She had found that comforting, even a bit exciting. The touching had come later. Just a touch to get someone's attention, then a nudge to share a private thought. When they began dancing it seemed almost second nature to take her hand, following her on and off the dance floor. Earlier, around the pool and Kara's employees, everything she did was forced; she felt on display. Not by Kara, who had spent most of her time shielding her from "the guys and their bull," as she described her self-imposed duty. The sweet part was realizing that she acted the protector for all the women present. *So the duty comes naturally to her. Interesting.*

Now it felt natural to slip her arms around her. If anything, Kara was the most responsive and polite dance partner she'd ever had. She never overstepped boundaries but the way they moved together…

Yes, they were from two different countries, they were at opposite ends of the spectrum on everything from social standing to income, and the sexuality scale too, yet something was so easy with this woman. Even during Kara's "bouts" as her sister had described them, those moments where the sadness seemed to creep in, Madeleine was starting to understand her situation. In a way, they were both at the same place in life. She was standing at the end of one big story arc that hadn't delivered the happy ending. Her career here in Vegas was over. She had known it for the last few years. What was the buzzword these days? Even Kara used it. Pivot? That's what she had failed to do, pivot and take her dream in a new direction. Now it seemed hopeless and definitely too late. Between Joanne's nervous jabbering and Kara's own more reticent input, she knew they were in the same place. Having grown up with parents uninterested in her dreams and an academic elite who wanted to bed her but not believe in her, she knew how that would have torn her to shreds spiritually if she had stayed in Minneapolis. She couldn't imagine being there all these years and still standing.

Abruptly, Joanne gave her the signal that it was the end of the night. The script called for Madeleine to return to her hotel suite alone. Her excuse was an early breakfast meeting. Not really wanting to follow the script but understanding it was her job, she announced to the group, "I hate to call a perfect evening to a halt, but I have a seven a.m. breakfast meeting."

The guys whined, and even Joanne said she was sorry to see her go. Uncharacteristically, and totally off script, she turned to Kara, "One last dance?"

It was already after two a.m., and the music had slowed drastically. She wanted to leave Kara thinking about her and nothing else. It wasn't part of the script, but for some reason she couldn't leave without having her in her arms one more time. It was a pleasure to dance with this woman. How was it that a woman, this woman, could fit her so perfectly? And the director was right. Like most of the world, she had equated pants-wearing, short-haired lesbians as the dominant partner and expected her to act that way. But Kara didn't act like any man she knew. Yes, she was shorter than her, noticeably so with Madeleine in heels. She had never known a man who didn't complain about it, but Kara seemed to enjoy it, almost delight in it. She even mentioned how lovely her designer shoes were. Yes, they were magnificent and worth more than she could make in a month but who says nice things like that? Certainly none of the guys she dated. Some would comment on how great she looked but always with their eyes on her ass or tits. When Kara complimented her, which was often, it was always delivered eye to eye.

* * *

Kara had kicked off her shoes and socks and was pacing around the darkened suite, drink in hand, something she sometimes did when she needed to think. Now, at the large window overlooking the Bellagio fountain, she was trying to imagine the music the water was currently choreographed to. Lost in her own thoughts, she didn't hear Joanne stomp in from her bedroom.

"Why are you still up?" Joanne looked cute, little kid cute, in pajamas with little bears playing hockey, her travel pillow clutched to her chest.

"Sorry, kiddo. I just couldn't sleep. Want a drink?" Kara offered, holding hers up.

Joanne visibly blanched. "Goodness gracious, no. I've still got a good buzz going. No need to overdo it. Now a hot milk I could do. Too bad we're not at home."

Kara grabbed the phone and ordered two hot milks from room service.

"I can't believe you did that or that they'll do it."

Kara took a seat on the arm of the couch where her sister had curled up. "This is Vegas. I'm sure hot milk at four a.m. will not cause a stir. Hell, it's probably downright pedestrian for these guys."

Jo harrumphed, then asked again, "Why are you up? Really?"

"Stop worrying. I'm always up. Frankly, I can't remember a night I've slept more than a few hours."

"Kara, you can't live like that. Have you seen a doctor?"

"Yeah. She wasn't much help. All she could offer was sleeping pills or antidepressants." At her sisters' big eyes, she admitted, "I'm taking the antidepressants but sleeping pills…"

"Did you tell her about our mom?"

Kara nodded. "She thinks the depression is just a side effect of the work situation. I told her I was leaving. She seemed to think that's a good idea."

"Kara, please…I know it's been hardest on you. Everyone does but can't you see how it's almost over? I mean Dad retires on Saturday. Don't you want to take over?"

She was quiet for a long time. "That's what everyone said last year and the year before. Even if he does retire this time, I don't trust him."

They sat in silence. Even Joanne, Daddy's favorite, was bewildered by her father and his unwillingness to relinquish control. And Kara was tired of being micromanaged.

At a light rap at the door, Kara let the room service waiter carry in the tray with their order. He set it on the coffee table, explaining, "They put your steamed milk in a warming carafe, and I warmed two mugs."

Thanking him, Kara signed the guest check on his electronic tablet, then handed him twenty. He smiled widely, nodding his way out.

Joanne was pouring out their drinks. "Yum! They put vanilla in it. Oh, and nutmeg too."

"I thought we could add some Bailey's, but I think I've already had more than enough."

"At least you worked most of it off on the dance floor. I'm going to have to get Zack to take the kids to soccer all month. I'll need that extra time in the gym just to get back in shape."

"Ugh. Don't be a gym queen. Besides, I saw you dancing. I think the guys had you up most of the night too. So stop pretending you've been a bad girl." She grinned, adding, "Unless this is all about you dancing with men who are not your husband?"

Joanne snorted, pouring herself another helping of warm milk. "And what about you? Spill already. It looked like you were having a great time with Madeleine. I thought that would have made you feel better."

"It did, she did. It was..."

When the long pause began to drag on, Joanne pleaded, "Kara, come on. I know I'm not Dougie, but I'm an adult too. Talk to me, please?"

Kara filled her own cup, stalling for a way to explain. "Madeleine is beautiful, graceful, and so much fun, but on Sunday she'll fly back to her perfect life in Minneapolis, and we'll return to Toronto and our... Look, I know you love the old man, and I respect that. He's always been there for you, he's never let you down. He's great with your kids, and that's perfect. It's just not what Doug and I have endured. I'm not asking you to admit our father is anything but perfect but..."

"I know. It's okay. Zack and I talked a lot about it lately. He sees how Dad is with you and Doug, you especially. I'm sorry, Kara, I should have listened a long time ago."

"I know you like to play peacemaker, but you really need to stop. You've got enough pressure on you without carrying my baggage. Come on, kiddo, it's not exactly in your job description."

"Like much of anything is."

"What?"

"That's a discussion for another day. Right now I want to hear all about dancing with Madeleine. Did you like it?"

"It? You make her sound like a sweater. And just to save you from explaining, yes, I like *her*. She's really nice. Easy to talk with and fun. The truth is, she's exactly the kind of woman I could fall in love with."

That comment stopped her sister in her tracks. "I... Have you ever been in love? I mean, I know you've had girlfriends but what about love?"

"Fall on your knees, hearts and flowers love? Once," she admitted. "It was a hard lesson."

"Lesson? Lesson! Oh my God, Kara. Real love isn't a lesson, it's—"

"Don't go there, Jo," she begged, pouring herself another small cup of warm milk. Jo lifted her feet, and Kara automatically eased herself under them. Jo had been lounging with her feet in her big sister's lap since she was a toddler. It was her comfort tell. Whatever was going on in Joanne's mind, she was in her element. Maybe her father had been right to dead-end Joanne into managing events. She did love to pull strings, loosen buttons, and get everyone to have fun. And she could admit she was having fun. Certainly, meeting someone like Madeleine had changed her own mood. "There was someone. Beautiful, smart, really smart, and she came with a chip on her shoulder. A big, big chip."

"Don't tell me, another gold digger?"

Kara shook her head. "On the contrary. She was exceedingly ambitious but in an unfocused way. Still, she knew she wanted more, a lot more, and I wasn't going to get her there. Maybe I could help in some small way, but she truly believed neither my wealth nor social clout would help her reach her dream. Don't get me wrong. She was brilliant, fun to be around, smart, funny, we could talk for hours and hours, but I always knew she had no plan to stay."

"Did she say that?"

"Sometimes it's what a woman doesn't say that tells you everything you need to know. Like Madeleine, for example. You know she's straight?"

"What!" Joanne sat up in a flash, milk dribbling from her gaping mouth. She sputtered out her questions as she grabbed the linen serviette from the table. "What…how…did she tell you that? No!"

"No. She didn't tell me. She didn't have to."

"Then—"

"Joanne it's okay. So you scoped me a straight girl for a date. I like her, and she seems to enjoy takin' a walk on the wild side."

Jo still looked confused, even worried.

"Hey, give yourself a break. She's a lovely straight lady who's in town at the same time as us and is probably enjoying a date where there's no expectation for it to end in bed."

Brow wrinkled and her travel pillow pressed hard against her chest, Joanne asked with a hint of innocence, "Did you, you know, want…"

Kara gave her sister's feet an affectionate rub to reassure her. "I'm not sure I could. I mean she is beautiful, and I'm attracted to her but…I don't think I can do casual anymore. No, I can't. I'm at a point in my life where, well…if it's not the real thing, why bother. Besides, we live in different cities, in different countries, and that's on top of her being straight. Which isn't an impossibility but it wouldn't be right for me to use her just like all the guys who have trampled her heart."

"You don't know that. Maybe she has huge demands at home and never gets time to explore her…you know."

"Sexuality, really?" Kara grinned at Jo's discomfort.

She shrugged it off. "Still, you like her right? Like her as if, as if she was, you know, interested, you might be too?"

She shook her head. Joanne was like a dog with a bone. Maybe that was why she gravitated to the job of family peacemaker so naturally. "Okay, then yes. If she were a lesbian, and if she was attracted to me, and if she was interested in pursuing something long distance or even just discussing the future, then yes. Yes, I would…you know. Hell yes. At one point last night, we were standing in the crowd at the bar, and she snuggled up behind me. It was…she was just trying to get close enough to talk but holy cow… Yes."

Jo rested her head on the arm of the couch and reached for her sister's hand. In a faraway voice, she uttered, "I think I understand."

CHAPTER SIX

Madeleine, desperate to cure her hangover, ordered poached eggs on dry toast from room service. Thinking about last night, how much fun she'd had and just how comfortable she felt with Kara had been her only thought for hours. Somehow, that woman made her crazy and happy at the same time. Maybe it was all part of the gig, this fantasy girlfriend experience. She had to admit it was fun the way things were playing out. It'd been some time since she'd done the new relationship thing, the getting to know each other. Trying to compare it to her own dating experience, she could admit dating guys was completely different. Being a woman—was that what made the difference? Was love different too?

Thinking about her past experience, she knew she'd been in lust, but not love. Her relationships had usually started at a party or a bar. One thing would lead to another, and they'd be in a relationship. It would just happen, rarely with her initiative. Some guy would get her in the sack and then imagine that made for a relationship, and she was just as much to blame for all the failures. It was always easier to have a boyfriend than not. Now she was going home, no career, no boyfriend, and the only person she could admit to truly connecting with in these past ten years was the subject of a scripted lesbian fantasy.

* * *

Kara stood on the stage of the ballroom, finally set for her presentation. She had just finished the sound check and run through her slides. She was ready to present her pivot argument scheduled for tomorrow afternoon. For the rest of the day, this room would be used for sales lectures and presentations from individual segment leaders.

She folded her analytics notes away for tomorrow. She was finally going to get her chance to prove her father wrong. But it felt like too little, too late. So what if they changed their tactics and pulled their asses out of the fire? So long as the old man was in charge, it was all for nothing. She considered him a caricature of right-wing politicians who believed the lies they were constantly telling. She had been hoping for years that the board would see his rhetoric for what it was, narrow-minded and out of date. He would never change, but lucky for her, she was through with Wexler-Ogelthorpe. She had made it clear to her siblings: this was it. She'd deliver the analytics and her pivot plan with the deep dive results and let them live from here on with the mess her father had made.

She wasn't expecting Madeleine. When Jo escorted her into the closed room past security and the A/V tech, she had to smile. The woman was just as stunning in her power suit as last night's little black dress, but it was the lopsided grin that Kara liked the best.

"I was just telling your sister I'm finished for today, and she dragged me in here promising I wasn't interfering."

"Interfering? Not at all. You've saved me from driving the A/V tech mad with repeated rehearsals."

"I was wondering what your schedule is like for the day. Joanne was just telling me I may be able to save you from, what did you call it, a boring old-boys buffet?"

Kara wanted to groan, but Joanne's description was apt and a little funny. "Actually, what I'm feeling like is a little adventure. These are the last days before they shut it down, so anyone for a ride on the roller coaster up at the Stratosphere?"

"Not in this lifetime!" Madeleine quipped. "But I have a counterproposal you might enjoy. How about a visit to Lake Mead? It won't provide the same adrenaline rush, but I promise to make it fun."

Joanne, without waiting for Kara to even consider the invitation, accepted for her. "She says yes! Don't you, sis? You love lakes and stuff like that." She went on to proclaim Kara free all day but to be back in time, with Madeleine if she was interested, to rejoin the group for a late reception for the account reps. "It's a mandatory thing. Everyone will be there."

Kara wasn't interested in attending anything considered mandatory, but Madeleine for whatever reason took it upon herself to tell Joanne they would be back in time for the reception. "We'll be there, I promise."

Kara just nodded. If Madeleine and her sister Joanne wanted to manage her life, so be it. As long as they weren't ordering her to eat her vegetables, she was happy to let them take charge.

Enjoying the hot Vegas sun, Kara was waiting in front of the hotel when Madeleine pulled up. She had asked for an hour to get changed and pick up a rental car. Kara had been expecting the usual nondescript Ford, not the purring Shelby Cobra. Madeleine offered her cheek for a quick kiss before dropping the transmission into first gear and turning south on the Strip.

"I want you to know this isn't something I usually do. Renting something like this, I mean. It's just that the minute your sister said you had the rest of the day free I couldn't help it. I called one of those fantasy car rental places. I was lucky. The Cobra had come back early." Nearing the last hotel before leaving the Strip, she pulled over, offering to let Kara drive. "For some reason, I can't enjoy the view and drive at the same time." But she wasn't looking to the mountains or the hotels, only into Kara's eyes.

Overwhelmed by the intensity of Madeleine's gaze, she obfuscated. "You're really giving me control of a vintage race car on an open highway? Please tell me you got the extra insurance?"

Madeleine just laughed, and went around to the passenger side. "I even got the 'Forget About It Clause.'" This she delivered with a perfect Jersey accent. "If we get too hammered to drive, we call the eight hundred number, and they send a limo to fetch us and a driver for the car."

Kara gave the accelerator a try, grinning as the engine and RPM gauge jumped to life. "If I get a speeding ticket in Nevada, will they dock points off my license in Ontario?"

"Who cares?" Madeleine laughed. "Just put the thing in gear. I'll navigate, you avoid the tickets, but when we get caught speeding, and we will, I'll pay the fine, you risk the demerit points. Deal?"

Kara was grinning up as storm too as she downshifted into first, "Deal!"

By the time they hit the I-93, it was obvious they couldn't talk in the open roadster with Kara pushing her speed. Still, Madeleine felt comfortable. Absent was any hint of awkward silence. In some ways, it was as if they already understood each other. It was interesting; she couldn't recall that same sensation with any of her past boyfriends. Easing back in her seat, she knew she could relax and even at their high speed, enjoy the ride through the vast, harshly beautiful desert landscape. Wanting to maintain a connection with Kara during the long drive to Temple Bar Marina, she reached over, taking the opportunity to rest her hand on Kara's thigh. She surprised herself when she realized what she'd done but not so much that she wanted to pull her hand back and sever the connection.

When they finally pulled off the highway and parked the car, Kara naturally took her hand as they walked to the restaurant. It felt good, no, natural to hold her hand. If anything, the connection gave her a sense of comfort and a little tingling of excitement, until they reached the door. The sight of patrons and staff reminded her the world was watching, and she dropped Kara's hand.

Madeleine knew immediately she'd made a tactical error. Of course, Kara would be one of those women who paraded around, fearlessly flaunting her gayness in everyone's face. Well, she didn't have to live here when everything was said and done! *And neither do I.* That thought, and her own homophobia, troubled her deeply. Was she one of those people who wanted rights for everyone else but didn't want to share the privileges of those rights? When they took their reserved table, a really sumptuous and private sitting area with a couch and coffee table, her face had clouded as darkly as Kara's. "I'm sorry. I don't know why I did that."

"You were fine last night at the bar, but I noticed you're more reserved in the casino. Hey, no judgment. We all have to find our comfort level. Especially these days."

Madeleine was shocked by the sudden rush of tears over her kindness.

Kara hurried to her side, sitting close to her on the couch, laying a comforting arm around her shoulders and, from somewhere, finding and offering up a pressed and clean white hanky. *A hanky!* Reining in tears she accepted the hanky, carefully touching up her eyes before politely dabbing at her nose.

"Oh brother! You're one of those?"

"One of those? One of those what?" Madeleine challenged before recognizing the playful smirk on Kara's face.

"One of those delicate women who can't blow her nose in public." She challenged, "Go on, give the old schnoz a great big blow, you'll feel better." Kara was making faces. "Come on, I promise I'll let you know if you have any Klingons. Scout's honor!" she said, grinning and offering a three-finger salute.

Madeleine started laughing and of course snorted, adding to her embarrassment and the comedy.

"Come on, Madeleine. You're a big girl, in command of your big world. You have the power in you. You can blow your nose in public with the gusto of an unapologetic toddler! Come on…blow that nose…blow that nose…"

As she chanted on, Madeleine didn't know if she should laugh or cry. Almost mumbling under her breath, "If I was in control of my world I wouldn't be in this mess." She unfolded the hanky, took a big breath, puffing out her cheeks and clearing her sinus cavities for all the world to hear. Still embarrassed, she appreciated Kara's kindness. There was no denying the woman was all smiles and jokes but something subtle had changed. She panicked thinking she had snot on her face and dabbed nervously until Kara stopped her.

"Stop. You're perfect."

"But you're not. What happened, two seconds ago you were… This mess…Kara, I wasn't talking about you. I—my life—my career. I'm at a crossroads, and I'll admit it. I have no idea how to move forward. But I don't want that to ruin our adventure. Forgive me?"

"Forgive you? Madeleine, you don't need to ask permission to be human, to have problems or concerns. We're friends, aren't we?"

That question caught her off guard. She'd never had a boyfriend whom she would categorize as a friend. Was that what lesbian relationships were like? Did they build on friendship or just fall into bed like she usually did?

"Hey, I'm cool. Whatever you need."

Madeleine just wanted to change the subject.

From their private dining room, they enjoyed an unobstructed view of the vast blue of Nevada's huge Lake Mead. The weather was perfect and the restaurant's Nana doors were fully retracted, allowing the light breeze to blow through. "Kara, you are so kind. It's sort of new territory for me." It was interesting to watch the range of emotions that played across the woman's face. They were still sitting close together, and while Kara had moved away somewhat, she hadn't removed the hand resting on her shoulder.

While they waited for the waiter to deliver their drink order, Madeleine for the first time let herself feel what it would really be like to let the world see her as a lesbian, a lesbian in a loving relationship. Drinks having arrived, and while the waiter jabbered about specials, when the dinner service would start, and the afternoon entertainment, she couldn't help but try a little test, leaning into Kara and placing her hand back on a firm thigh.

He did notice that, but instead of faltering or backstepping, he gave them a wide smile. "It's so nice to have family in the house," he said, and was gone.

For a moment she actually imagined he was pleased to be serving someone from his family. Well, that wasn't her, and Kara hadn't... *OMG! I have lots of gay friends. I know what that means. Madeleine...sometimes...*

"Madeleine?" Kara asked gently. She had moved her hand to wrap her arm around her shoulders. It was comforting and didn't make her feel creepy the way many guys did, the way they would drape their arm over her shoulder like it was too heavy to lift but light enough for her to bear. What upset her most was the way they would dangle the hand of that arm right in front of a breast. It was like they were killing three birds at once: the public display that said *she's my property*; dropping the weight of their appendage as a reminder that she was to carry the load of their relationship; and the lecherous part that always made her feel like meat: "I can have this whenever I want." There was also the constant risk of being publicly embarrassed. How many men had enjoyed putting her in her place? And how many had she let pull that crap, always laughing it off while seething inside?

Half of the reason she hadn't wanted this job was her worry it would be just as bad or worse. She had worried Kara would be some big tough dyke with short stubby fingers always busy with an even shorter stubbier cigar. After she had signed the nondisclosure agreement, they had shown her a complete workup on their client including pictures from the company website and her social media accounts. While Kara was nothing like her worst scenario, she would have easily pegged her as a lesbian just by the haircut. She could also admit she would have revised that first impression had she been briefed on her career first. It was illogical to think lesbians couldn't be successful business leaders. "Do you ever have people assume you're straight just because of your work?"

"All the time," Kara answered. "Everyone presupposes the world through their own lens. It's natural especially when we get down to our reptile brain."

"Reptile brain. We don't have a reptile brain."

"Actually we have three brains. The first one we gained millions of years ago, back when we crawled out of the ocean to adapt to life on land. That's our reptile brain. It's back here." She touched a region at the lower back of her head. "Then, about four hundred thousand years ago we gained our primitive middle brain." She tapped the back of her head toward the top. "Finally we got really smart and grew our modern brain up here, the prefrontal cortex. The thing is, we have this amazing supercomputer at our disposal, but most of us fall back on the old reliable primitive brain even though we have a better tool available."

"I had no idea. Did you learn this at school or just take an interest and teach yourself?"

"I have a degree in communications, but I can't say I've ever used it. Being the boss's kid, I was tutored since I was oh, fourteen or so, on the reality of modern advertising. I started reading everything I could find to help me understand why smart people could be so easily persuaded to do stupid things."

"Uh-oh, I'm scared to hear your conclusion."

"Uh-oh is right. We could be here all year if I get into it. What I'd really like is to hear about is you. It wasn't like we got to talk much last night. Although," she smiled, cuddling in just a bit closer, "I must admit I've never danced so much in my life. Thank you for that."

Caught off guard by this woman's constant gratitude, she couldn't hold back the smile or the blush. "You're not like anyone I've ever met."

"How many crazy Canucks do you know?"

"More than you'd think, especially if you're speaking of the hockey types." At Kara's incredulous look, she added, "I'm from Minnesota. We know about Canadians and hockey." She closed her eyes, taking a deep lungful of the soft warm desert breeze. This was nice. No, this was starting to feel like a perfect adventure. It would be so easy to befriend this woman.

"Tell me about your crossroads. I want to listen," Kara promised.

That caught Madeleine. *I want to listen.* Men would say, I want to help, I want to fix it, I want to make it better. They didn't want to listen to her opinions and choices, much less her feelings. It was exactly what had driven her from her family home. Her mother always wanted to do something to help her, fix something, anything to have peace, without regard for the cause of her problem or her actual feelings. Kara didn't want to fix her life. She didn't seem to be interested in telling her what to do. She wanted to listen, *Listen? Who does that?* "You don't want to listen to me whine about my failing career. Besides I'm not ready for advice, no matter how well intended."

Kara just smiled in that gentle way of hers. "I would never assume to advise you on your career or anything really, unless you'd like to run a national or global advertising campaign, then I'm your woman."

Affected by the sincerity and feeling a little naughty, she couldn't stop herself from saying, "You're my woman? Hmm, let's see..."

The waiter chose that exact moment to make an appearance. He set out place settings and delivered a rather large hors d'oeuvre platter with a flourish before dismissing himself.

Madeleine leaned forward to sample the assortment. Sitting back to comment, she turned and met Kara's lips. It wasn't their first kiss. Kara had given her a peck at the car when she picked her up, and they had shared a few teasing kisses late last night on the overheated dance floor. Taken by surprise, she offered a perfunctory kiss in return. She could feel Kara's disappointment as she resumed her place and suddenly pulled her back into her arms and corrected her lame kiss with a fire-breathing attempt, leaving her out of breath and her own legs weak.

"Wow," Kara said quietly. "I did not see that coming."

"Did you...was that..."

"Madeleine? Please forgive me if I'm out of line, but as much as I'm enjoying our time together, I have this idea in my head. I keep thinking you haven't dated a lot of women, maybe none at all?"

Trying to look sentimental or at least mysterious, she toyed with the comment. Her attention focused on topping up their wine classes, she deflected, "So you liked the kiss?"

She knew Kara was watching her. She waited almost breathlessly for her answer, not knowing why it mattered so much. When it didn't come, she knew Kara wanted to see her eyes. Turning, connecting, she listened.

"Yes. I liked it. I'll warn you though, a woman who can kiss like that is dangerous."

Piqued and leaving the "dangerous" comment, for now, Madeleine asked, almost in disbelief, "Not all women can kiss like that?"

Kara gave her a teasing grin. "You tell me. What's your experience?"

Staring at the hors d'oeuvres again and wondering just how to answer the question, her head fell when Kara started to laugh. It wasn't a mean laugh or depreciating in any way, but clearly, she'd blown it.

"You are so busted!" Kara raised her glass. "Here's to Madeleine's walk on the wild side. I can only hope that while you're visiting, you might find you like living with the other team."

Madeleine couldn't control the blush. "You're not offended?"

"Me? Oh, Madeleine. All you need to know about me is that when a beautiful, smart, charming woman plants a kiss on me like that, well, you can stay as long as you like. And," she warned with her brilliant and mischievous grin, "you mustn't worry. I'm a gentlewoman in all respects; content to be your host for this outing or, well, I'm happy to just listen, too."

Face still flushed, she nodded, finally asking, "How did you know?"

"Until now, I didn't for sure."

That got a rise out of Madeleine.

Smiling, Kara moved a little closer, her arm around Madeleine's shoulders again, and said quietly, "It's the little things that tell me you're uncomfortable at times. That's okay. Everyone has their own comfort level." When Madeleine wouldn't look at her, she offered with no hint of disappointment, "Would you like to talk about your career crossroads? I'm a good listener with a great advantage over most others. After Sunday, if you want, you'll never have to see me again."

"If I want?" She needed a moment to gather her thoughts. Finally, she conceded, "You're right, I don't know a lot about women. But most people would look at an…encounter in Vegas as a no-strings-attached fling."

Kara fussed with her wallet, then said, "Here's my card. As you can see it clearly says, 'Not Your Average Bear.'"

Madeleine examined the card. "It says no such thing."

"It doesn't have to. It's been my tagline for a good seventy years."

Rolling her eyes, she offered the card back, "I do believe it's Yogi Bear's tagline. Besides, you are not seventy. I'd be shocked if you're even nearing forty."

"Thirty-four," she answered, pressing the business card back into Madeleine's hand. "You keep that. Think of it as your 'get out of jail free' card. If you ever need me. Call, write, swipe, whatever you like."

"And in return?"

Kara smiled, but her look had saddened. "I'm not a *quid pro quo* kind of gal. Madeleine, you've made what I imagined would be the worst week of my life into a complete delight. I'll always be thankful for your friendship. Much as I enjoy your company and forgetting the fact that you are one hell of a kisser, I would never dare presume more."

"So…I'm a good kisser?"

"You, gorgeous Madeleine, with your Riddler Red hair and your mesmerizing green eyes, are the best kisser I have ever had the pleasure of experiencing. A skill like that could upset the balance of lesbian life on earth."

"And all this time, I assumed it was just men who couldn't kiss worth a damn. Damn!"

That had them both laughing when the waiter reappeared. He explained the afternoon's entertainment was an open mic and the first act was ready to take the stage. The private dining area they occupied could either be closed off from the stage, or the divider panels pulled back so they could enjoy the show. Madeleine astonished Kara and the waiter with a request to take the stage herself. The waiter, delighted, opened the glass divider, and left, promising to add her name to the list.

Soon Kara sat hypnotized, along with the all the staff and patrons, as Madeleine sang, entertaining them in the midday sun with the breathtaking view from the Temple Bar Marina behind her. She was a natural with the crowd, funny and kind; she had everyone eating from the palm of her hand before she even started her first number, an upbeat and playful version of Belinda Carlisle's, "Mad About You." The applause that followed more than demonstrated the room's appreciation and Kara's too. She was only supposed to sing one song, but the place loved her, and the host invited her back up and no one was disappointed. After a few seconds conferring with the three-piece band, she had everyone and Kara too swaying to "It's All In The Game."

Not good with music, after all that's what she paid her composers and her music people for, Kara used an app on her phone to find the song title and the name of the original artist: Tommy Edwards, 1951. She bet it didn't come close to the way Madeleine's rendition set the place in flames. God, the woman could sing. And it wasn't just her voice, it was the presence, the entire package. She commanded the stage like she'd been born there, and everyone was falling for her. When the number finished, she and the guy on the piano played at fighting for his bench and had everyone laughing. Kara could only grin with pride.

The best was her third and last number. Now sitting at the baby grand, Madeleine locked eyes with her, delivering a song she knew from Diana Krall. Her app said "The Look Of Love" was a Burt Bacharach composition and first recorded by Dusty Springfield in 1967. Madeleine's rendition was slower, steamier, and much, much more sensuous.

Kara sat entranced. *Uh-oh. I'm in trouble.*

CHAPTER SEVEN

That evening, Kara stepped off the elevator surprised to see Madeleine already there, ten minutes early. "I'm so sorry you've been waiting. Why didn't you call?"

"I just stepped off the elevator too, and I certainly didn't want you standing here alone while your account reps march past."

They were headed for a ballroom. Everyone would be there, everyone with any clout in the company. Kara hadn't planned on attending. After all, she had already quit, so this sucking up reception held little value for her. That plus her father would be in attendance removed the last ounce of appeal. But once again, Joanne had talked her into it. And she'd convinced Madeleine to join her too. She did wonder why Madeleine would volunteer to accompany her for such a crap duty, but she was thankful. It wasn't that she didn't like the national account reps. Most were a little too driven for her liking, but they brought in the work even though her father's management style and shortsightedness robbed them of potential clients and commissions. It would be interesting to see who was sucking up to the old man this year and who, like her, wanted fresh blood.

As they strolled the long corridor toward the reception room, Madeleine slipped her hand into the crook of her arm. "It won't bother you, will it?" she asked, her face apologetic as her gaze flicked to Kara's arm and her hand.

Stopping, uncaring that she forced other guests to walk around them, Kara took both her hands. This was important, and she wanted to be clear, to be sure Madeleine understood. "You could never do anything to bother me. As far as this crowd goes, there isn't a single person who will be bothered or surprised to see you with me. Well," she joked, "there'll be questions as to how I met someone so amazing. These guys can be a little forward. Still, if someone says anything untoward, you have my permission to slap him upside the head."

"Untoward?" Madeleine laughed, her grin reaching all the way up to her eyes. "I take it you've had offers to help you switch teams?"

"All the time," she said with a groan, and taking Madeleine's hand, led her into the reception, giving that soft hand a reassuring squeeze. They passed through the open double doors to the gathering of media sales professionals. Even though there were several female account executives, it always felt like a sausage party to Kara. What was it with men? It was like a gathering of roosters, all of them cocksure and strutting around crowing over their accomplishments.

A waiter arrived offering flutes of champagne. That was new. Looking around the various chatting groups, she noted that the West Coast boys hadn't arrived yet. That was too bad. She could always count on them to shield her from the old man, not to mention various right wing nutbars among the group.

"There's my girl!"

Kara almost choked on her champagne. The sound of her father's voice always raised her hackles. "Here we go," she warned Madeleine, squeezing her hand again and leading her to a group of men surrounding her father. As usual, he was dressed impeccably in a Saville Row suit. And just like his attitude it was just slightly out of date compared to the trove of men in much more fashionable skinny suits. His shirt too was expensive but off the shelf and compared to the suit, seemed low rent. She might have given him points for the silk tie but knew that since her mother had left him, Joanne had taken on the duty of picking up the shirts and matching the ties for him. In her eyes, he looked like a bespoke wrapper covering a grizzled artifact. With his sallow complexion and hollowed, mean looking eyes, no one would mistake John Wexler for being in his prime.

"Madeleine, may I present my father, John Wexler, and this is his merry band of men. Dad, I would like you to meet my good friend Madeleine Jessepp."

Madeleine smiled graciously, offering her hand to the senior Wexler. "I'm pleased to meet you, John. Kara's told me so much about you and Wexler-Ogelthorpe."

"Funny. She's never mentioned you." It wasn't meant as a question. It was delivered with clear disdain and absolute dismissal.

"Dad!" Kara warned in a deep growl. "Madeleine is my friend. She's a rep with Norstar Conventions out of Minneapolis and is here for pretty much the same reasons we are." There was no joy in her voice. Something about the malicious spark in her father's dark eyes had pushed her right to the edge. She braced herself for his second swing. It would usually be some spittle-laced insult about her suit, her self, or her sex.

"Well then." He gave Madeleine's offered hand a quick, limp shake before raking his eyes over her, head to toe. "Welcome to the party," he said, leering.

Madeleine, the picture of perfect etiquette offered, "I look forward to chatting once Kara's had the opportunity to greet the other guests." She snaked her arm through Kara's and led her toward the next group.

Kara, more than delighted and surprised by Madeleine's bold move, suppressed a smile. She was introducing the account reps from New England to her when she overheard her father boast to his ass-kissing followers, "Now that, gentlemen, is pure Vegas gold! Account rep…huh!" He laughed loudly. "So, what's the going rate these days for a first class piece of Vegas pleasure?" There was no pretending whom the comment referred to when he added, "Maybe they offer a father-daughter deal."

Madeleine ran from the room.

It was the last straw. The dam broke and all the pain and anger Kara had been harboring year after year came pouring out as she moved on him. "You bloody asshole!" A furious, solid right hook followed her words, landing on her father's nose. Bone cracked, blood and snot blew in every direction, her father reeled backward, mouth agape. Hands grabbed her arms, pulling her back while she screamed obscenities. Only the arrival of her brother and the West Coast boys put an end to the bedlam, with them dragging her struggling, enraged body from the room.

Shaking off their physical restraint, still seething, she apologized to them for losing her cool. "Stop! Stop already. Just…just leave me alone," she said, and sprinted for the elevator.

She wanted to go to Madeleine. To explain. Apologize. Mostly she just wanted to make sure she was okay. But she had no idea where Madeleine would be, whether she was staying here at the hotel or somewhere else. It had never occurred to her to ask. She would return to her room and call her. The least she could do was make sure they could have a quiet conversation without the noise of the casino or dipshit men around her. It wasn't until she reached her suite and closed the door behind her that she started to shake from the crash of her adrenaline rush.

"Oh my God! What happened?" Joanne, dressed in a business suit but still in stocking feet, disappeared into one of the bedrooms returning a moment later with a fresh towel. "Your hand! You're bleeding…"

Kara flinched the moment the towel touched her swelling hand. Obviously, she had done some damage not just to her father's face, but to herself as well. "It's not my blood," she said without emotion but feeling as if her own blood were draining away along with the adrenaline.

Holding the towel-wrapped hand as if it were an unexploded bomb, Joanne hissed, "What did you do?"

Eyes closed and leaning against the door, she shook her head, declaring, "I just personally delivered my resignation to our father, and there's no taking this one back."

* * *

Madeleine was pacing the living room of her suite. Still steaming from the insult, she ignored the director as he spoke insistently on his cell phone and did his own pacing. He was taking a report from someone else on what had happened, working with God knows who on updating the script. As far as she was concerned, they could shove the script up their asses. She wasn't a prostitute. And she wasn't playing a prostitute. Even if she were, there was no way in hell she would put up with that crap from anyone.

The director tabbed off his phone and turned to her. "We may need you to reach out to her."

"Are you kidding me? After what—"

"I know you're upset. That makes perfect sense." At her harsh look he added, "Frankly, my dear, if it had happened to me, I might have wilted on the spot, or screamed and cried like a baby. Either way, you handled it magnificently."

Still not ready to hear him, she nodded absently, pacing with her arms wrapped tightly around her chest. "Tell me that was not part of the script?"

"It most certainly was not! But…and this is a big but…now that it's happened, we can make it work for us."

She turned on him. "Are you kidding me? There is no way in hell I'll let that bastard get away with insulting me like that!"

"Oh, my dear you mustn't fret. That's already been taken care of." At his mischievous smile, she froze, wondering what he meant. After all, this was Vegas. "Oh for God's sake!" The director rolled his eyes. "It's nothing like that. But it may make you feel better to know Mr. Wexler, is, at this moment en route to Cedars Sinai with a broken nose. Delivered without mercy at the hand, or should I say fist, of your love interest. That, I would conclude, is an excellent indication that you're close to delivering on the performance expectations of the script. Brava, my girl. Brava!"

A little confused and more than a little shocked, Madeleine stumbled into the nearest chair. "She defended me?"

"Oh, my dear. Your lady didn't just defend you, she called him out, then punched him out. The way I hear it, it took half the men in the room to pull her off and prevent her from killing him on the spot. The man was lucky to escape with just a broken nose. That certainly sounds like the work of a woman who's found her mojo."

"She defended me," she repeated. What a strange experience. The truth was, working in a town like Vegas invited a high level of inappropriate behavior. "What happens in Vegas, stays in Vegas" was the mantra most men took far too seriously, often assuming everything was up for grabs. It wasn't as if she hadn't met or even dated guys she would've called gentlemen, but the work, the industry, and certainly those men with any power, assumed the rules changed simply because they were in Las Vegas. Thinking about it now, she could admit it wasn't the bad behavior of most men or her failing career that were driving her to leave. It was the constant aching comprehension that she was alone without someone with whom to share her aspirations. Picking up her phone she tabbed to Kara's number, wondering if she would pick up or let it go to voice mail.

"Madeleine! I am so, so sorry. Are you all right? That should never have happened. I am so sorry. That bastard was way, way out of line. I hope you know I wouldn't put up with that. Never. You don't deserve that. No one deserves that, you don't deserve that, and I am so, so sorry—"

"Kara. Kara stop! I'm okay," she insisted, pleased by the sound of Kara's deep and unbridled concern.

"Are you?" Kara asked, her tone gentle and apprehensive.

"Is it true? Did you hit him?"

There was silence on the phone, the kind that carried more tension than white noise. "Yes," she finally said. "I know that's reprehensible behavior and I'm embarrassed, but I'm not going to apologize."

"Don't. Yes, I know it's inappropriate, and I can't even begin to imagine how much trouble you're in right now." Finally, she asked, without waiting for the director's cue, "Where are you? Can I come to you?"

"Eleven oh five."

"I'm on my way, honey." It slipped out automatically, and she didn't think twice about it. She was back on her feet and heading for the door before she remembered the director was standing there with his modified script in hand. "I don't care what you say or what that thing says. I'm going to see her. I have to be sure she's all right." She didn't wait for a reply.

Kara's sister was staring at her as she put her phone down.

"People want to talk to you." She held up her own phone. "Zack's downstairs. He says Samantha will handle it if you want her to represent you." Their sister-in-law was the agency's contract lawyer. She also had issues with her father-in-law which explained why she was offering to manage things for Kara and not the other way around.

Kara nodded, agreeing that Samantha was the best choice to settle things down. "Jo, go to the hospital. Check on the old man."

"But what about you?" She nodded at the towel-wrapped hand.

"Just tell me if he's pressing charges."

Joanne shook her head. "The sheriff suggested it, but Zack says he laughed it off." She stood, looking forlorn and confused.

Kara knew this latest fight would be hardest on Joanne. She adored her daddy and respected her big sis. It was the ultimate no-win scenario. "Tell you what. You find me the Tylenol and get your shoes, then get the hell out of here. My date is on the way up. Having my little sis here will cramp my style, even without functioning equipment." She held up the towel- wrapped hand.

"You! You're just as big a pig as he is!" Jo was smiling as she delivered her accusation. She disappeared into her room, returning with a family-sized bottle of pain-reliever and her designer heels. Someone knocked at the door. "Oh my God, what do we do?"

Still a little shaky, Kara moved to the door. "Keep breathing, Joanne. It's probably just Madeleine." She opened the door to Madeleine's concerned look. She was carrying an overfilled bucket of ice.

"I had a feeling you might need this," she said as Kara held open the door. Madeleine took her good hand, pulling her toward the couch and only then seeing Joanne. "Oh thank God you're here. Have you checked her hand?"

"Not yet," Joanne said. "I was so busy worrying about everything, then I saw the blood... Madeleine, can you take care of things here? I need to go to the hospital."

"Don't you worry Jo, I've got this," she promised. "Text me an update when you can."

At the door, Joanne stopped, half in, half out. "Madeleine," she uttered, "I'm sorry about what he said. He's not really a bad guy, he just gets like that when he's around his men. Still, it wasn't right, and I'm really sorry."

"Joanne, I want you to hear me and listen to every word. You are not responsible for your father's actions. You're not responsible for your husband's actions, or even your brother's actions. Or even for this one," she said tipping her head toward Kara. "You are only responsible for yourself. And you have been nothing but a friend to me so don't apologize. Got it?"

Jo nodded, then left, leaving Madeleine and Kara alone. Not quite alone, they still had the elephant in the room and Madeleine knew it would be her job to dismantle it. "Kara, I meant what I said to your sister. You are not responsible for his actions. Still, having said that, I have to admit I'm overwhelmed. I know it's silly. It's like I'm in some B movie from the sixties where the boy stands up to protect the girl's honor..."

"I'm still sorry. He was fucking wrong, and I won't have him or anyone else talk like that to you. Look, Madeleine, I know we're not really a thing. Still, I really like you. Even if it turns out we never see each other again, I would still have done the same thing. It's just, I guess hearing him put you down just brought up everything I hate about him. Maybe it was everything I hate about the world these days."

"Honey, don't be like that. I know the world's a little strained. Okay, that's an understatement, but it doesn't matter. You stood up for me, and I'll be honest, that's just never happened." Taking Kara's good hand, she led her back to the couch and sat her down, perching on the coffee table across from her. She reached for the hand wrapped in the towel, carefully opening it up to inspect its condition. "Oh, honey. This looks bad. Maybe we should go to the hospital too?"

Kara shook her head. "I don't think anything's broken. Even if it is, I'm not going to walk around with those stupid finger splints on. I think your first intuition was right. All I need is a little ice, and the Tylenol," she added, lifting the bottle Joanne had left behind.

Madeleine was up and off to the bar where she collected bottled water and dished out the pills. Then she headed for the bathroom, soaking a washcloth in cold water and grabbing more towels. Back in the living room of the opulent suite, she sat down next to Kara and placing the wounded hand in her lap, began her careful ministrations.

Mostly quiet, Kara sat, deeply concentrating on Madeleine's face, her gestures, and the tiny line at the corner of her mouth which would deepen whenever her brows tightened. What an incredible beauty. How many ad campaigns had Kara run, dissatisfied that she couldn't find someone with the type of appeal that both men and women would react to? The thought made her question whether her ideal woman was based on a form of advertising or her own attraction to Madeleine. "Why did you kiss me?"

Pausing in her work, Madeleine searched her face for an answer or perhaps the cause of the question. Turning her attention back to the wounded hand, she finished cleaning up the blood that had clearly come from someone else since the skin on Kara's knuckles wasn't broken, adding ice and wrapping a fresh towel around it. Finished, she sat back, still protectively holding the towel-wrapped hand. "You're not like anyone I've ever met. Honestly, I don't know why I kissed you. I just, I just wanted to."

It seemed such a strange idea to Kara. Attraction. She'd been attracted to plenty of other women, hadn't she? Yes of course, but had it been like this? No. Never. "Did you like it? Kissing me, I mean?" She watched a slow smile spread over Madeleine's face, followed by her rising color. "I'll take that as a yes."

"What about you? I mean, you're the one with the experience and..."

Kara leaned in, offering the soft renewal of the enticing kiss they had shared in the restaurant, not to mention the mini-make-out session that followed outside in the parked Cobra. Coming up for air and leaning back she finally admitted, "I could kiss you forever."

"You mean that?"

"I realize you don't know me well, at least not yet. The one thing I can guarantee is I will always tell you what I mean. And you can ask me to explain anything you want, any way you like."

Madeleine was quiet for a long time. She still held Kara's hand, but her eyes roamed the suite as if looking for an answer. "Is that your room?" she asked. When Kara nodded, she was on her feet, gently tugging the towel-wrapped hand. "Please tell me you're not in too much pain?"

Caught off guard and a little overwhelmed, Kara's comprehension was slow. As the meaning of the question dawned on her, she watched as Madeleine's smile traveled from her mouth to her eyes. "No pain. Just a little awkward," she confessed.

Unperturbed, Madeleine led her to the bedroom, closing the double doors and locking them. *This isn't called for in the script. So no one can call me a whore!*

Then she stalled, extremely aroused but unsure how to proceed. Kara, still holding her hand, led her silently and sat her on the edge of the bed. Stepping between her thighs, Kara leaned down, and holding Madeleine's face in her hand, she locked eyes with her and said, her tone kind and reassuring, "You can change your mind any time. All I need is your honesty." Then delivered a soft, tentative kiss.

The promise of the passion behind the gentle kiss was more than enough to push any hesitation from her mind. So when Kara pulled away, she felt disappointment. Then understood. She was waiting for a reply. Kara needed her to say she wanted this.

"Kara," she said, "please, you're torturing me."

That made her smile. There was no denying the kindness in her eyes. *Get on the bed and get on me* was all she could think. But Kara stepped back and slowly began to unbutton her shirt. Dumping it unceremoniously on the floor, she followed that with her bra. A moment later her pants. Then she stood. Waiting.

Standing, Madeleine reached for Kara's hands, lifting the unwrapped one to her face. "You're beautiful, Kara Wexler."

Beautiful was not a description that ever applied to Kara. Even with her workout schedule and weekly rowing practice, working sixty hours a week in an office had added pounds around her thighs and hips. No, with her mousy brown hair, and the extra twenty pounds she was carrying, she would not be considered a beautiful woman by any standard. "I'm not beautiful. But this is me, and God knows you are gorgeous and the most amazing woman I have ever met. The truth is, I don't want to disappoint you."

Those words almost made Madeleine cry. When had a lover ever cared about her needs? Moving closer, she wrapped her arms around her. If her words were not enough, she'd show her.

There was something about kissing Kara. Exploring her mouth, and feeling her tongue explore her own was earth-shattering. The feel of the woman in her arms was the end of her composure. Her knees began to buckle. Kara held on, her strong arms lowering her to the bed. Kara unbuttoned her blouse and discarded it along with the pretty lace bralette. Kara was on her knees, kneeling between her legs, still kissing her, still holding her. Kara's good hand traced over her small breasts. She moaned her pleasure through their kiss. Finally, Madeleine said, "There's not much there."

"They're perfect, you're perfect."

Madeleine nodded, unwilling to trust her voice. She unzipped her slacks and allowed Kara to pull them off. For a moment she braced for that inevitable disappointment the first time getting naked with someone. Suitably dressed in heels and makeup, there was no denying her beauty and grace. But in bed, naked, she believed she was just a skinny, awkward, flat-chested girl guaranteed to disappoint. Kara, it seemed, harbored no disappointment. If anything, the hitch in her breathing and a slight tremor in her hand were all signs this would be different...

With an almost feral grin, and one hand still wrapped in the ice filled towel, Kara stepped between her legs again. Lifting her chin, she delivered an almost chaste kiss. "I want you so badly but I don't want to rush. Will you promise me something?"

Madeleine nodded, not trusting her voice.

"Don't do anything to please me. I mean, I know you will. It's not like that. It's just..."

"It's just that I'm straight and straight women have a habit of working hard to please their partners who rarely understand the concept of doing the same." At Kara's nod, she slid back on the bed, then pulled her to join her.

Instead of lying down beside her, Kara moved like a predator, over her and on top of her. She imagined it would feel strange or uneven to have the shorter woman on her. Yet, the immediate feel was overwhelming, soft, encompassing and oh so fitting. The feel of her thigh sliding up between her legs, her lips tracing her neck and working toward her mouth was almost her undoing. "Oh God Kara. How is it you just feel so perfect?"

Kara's head lifted, their eyes connecting. "You fit me." It was said with such simplicity and sincerity. "I want you to feel and do everything you want but first, I want you."

Madeleine wouldn't argue but she did want to run her hands through her hair. Grabbing her face, she promised, "You can have everything but I have to touch you too. I need to connect." That seemed to be the right thing to say, judging by the searing kiss Kara delivered and the roll of her hips that followed. For a moment she considered just drifting away to her happy place and letting her continue as she pleased and at that moment she realized that was how she had always coped with sex. Except, for the first time ever, she didn't want to cope. She wanted to revel with Kara, together.

She let herself feel everything as Kara's mouth migrated to her chest. No one had ever spent so much attention there. The pleasure was unexpected. As Kara teased and laved her nipples, she found her own hips answering in kind. "God!" It just popped out. "I want you inside!" The thought, the words, her verbalized need were all new. The best part was Kara's own verbal cues. She wasn't a talker so much as simply letting every sensation escape as moans of pleasure.

Kara warned her. "I'm not so good with my left hand," and said no more. Madeleine's thigh slithered up Kara's body almost of its own accord. Looking down she could see the glistening sheen Kara had left there. "Are you wet?" It just slipped out. It was as if she had no filter and a part of her knew she didn't need one.

Kara just groaned. She wanted to wrap both legs around Kara but the thought of losing the feel of her thigh against her warmth, her need, was beyond her thinking. Kara's hand was between her legs. Her fingers tracing a painstakingly slow path between wet lips. She didn't aim for her clit or make the mistake of past lovers thinking it was some sort of switch. Instead she teased, tracing around, playing with her touch, her pressure, skirting back and forth between her opening and her every wet inch.

Madeleine broke breathless from her kiss, rocking her hips and begging, "Honey please, please…"

In response, Kara teased gently, "Please? Tell me."

"Please," she half moaned, half begged. "I want you inside, I mean right there, I… I don't know what I want," she gasped, rocking her hips, the need overwhelming. "I feel like I need you everywhere."

The long pleasing moan she heard in return did nothing to ease her crushing desire. Before she could beg again, fingers one by one slid into her while a thumb pushed up along her swollen flesh to rest against her clit, delivering the most pleasure that she had ever experienced there. It wasn't all. Kara's mouth had migrated back to her breast. Then there were her fingers, buried deep inside. Instead of pumping in and out, they were gentler, curling and enticing an all new type of pleasure. Her back arched, her hips bucking for more contact, more Kara. If the sensations of her touch were overwhelming, the orgasm that broke was her complete undoing. "Oh my God. Honey. Baby. Kara!" She couldn't think, couldn't form a coherent thought. Had that ever happened before? She'd had orgasms, hadn't she? If she had, why hadn't they made her brain melt like this? And her body too. It was as if Kara knew some secret about her body, her pleasure, she had never discovered herself. She wanted to talk, ask questions, or maybe just touch her. Yes, she wanted to touch Kara. She wanted to deliver the same pleasure she had received. Could she? Before she could consider how to do that, she felt Kara slipping away. *No!* Please, she wanted to beg. She was used to men rolling over once they were satisfied but she never expected that from…

Kara wasn't leaving her. If anything, it was the opposite. She wanted to argue, tell her it was her time but her brain still hadn't returned her ability to articulate her thoughts. Other than moans and inarticulate words and phrases. "Oh!" She had moved down her body. Lavishing her breasts again before moving lower, much lower. She was between her legs. Her tongue tracing the path her fingers had established. And those talented fingers were back inside her, resuming their slow motion, curling and pressing some spot she never knew existed. "Oh my God, honey! Oh God!"

Kara's tongue had found her clit but instead of latching on or flicking at it the way the few guys who had tried this had, she knew exactly what she was doing. She teased all around, licking at a pressure point along the side she never even knew existed. The effort drove her hips up and it was all she could do not to crush her head between her thighs. Words, sounds, and incoherent noises escaped her mouth and without thinking her own hands latched onto her own breasts, pinching her nipples and copying what Kara had done. It wasn't as if she wasn't experienced in pleasing herself but like her male lovers, she had learned to ignore her breasts. No more. "Fuck!" Her orgasm was so close and so, so not like anything she expected or experienced. "Fuck! Fuck! Fuck, honey! Oh my Godddd!" She was bucking so hard she couldn't believe Kara could hang on. Her towel-wrapped hand had migrated to her belly, her strong arm the only thing keeping them on the bed. Her head swam, all thoughts long gone. It was only them, this thing, Kara. Her orgasm broke, she felt something release, maybe it was everything, as if the entire world had disappeared. She reached down for Kara, desperate to have her in her arms, close, tight, holding her, keeping her from completely falling apart. The involuntary tears that followed were so unexpected and so unlike her. She couldn't understand it and wouldn't try.

Kara was holding her, soothing her. "I'm right here. I won't let go. You're safe, you're perfect, you. Oh Madeleine. Don't hold back. Let it out. I'm right here."

Wiping at her eyes, she imagined she should feel embarrassed but Kara was so kind, so understanding, "You're not..."

She smothered her mouth with a gentle warm kiss before saying, "You are absolutely amazing."

Her warm kisses had migrated to her cheek then her lips seemed to rest there as she continued to hold her, soothe her. Kara gave her time to come down, time for her mind to digest what had just happened. Time. They were each clinging to one another, arms and legs completely intertwined. It had never been like this and something inside her, something that recognized her need, desire, snapped. She carefully rolled Kara on her back. She wanted her like she never wanted anyone before. "I need you," she said, staring deeply in her eyes. The openness and the acceptance she saw there was more than rewarding but it was the need she truly recognized. "And now I'm going to show you how much."

CHAPTER EIGHT

Joanne had started her day at the break of dawn. First breakfasting with her sister-in-law to be sure all the legalities of Kara and their father's disagreement were settled, then racing to see her father who had been forced to spend the night under observation at the hospital. She had been worried about that, but Samantha had assured her it was more about the hospital avoiding malpractice suits and cashing in on the generous Ontario Health Insurance Plan than any worries for his recovery. Now, standing in the center of Madeleine's suite, she was pleased to see it jammed with racks of clothing and a myriad of accoutrements associated with putting on a show. That was comforting. It meant this woman really was what they said she was and hadn't been planning on jumping her sister's bones. The situation was bad enough without adding that mess to the mix. "I'm so sorry. I know he can be an ass, but he doesn't mean anything…"

"Really?" Madeleine's harsh reaction was unmistakable. She'd known plenty of women like Joanne. Little mice who scurried from the heel of their men. "Don't you dare come in here and make excuses."

"Please," Jo begged. "I'm so sorry. Please, please, I'll get him to apologize. I promise."

"You are not his mother. For God's sake, woman, please tell me you don't put up with that kind of crap all the time."

Collapsing in a nearby upholstered chair, Joanne looked like she wanted to explain, but her face said everything. Her father was a misogynist SOB, and there was no changing that. "He's not like that when it's just me. I…I don't know why he's always such an ass with Kara. Sorry. I…are you going to quit?"

"Quit?" For a moment Madeleine had forgotten this was an acting job and not actually her life. This wasn't her problem, and suddenly she could see just how horrible it must be for Kara to try and work with the man. At least she herself had escaped her family's harsh criticism and to be honest, it had never been too bad. "Why does she put up with it?"

Joanne colored.

Instinctively understanding that this was going to be a tough conversation, Madeleine hit the minibar, pouring them each a drink. Taking a seat on the couch, she waited patiently for the woman to answer. Maybe this was off script, but for the amount of money they were paying, she figured she could at least listen.

"I guess my sister has already told you all about it."

"No actually, she hasn't said a thing about your family. She did mention intending to carry through with her resignation. But that wasn't until I told her I was looking for a job with a lot less travel and I was thinking of relocating. She said she was too, explaining she wanted out of the family company. She believes it's the only way to prove she is any good at her job. Now I kind of understand why."

"My father has always treated me like a princess. It's obvious, I'm the youngest—I guess that qualifies me to always be his little girl. Kara's the oldest. I think he was disappointed when she was born, he wanted a son. According to my mom, he was loving but disinterested. Dougie came along a year later, and Mom says he immediately started acting like Dougie was actually the first born and a friggin' genius. As Kara and

Dougie got bigger, it was always a competition. I think Kara got especially supercompetitive just to get my dad's attention. Still, Doug could do no wrong, and Kara was, well, she just made Doug look like a slacker. Which, to be honest, he is."

At Madeleine's incredulous look she defended her opinion. "It's not a secret. Even Dougie will tell you the same thing. See, he's never had to work at anything. Well, he tried in the beginning but he isn't Kara, and the comparisons were hard on him. Dad too, I mean he was hard on Doug too. We did internships every summer. Well, they both did. I just kind of trailed my dad around when I was old enough. I liked to pretend I was his secretary, but Kara worked every department, even custodial. I guess the difference was, she wanted it, and Doug could care less. I'm sure he'd have walked away by now, but Dad still has control of his trust fund."

"Is that how he controls your brother?" At Joanne's embarrassed nod, she asked more pointedly, "What about you, Jo? You don't seem like the kind of woman who would play that game."

"I..." She stalled, and finally, uncomfortably admitted, "I received control of mine when I got married. Actually, Dad was going to give Zack, my husband, control of my trust but the law wouldn't let him. Plus, my grandmother, mother, and even Kara threw up a huge fuss. So he sent me on an investing course. That was good. I mean it gave me some confidence."

"What about your husband? How did his ego take that?"

"He surprised me. He was so relieved. He said he knew the money would come with the marriage but he figured the worst part would be sending the kids off to some snooty private school. Managing his wife's money was downright Edwardian."

Madeleine was contemplative, considering everything Jo had shared.

"If you're wondering, Kara got control of her trust when she was nineteen. Eleven years before Doug was supposed to get his."

"I don't want to snoop into Kara's private life, but I'm intrigued that she managed it with your father involved."

"Does that coffee maker work?"

Confused by the change in subject, Madeleine had to turn and look to where Joanne was pointing. "Ah yes. I think so. Is that what you want, coffee?"

"Oh I'll get it," Jo offered casually, as casually as if the suite were her own home. "Let me make us some decent coffee before we go on." She continued as she moved to the bar area, "I love my sister, but she does this thing where she can see things no one else can. I mean she gets so excited it's hard to understand everything she sees, and forget trying to slow her down. Anyway. When she started university she had this idea she would join the militia, you know, in case she ever wanted to run for office."

"Join a militia? I would think that would be the last thing any politician wanted on their record. I can't even imagine what a liberal lesbian would be doing in an anti-government—"

"No, no, no! It's not like that at home. Umm, what would you call it here?" She hemmed and finally came up with, "Oh yeah, like the National Guard. That's what it is, kinda. Anyway, she was going to join. So I went with her to find out about it." She turned and smiled at Madeleine's raised eyebrows. "Okay, so I was only eight, but she had to babysit me and I was a brat, so I got to go everywhere with her. Anyway, after talking with some guy and watching them march around the armoury…you do have armouries, don't you?"

"Yes, of course. Did she join?"

"No, not that one. Instead, we went to Fort York a week later, and she joined the Communications Reserve. It was right up her alley, but that wasn't the point. When we were wandering around Moss Park Armoury, she spotted this old building for sale just around the back. It looked like it was going to fall down and all the corner bricks were broken. And when I say old, I mean something from Victorian times. Something just waiting for the wrecking ball but she could see what no one else did. We went to the city archives, then a special map room in the original York Town Hall. I didn't even know we had a Town Hall from when the city was named York, or that it was a hundred years older than Old City Hall. Then she took me to Ottawa. That was my first big girl trip. No parents, no nanny, just Kara and me. How do you like your coffee?"

Caught trying to imagine what a young Kara was like, she answered, "I'm good with black."

"You and Kara, I swear… Anyway. We went to Ottawa and she found what she was looking for in the National Archives. Turned out the old building used to be the Queen's Printers for the Dominion. It's carved into a stone lintel above the horse carriage gate. I never noticed it, but she did. So we came home, she took all the old plans and history of the building to my dad. She wanted to buy it and turn it into lofts."

Madeleine accepted the coffee from Joanne. By her old entertainer schedule it was still extremely early, before noon. The smell of the fresh brew was energizing. Joanne was energizing too, sitting with her and gabbing away about her sister and their life. It was nice in a way. She couldn't honestly remember the last time she'd sat and gabbed with a friend. "I can't imagine what your father thought."

"Oh, he was an ass, wouldn't hear of it. Even I can admit that. But Kara was determined. She drew out the plans and costed it out herself. It took most of the summer. I don't know how many trips we made out to Scarborough, to the old Lansing Build-All company so she could talk to the old guys there, ask about materials and comparisons in construction techniques. God, it would bore me, but she let me run around the store. I'd spend all my time out in the garden center picking out flowers and plants, even the patio furniture for my dream home. The difference between Kara and me is, what I dream, she can make. It took me a long time to realize that, but I must say that summer was so much fun. We visited stone yards and glazing manufacturers. We talked with the city engineer and the local heritage council. Well, Kara talked with them all, I just nosed around or played Ms. Pac-Man on my Gameboy. Anyway, at the end of the summer, she presented the whole thing, with costings and income projections, even the sign-offs from the city but…"

"But your father said no."

"Actually, she skipped him and went right to our grandparents, and they said yes, but with your father's approval and oversight. When he said no, my mother stepped in and promised to help.

That just made it worse. Anyway, school started, and a big developer made a play for the building."

"That must have been crushing for her, after all that work."

"You would think so but Kara, well, she's not so good with being told no. And she was mad as heck that they were going to take the place down for a new building so she went to the city engineer and he helped her apply to city council to declare the building a historic landmark. When they did, the developer pulled his offer. I guess that gave her some confidence. She went to our bank and applied for a developer's loan and they gave it to her. It took a year but holy cow, Madeleine. You should see it! The first two floors use the old brick warehouse as the façade, but the engineers designed something, she can explain it, it let them put these huge steel beams in and they basically hold up the four floors added on top.'Course, that's a very long explanation for how she got control of her money."

"Except you didn't explain that part," she reminded her with a smile.

"Uggh! You're right. So, she gets the loan and Dad runs around telling everyone she's fucked up big time and he doesn't think it would be right to bail her out. By the way, he bails Dougie out on a daily basis. Anyway, she doesn't care. She goes to school and runs the building project and a year later she hosts an open house and everyone's standing there while Dad's all like, 'Well, you wasted your money, you'll never get it back. We might be able to lease some of this space from you, but you'll have to accept the loss.' And my favorite, 'Suck it up, kid.' Just then the real estate agent rushes up to Kara and says she's got a bidding war going on from rental applicants and would she mind leasing out the whole building? I remember the silence, my dad speechless. Then my grandmother wraps her arm around Kara. 'Kara, your grandfather and I are very proud of you. We'll get out of your hair now, but please come by for Sunday supper. I think it's time you sign those papers to take control of your trust fund.'"

Madeleine set her coffee cup down, exclaiming, "Your grandmother sounds like an amazing woman."

"They both were, really. Since we lost them, Dad's been a lot harder on Kara. I think he believes she's the reason Dougie hasn't done better for himself."

"From what your sister tells me, he's extremely happy with his circumstances. Does he hold her in contempt too?"

"Dougie? Naw. He likes the social clout that comes from working in a big advertising company, but that's about it. His only thing is Samantha. As long as she continues to work, he'll work, and she's driven. She wants a seat on the Supreme Court, and Doug will happily follow her to Ottawa and be her happy social secretary husband. Until then, he likes playing number two at work. Between you and me, he can't wait till Dad retires or Samantha is offered a Bench seat. All he really wants to do is play house husband and daddy daycare. That's if Sam ever decides to have babies."

"Will he be disappointed when she doesn't? I mean, I don't know the lady, but from our conversation yesterday, I got the impression her career is all that counts."

"Me too, and Doug would handle it. If it makes Sam happy, he's all in."

"That's so unusual," she said, grabbing her empty cup and Joanne's. "Another?"

"Bend my arm, already," Joanne joked. There was such colloquial joviality about her. Not to mention a sweetness. "Do you mind if I ask a question. You know, a personal question?" Jo asked.

Madeleine nodded, wondering where she was going with this.

"You like her? My sister, I mean, and not just because you have to for the job."

It was a question she'd already asked herself many times today. While she was willing to answer it honestly, she was more curious to understand Joanne's motivation. "Why do you ask?"

Joanne appeared caught in the crosshairs. She stood, taking an inordinate amount of time to straighten her summer jacket, her defense against the extreme air-conditioning. "I… it's just you're doing great with Kara. Frankly, I wish you lived in

Toronto. She could use a friend like you. Please don't quit." She made her way toward the door.

"Quit?" Once again, Madeleine had forgotten this was a job. They'd been discussing family, something a sibling and love interest might normally do. Now she had been reminded, ever so subtly, that she was not Kara's love interest, but her paid escort.

She showed Joanne out, assuring her she wouldn't "quit" on them, then collapsed into a chair. "Too bad I don't live in Toronto? Yeah right! How would that work? An envelope on the bedside table? Or maybe she'd offer to put me on the payroll. I can see my green card application now, 'Yes, I've been offered a full-time job as a paid mojo maker.'"

What have I done? I spent the night making love with a woman. A woman! And it was sublime. She was sublime. What have I done?

* * *

According to the conference schedule, today's scheduled pool reception was for families and would be a lot more enjoyable than entertaining account reps. After last night's brawl, Kara wasn't planning on attending but Joanne, as always, talked her into it. Stepping into the elevator, she decided this might work to her advantage. At least she would have a much better idea of who was ready to take her side and just who exactly was coward enough to continue hiding behind her father.

When the elevator opened, Madeleine was standing there. Kara began a stream of apologies for Joanne asking her to do this.

But her apologies were smothered by a long passionate kiss from Madeleine. After coming up for air, she contended, "I wouldn't miss this for the world."

Kara, lost somewhere between her lips and the bathing costume on her lush body, was at a loss for words. Something no ad executive ever wanted to be accused of, yet in Madeleine's presence, it seemed inevitable.

"That's enough, you two!" Joanne interrupted, giving her sister a gentle jostle.

Kara hadn't seen Joanne when she got off the elevator, only Madeleine. Who would, between the oversized sun hat, the designer shades, and the sheer wraparound which did little to hide the bikini underneath? Kara had immediately lost track of the rest of the world. She was starting to consider it hazardous to be in Madeleine's company.

Joanne too was dressed for the pool, explaining to the still-confused Kara. "We're about to make a statement. And don't worry, I brought your bathing suit," she added, lifting the oversized pool bag. "Now let's go kick some pretty boy backsides!"

Grinning at Jo's stance, she fell in line, delighted to find Madeleine in step with her. Even more delighted when Madeleine's hand slipped into hers.

So delighted she stopped in her tracks, almost causing a pileup of guests and patrons making their way through the casino. All floor traffic in the hotel was routed through the casino, the ultimate flow pattern for casino profits, but a traffic jam occurred whenever someone stopped walking. Madeleine tugged her away from the traffic flow to stand between the roulette tables, as Kara said shyly, "I missed you this morning."

"Hey!" Joanne was back and looked madder than hell. "Keep up you two. I ain't walking out into that poop storm alone."

"Poop storm?" Kara questioned.

"You know what I mean. Now come on. Dougie and Samantha are waiting with Zack by the entrance to the pool. We're all going to walk out there together. Show of force!" She turned, checking over her shoulder to be sure they were following this time. "I swear, you two are worse than my kids!"

Madeleine squeezed her hand. "I didn't want to wake you. You looked so peaceful and... And I didn't want to run into Joanne. I have a sneaking suspicion she's an early riser."

Kara chuckled, agreeing. "That girl is an early everything."

CHAPTER NINE

Kara was standing with the audiovisual technician at the back of the room as the account reps filed in. She looked to be in deep conversation with the young man, the kind that intimidated others from interrupting. In reality, they were talking about the latest *Star Wars* offering. She didn't like being distracted before a speaking engagement, especially when presenting a heavy duty technical analysis like this one. So, getting into a heated debate with the kid on the sound board was usually all it took to ensure she was not pestered before the presentation. They would clobber her with questions afterward, but that was to be expected. If anything, the number and caliber of questions were always the best way to gauge the success of her presentation.

When her watch showed the appointed hour, she gave the A/V technician a brotherly shoulder pat, conceding, "I think you're right, but we'll have to see."

"Yeah. The next movie should settle things."

Proceeding to the stage, Kara was now all business. Having her sister and Madeleine in the front row gave her confidence a boost. Not that she had issues in that department. But having Madeleine close by and smiling her support made her feel a little bit cocky. That was good. It was probably her best stance, considering all the rumors flying around after last night's debacle. Her father wasn't present, but he never was for these things. He would always slough it off, explaining he had no time or patience, but would read the report. He never read the report. Not in all these years. And not showing up didn't mean anything except Dougie was absent too.

It took longer than expected to deliver her analysis. It wasn't the presentation that ran long, but the question and answer session that even burned through most of the scheduled dinner break. She wasn't surprised that the first question was how they could turn around the company's sluggish performance. She took her time explaining how they could address each issue they were facing, where to cut their losses, and where to turn their attention to maximize the company name, leverage industry capital, and stage the most radical rebirth the company had seen since the advent of cable television. When she stepped from the stage, everyone was on their feet clapping and cheering, a startling contrast to how these things normally ended. Usually, after she delivered her analysis of the past year, her father would show, taking the stage and discounting the numbers with his alternative facts. She couldn't guess what was going on behind the scenes now, but the response meant her analysis had been heard and taken at face value. The men and women in the room were concerned. More than that, they wanted to see change as well. It was an interesting fact that humans resisted change except when it came to their income. When she demonstrated that their commissions might grow by as much as three to four hundred percent simply by changing their format strategy, she knew they were invested and willing to make change work.

Off the stage and standing with a large group of senior reps and a few enthusiastic juniors, Madeleine and Joanne stood at her side as she answered question after question, taking the time to reassure each and every one. Finally, forced to give up the meeting room for another group, Madeleine suggested the senior reps join her, Kara, and Joanne in the hotel bar for a chat. It was the right thing to do. It had never before occurred to Kara to invite these people to join her socially for a more casual conversation. Somewhere in the back of her mind, she realized she'd avoided doing it, worried it would cause a division between those who would consider it disloyal to abandon John Wexler for the opportunity to listen to his daughter's strategy and creative ideas. In truth, she felt none of the account reps really knew her. They exchanged emails, most of them on a weekly basis, but they'd never socialized. Kara believed in focusing her attention where it would have the most effect. She worked hand-in-hand with the creative teams but rarely dealt directly with the account reps.

Back in Lily's Bar, everyone stood around in a large group listening intently while Kara shared several ideas for new campaigns for existing clients and ideas to bring in future clients. It was what they needed to hear because they asked question after question. Her every response was reassurance that the opportunities she envisioned would work for them. When Dougie joined the group, with Samantha and Joanne's husband in tow, he set her more at ease by offering his support. As much as it was great to hear, she was a little confused. After all, Dougie knew she had no intention of staying with Wexler-Ogelthorpe. Still, as promised, she'd kept that fact from everyone else. It was reassuring and even heartwarming to see how much these guys wanted to change and how much support they were offering. After all these years, it was quite incredible even if it was too late.

She did feel bad for them. There was little hope that her father would carry out the changes she had offered. She knew from experience her father would only consider changes which served him best. He'd long lost the pulse of their consumer base. The only hope going forward would be for Doug to lead the charge. Looking at the group, seeing their expectant faces, listening to their ideas and support, she realized she was doing more than misleading them. For the first time since submitting her resignation, she had to ask herself if she was doing the right thing.

Yes. Working for her father had become impossible. But the thought of stepping back and watching Wexler-Ogelthorpe go down the drain… It wasn't just the years of creative work she'd invested, it was these people, the men and women who brought them clients with one need in mind: help buyers find their products or services. She sat watching and listening while Dougie described one of the new campaigns Kara had created. *It's not just about me. If I go and they don't replace me with someone willing to take on John Wexler, there won't be a Wexler-Ogelthorpe to fight over. What will happen to them? And not just the sales reps. What about our graphic artists, copywriters, team leaders, production assistants, even the kid who does the Tim Horton's run? What I do, what I choose, doesn't affect just me. If I quit, I'm not just quitting the job. I'm quitting them.*

Madeleine gave her arm a little nudge, asking quietly, "You okay?"

"Yeah," she muttered, adding under her breath, "Something just occurred to me. Maybe we can talk about it later? Along with the family?"

Madeleine nodded, delivering that perfectly understanding smile. "Absolutely."

Madeleine suggested the restaurant, sticking to the script even though the reservation was probably for two. All she could hope was that whoever was pulling strings had added the appropriate number. Sure enough, when they reached the restaurant, they bypassed a long line to find a table for six ready and waiting. Madeleine had to smile. It was nice to have clout in Vegas.

Sitting through dinner with the Wexler clan was a learning experience. There was the standard sibling rivalry and jokes involving shared stories from their childhood. But mostly there was love and respect. It was also clear to Madeleine that Douglas Wexler was as much in awe of his big sis as baby sister Joanne. She almost bristled at the realization. It was a lot like hero worship, which she didn't buy. No one was that perfect. Still, there was something about Kara. She didn't want to accept her as the innocent woman portrayed in the script. When she'd first read it, and the background material, she'd decided she wouldn't like this Kara Wexler. After all, who paid for this kind of thing? Not prostitution, although she did have to ask herself what the hell she was doing last night. She had acted on instinct and instinct had led her to Kara's bed.

"Earth to Madeleine. Earth to Madeleine," Joanne repeated, bringing her back to the restaurant. "Where did you go?"

"I'm sorry. I was just thinking about how much I was enjoying myself. I can't remember the last time I joined in with family fun. Thank you for inviting me."

"Well, of course, we'd invite you," Joanne reassured her. "Anyone willing to sit through one of Kara's tech talks…"

Dougie interrupted, "What about tomorrow, Kara. What say you? Ready to take on the old man?"

Kara just groaned, but she didn't say no. He seemed to take it as a good sign. They all did, and Madeleine knew it was up to her to deliver. She worried Kara might be disappointed if there was no repeat of the previous night. Surely no one expected her to sleep with her again, but hell yes she wanted to. It was hard to look her in the eye. For some reason, it felt like Kara always knew what she was thinking. Chancing a quick glance, she colored slightly. Yes. Kara was watching her, and yes, Kara knew exactly what she was thinking, what she was wanting. *Yes, Kara. What say you?*

CHAPTER TEN

Madeleine accepted her offered hand with reluctance. After all, it wasn't as if she were offering to help her step into a small car or perhaps a boat. This was the roller coaster mounted precariously atop the Stratosphere Hotel, and it had taken some sweet coaxing to get her this far. "You can do it. I promise."

Sucking in a deep breath, she slipped into the seat beside Kara and allowed the attendant to lower and lock the safety bar.

Kara gave it a good shake. "See, nice and safe. Besides, we have other rides to try. There is no way I'm letting you miss all that."

"You! I've been avoiding this for years."

"Years?" Kara questioned, then let it slide, obviously deciding Madeleine was referring to all her Vegas business trips which she had alluded to many times, whenever she appeared to be too familiar with her surroundings. "Let me guess. This is the first time you met someone as crazy as me?"

"You are not crazy," she said over the noise of the night. "Just doggedly determined that everyone be as ferocious as you." The cars jerked into movement, Madeleine's hands white-knuckling the safety bar.

Kara placed an arm around her shoulders, her other hand covering Madeleine's. Leaning in as the cars traveled up, up, even higher, she advised, "Try not to anticipate what's coming. Just let the fear do its thing. The minute you stop trying to brace for what scares you, the fear abates, and it all becomes nothing but... ex-per-eeeee-ence!" This last word she delivered as they crested the top. Madeleine screamed so hard, Kara had to shake her head. As the coaster began to climb the next hill, she gave her a warm hug and kept her close. She could feel Madeleine start to relax, not completely but the apprehension was dissipating. "Don't worry about the next turn. It's all about the moment. Just let it happen."

And she did. As they began their downward spiral through the short vortex, she forced her eyes open, sucking in a lungful of the cool desert night air. She had stopped screaming, and the grin stretching across her face said everything.

When they pulled back onto the platform, she practically leaped from the car, her legs still shaking; she reached out to grab Kara's hand. A little too loud but excited beyond control, she said, "You! Oh my God! That was amazing! Come on!" She pulled Kara along with the exiting riders. Once clear of the coaster, she found a break in the crowd. "Kara Wexler! You... you..."

Kara pulled her face down, offering a stunning kiss of appreciation. "You did it! I am so proud and didn't I say you'd have fun?"

"Fun... You wild woman," she said, adding another excited and fiery kiss. "Kara if you care anything about me, you will take me back to the hotel and your bed right this minute!"

Kara grinned but didn't say a word. *My momma didn't raise no fool!* Then took Madeleine's hand and led her back through the Stratosphere and straight to the cab stand. In the short ride back to the hotel, Madeleine was so aroused, she swung herself over to straddle Kara's lap. With her hands holding her face she delivered a kiss so scorching Kara felt she would self-combust. It was overwhelming, her newfound confidence, her unbridled desire, and Kara adored every second. She melted into Madeleine, buoyed by her enthusiasm, craving her excitement and more than willing to let her have her way.

The driver cleared his throat. "Uh, that'll be fourteen bucks."

Kara shoved two twenties into his hand as Madeleine pulled her from the cab and rushed her through the casino. In the elevator they stood side-by-side, still holding hands and grinning as a gaggle of women from the dental hygienists convention giggled and shared stories from their evening playing the slots. A few feet from entering the suite, Kara slowed cautioning, "Shit! Joanne and Zack might be here. Will that be okay?" Madeleine gave her nonverbal approval, delivering another fire-breathing kiss. "Okay!" she said, as her key card opened the lock. She pushed open the door to find the suite all quiet. "Jo and Zack must have gone to that late show after all."

Not caring, Madeleine tugged her along to her room. "Good. That means less time wasted on pleasantries and more time for pleasantries between us!"

"Pleasantries?" she questioned with a grin as she followed her. Madeleine was holding both her hands, walking backward into the bedroom. Kara had just enough time to close the door before she found herself on the bed with Madeleine on top of her. "Oh..."

"I know. I can't believe how perfectly we fit."

Kara didn't have a chance to respond before Madeleine deepened their kiss, her legs scissoring with hers. She managed to get her hands on those perfect small and extremely sensitive breasts and the accompanying moan was all the encouragement she needed. She rolled Madeleine. She took no time with seduction, undressing her, worshiping her every inch. There was no time for any of it. Madeleine wanted her and now. She pulled away just enough to remove her shirt and sports bra.

Madeleine grabbed and unbuckled Kara's belt, hauling down her pants. Yes, Madeleine was in a hurry. She grinned at the she-monster she had unleashed. Last night Madeleine had been shy. Tonight she was a tiger who knew exactly what she wanted and wasn't going to waste time getting it. "Kara if you don't devour me right this minute I think I might die."

Taking her time and teasing each inch of her way, Kara slowly pulled Madeleine's pants down her long legs. "Did I mention you have the most amazing legs?"

"Let me guess," Madeleine gasped, now naked, "you're a leg woman?"

Kara took her time kissing and nipping her way back to her lips before lowering herself down to lay her body against the whole length of her, breast to breast, thigh to thigh. "Actually," she murmured, her lips making a circuitous route to those perfect little breasts, "I'm a brain woman first. But…you Madeleine… are the most beautiful woman I have ever met."

Her hips pulsing, Madeleine pleaded, "Kara honey if you don't touch me soon…"

"I want to be inside you."

"Yes!" she screamed.

Kara slid her fingers inside. It felt so perfect, so natural, and the woman—damn the woman was hot and…so wet. Last night's hesitation was gone; she was alight with passion. Usually content to play the top, Kara was highly aroused herself and struggled to focus on her. Her hips pulsed harder now, the action stirring Kara as much as her touch delivered. As if instinctively understanding or at least wanting to share, but not wanting Kara to sever her connection, she began to mirror her actions. "Honey please, let me touch you too."

Kara, more than willing to comply provided just enough room for her to slide her hand between them. At first, she seemed tentative, as tentative as she'd been last night. Renewing her determination, she rocked, arching and begging, "Come with me, honey."

She was overwhelmed by Madeleine's hunger for her and her own response. No other lover had devoured her like this; nor had there ever been a woman so intoxicating, alluring, and downright perfect in her life much less her arms or her bed. She screamed out her orgasm, taking the moment for all it was worth.

If she were to spend the rest of her life right here, with this woman, she would never miss a thing. As the satin sheen of sweat cooled on them both, she asked, playfully, "How is it you could be so perfect?"

Madeleine raised her head. She was used to hollow tributes from guys happy to say anything to get her in bed but this was unexpected from Kara.

Sensing something wrong, Kara stopped. Her face close to Madeleine, she said softly, "You must hear it a lot. It's no less true for me. Madeleine, you are brilliant, funny, just as smart as Samantha. I'm in awe. Whether you honed your people skill in business or were born with it, you have a gift... What I would give to see what you see. I have to hire a polling firm or order product testing done. You just *get* people. And I...I worship it as a skill. Then," she added, moving to Madeleine's side, their legs intertwined and bellies pressed tight together, "there are your looks. I guess it's something you hear a lot from folks not so interested in your brain?"

Madeleine nodded, finally trusting her voice. "I swear, in this town it's all people see. I don't want to be just a pair of legs and too small tits."

Kara brushed the hair from Madeleine's face. "I see it all the time in my job too. They divide up women's bodies like cuts of meat and then wonder why I reject those ad proposals. Madeleine, to me you are a whole being; mind, body, spirit, and all beautiful, and in case you don't know it, I rarely use that word. Truly, I never thought I'd find myself in the arms of a woman like you. Dougie would accuse you of knowing how to speak Kara, which you Madeleine, with your Bad Ass Red Brass hair, your long, lovely legs, and sweet, perfect breasts, quick wit and amazing insight are beautiful to me."

She was quiet, intent on Kara's face. Finally she said, "So you think my breasts are small?" When Kara started to laugh, she rolled her over and pinned her down. "You are in so much trouble!"

"Oh yeah?" Kara grin was instantly replaced by Madeleine's lips. The passion had returned and fired through her from head to toe. Last night had been about going slow, getting to know one another and pleasing each other. Tonight was about pure, unadorned passion. "I think they're perfect. You're perfect."

"Oh yeah," Madeleine teased, adding her own thoughts. "I love how strong your arms are and how gentle you are with me. God, I want to feel you all over me."

Kara took that as an invitation, rolling on top of her and delivering another fire-breathing kiss. From there it was easy to worship that long lean neck all the way to her shoulders and along her sharp long collarbone. When she took her nipple in her mouth, Madeleine's hips bucked up in excitement. It was pretty clear her past lovers had skipped this part, assuming size somehow influenced response. They couldn't be more wrong, and Kara wasn't going to waste the chance to let her really feel something, really let go.

"Perfect?" Madeleine asked, snuggling down so they could face one another. "I'm anything but perfect."

"You are to me Madeleine, never Maddie. You are to me."

* * *

The stroll through the shopping concourse at Caesar's Palace was nerve-wracking for Madeleine. She worried she might run into someone, either a performer she had worked with or worse, an old boyfriend. She knew Franco was nearby as a lookout for just that reason. She also knew that most people who actually lived or worked in Vegas wouldn't be caught dead here among all the tourists unless, like her, they were showing a visitor around. It wasn't the worry of people seeing them and thinking they were together. She was past that and wandered casually with Kara's hand in hers. It was just the outside chance that someone would recognize her and blow her cover. She was so close to delivering Kara to her board meeting and delivering on her contractual obligations, she was determined not to ruin it all now, although it would be a relief to bring this charade to an end.

All morning she had been telling herself to think of this as a simple performance. She was contracted to play a lesbian. She was a consummate professional and could handle any role and prided herself on her work. As long as she told herself that, she didn't have to think about the woman holding her hand. She didn't have to think about the night they had just shared. She didn't have to think about what it all meant to be with her, to make love with her...

Last night had been like no other. It wasn't that Kara was an outstanding lover; it was herself too, and Kara had said as much. They had made love and talked and made more perfect and passionate love. It was surreal and unlike anything she had experienced. Kara too had said she'd never had the kind of night they'd shared. What did it mean? It was so hard to figure out. How could she feel this way? How could Kara? After her long talk with Joanne yesterday morning, she knew Kara had no idea this was all fictional. *And it's all it can ever be.* Still, she struggled to stay in character and follow the script. She was supposed to take Kara shopping, not the other way around.

They had wandered through the shops, first on the casino level and later in the concourse. They had strolled, looking, talking, and basically kibitzing like any two lovers would. When they reached Cartier's Kara dragged her in, and at first she thought this would be her chance to buy her a gift as scripted. Except Kara was here to pick up her watch. She had dropped off her precious Santos-Cartier for cleaning and wanted to collect it before the board meeting. Apologizing, she explained, "It's my lucky charm. My grandmother gave it to me when I turned eighteen, and I've always felt it gave me luck, or maybe a little of her strength."

"I can't imagine you needing either."

She smiled. "And let's hope it stays that way."

When the petite sales rep returned to the counter, she had Kara's watch in an open box along with several other things. She set out the red boxes, explaining, "We have both the Trinity and the Amulette de Cartier in stock." Opening the red boxes, she placed them in order before beginning her sales pitch which Kara cut off.

"Let us have a quick look, please."

As the sales rep walked away, Madeleine remarked, "I didn't take you for the bracelet type."

"It's not for me. Tell me what you think of these?"

Not sure where this was going, she picked up the sapphire amulette. "This is beautiful, but it wouldn't work for Joanne. If it's for Samantha, it would be perfect."

"Really?" she asked, smiling, "I don't know anything about buying jewelry. Is there something that says, Samantha, yes, Joanne, no?" At the sight of Madeleine's lopsided grin, she pleaded with sincerity, "No really, I need your help. Please?"

Madeleine shook her head. "Let me guess. You've always taken Jo or Samantha when you wanted to pick out a gift for a girlfriend?"

"I've never bought a girl jewelry."

More than a little surprised, she eyed Kara, assuming she was bullshitting her, then she remembered: she doesn't even know this isn't real. In an effort to be helpful she picked up the amulette. It was a thin gold bracelet with a sapphire cut into a circle with a pie shape cutout and a diamond in the center. "Your sister is a classic autumn. Samantha on the other hand is pure spring." At Kara's blank look she explained, "Your sister's skin is like yours. You tan well and look good in darker earthy tones. If you're set on the amulette, order one with a garnet, or if you can afford it, a ruby. It would really suit her. For your sister-in-law, the sapphire would be perfect. I would categorize her a spring or maybe even a winter. The light wash of the blue would stand out perfectly on her light skin."

"What about the other one?" Kara asked indicating the Trinity de Cartier bracelets.

Madeleine sighed. "I have a hard time with it. I mean it looks lovely, but the cordage is just a little too urban chic for me. I mean, I can't see either Sam or Jo wearing it. It just screams soccer mom trying too hard to be cool."

Kara nodded her understanding. "I knew you could translate for me. We do use seasonal colors in our campaigns, but I've never applied it to buying a woman a gift. Tell me, I'm curious, what season am I and what season are you?"

"You I would put more in the summer range. You're much like your sister but more vibrant somehow—I'm not explaining myself very well." This she said in response to Kara's grin.

"I don't have a child-man for a partner and two rambunctious kids at home. And, for some reason, Joanne thinks she has to dress like she's in her sixties. Even my mom failed to loosen her up."

"So you thought you'd get her some jewelry to help?"

"To say my thanks to her and Samantha for their support these last few years. What do you think, the sapphire for Samantha? Now, what about Jo? Can I buy the same bracelet for her?"

"Well, if it's a different stone I think it's okay. Especially since they're both thank-you gifts. Now let me see..." She looked carefully through the other boxes, finally pulling two forward. "With your sister you want less color. I would suggest the onyx with the diamond or the mother-of-pearl. Both are pretty, and the mother-of-pearl with the diamond is very classy looking. I think it will suit her since she craves the mature look."

"Holy smoke, you pegged her perfectly. I told you I knew you were a natural at this people stuff. God, I wish you lived in Toronto. How I long to talk to someone who gets all this. Some days... Okay, tell me which one you would pick for you." At Madeleine's raised eyebrows she smiled. "Come on. Think of it as part of my tutoring. Go on. I've picked what I would get, but I want you to tell me what your choice would be and why."

Madeleine stalled, not sure what to do. She knew if she picked out a bracelet, or anything for that matter, Kara would buy it for her. That wasn't how this was scripted. She was supposed to buy a gift for her. She still wasn't sure how she was going to make that happen—then realized letting Kara do this would give her an opening to do the same. She looked over the assorted bracelets, not finding anything she could press on Kara. The woman liked things simple and usually just wore a watch. Taking Kara's from the box, she stalled for time as she strapped it back on Kara's wrist. "I can't choose. I want to see what you've learned."

"Hmm, let's see." She reached across the boxes, grabbing the one still unopened. "Here it is," she said quietly, holding it out for Madeleine.

She was afraid to touch it, to even look at it, but Kara was right. It was exactly the perfect match and the only one she would have chosen. "Why this one?" she asked, eyeing the green stone she couldn't name and the large center diamond.

Oblivious to the shoppers passing outside and the Cartier clerk standing nearby, Kara wrapped her arms around her waist, tilting her head up for a kiss. Without hesitation, Madeleine leaned in, feeling the desire to embrace and be embraced. The kiss while almost innocent, lingered on her lips. Finally, she sighed out the faintest moan of complete pleasure.

"It matches your eyes. The moment I saw it I knew I wanted to get it for you." She removed the bracelet from the red Cartier box, wrapping it around Madeleine's wrist and affixing the clasp. "It's a perfect fit."

"Kara I can't." The look she received bordered on sheer heartbreak. "I mean… It's just… I wanted to get you something too. Will you let me?"

Kara seemed more than surprised by that, maybe even confused. "You wanted to get me something? Even before this?"

"Yes, of course, honey. Why is that so hard to believe?"

"I… It's just. Well, no one ever wanted to. At least they never have."

"Oh honey." Madeleine pulled her back in for another hug, completely forgetting where they were or what this really was. For a moment all time stood still, and it was just her and Kara. She was like no one she had ever met or even imagined. Patient, kind, generous, and never truly loved. How could any woman not fall head over heels with her? Beckoning to the clerk, she asked to see some other styles.

"Actually, I already know what I want," Kara told her, smiling.

"You do?" That took her by surprise. Maybe she did know what was going on. She'd just said she'd never received jewelry from a woman; now she had expectations? *What the…*

Kara handed the clerk her credit card before explaining, "I saw something the other day. I wasn't sure I should get it but if you really want to get me something, I would really, really love this."

Madeleine nodded, accepting the gift bag with the empty Cartier box inside while Kara signed for her purchase. While they were chatting, she surreptitiously turned over the tag from one of the other bracelets still on the counter. She almost choked to see the simple thin chain bracelet was almost three grand.

"Ready?" Kara asked, reaching for her hand. "We have just enough time to visit the place they sell Indian Motorcycle stuff before I have to head back for my meeting."

They were barely three paces from Cartier's when it hit her. "Wait, you want some*thing* from a motorcycle shop? That's not fair! I just let you buy me a very expensive gift. Now you have to let me get you something special too."

"This *is* special, and it's not cheap. Look." They stopped at the window display outside the custom shop. "See, these are hand-crafted, and they are licensed, so it's not like it's some knockoff."

She pointed out the bracelet she wanted, and Madeleine had to agree it was very handsome, with a pewter pendant on a braided leather wrap. The band was the same color as her very expensive Santos-Cartier which she sported with pride. Madeleine shelled out three hundred bucks, and placed it on her wrist, which was a good idea since it didn't come with a box or even a bag unless you counted plastic.

They were quiet as they walked back to their hotel. The day was perfect, sunny but not as hot as it had been. It was funny how easy it was to be with Kara. She did worry she had somehow blown it by not spending more money on her, but she could also defend her position. She believed she knew Kara now, almost as well as her siblings did. In a way she was sure, even in their short time together, that she understood her better. Maybe it was the connection only a lover could have. *Is that what I am? Her lover?* It felt real in so many ways. Even now, it was so easy just to be with her.

"Uh oh. I think that supercomputer of yours is up to some serious processing. Any little side jobs you want to pass off to me?"

Madeleine laughed. It wasn't funny. The joke was in how Kara asked. Most people who cared to inquire into her deep thoughts would have made some sort of quip about her pretty little brain overheating or some such crap. "I'm going to miss you." It slipped out before she could censor her thoughts.

Kara squeezed her hand. "Me too. How about you join me for a quiet supper, and we can talk, just talk." While Madeleine offered up her most gracious smile, she didn't answer. Kara, no fool, caught on and stopped her just feet from the casino entrance. "Hey. No worries. Whatever you need to tell me I can handle. Just promise me you will tell me."

She moved them out of the entry and behind a pillar into the shade. The kiss she delivered was Oscar-worthy. If only it hadn't worked as well on her as it did Kara. "Honey, you need to get to your meeting and so do I." When that didn't appear to be enough to reassure Kara, she added, "I promise. We can talk after."

Kara sucked in a breath as if she had forgotten to breathe. "Good. Very good." They walked together as far as the elevators.

Madeleine pulled her aside one more time. "Honey, I just want to wish you luck. I know you don't need it. You're amazing and you've got this. Whatever happens, remember I'm so proud of you and I believe in you. I always will."

What she didn't say was "thank you," or "I feel things for you," or "goodbye"—but that's what it was. She kept her emotions in check as she worked to make sure Kara was suitably ready and enthusiastic about taking on her board of directors. She savored their last moments together knowing they would be the last, then sent Kara off as scripted with a smile on her face and her fight restored. She had her groove back. That's what they wanted, right?

Yeah right. So why do I feel like I just betrayed the love of my life?

CHAPTER ELEVEN

It was exactly two p.m. Start time for the annual Wexler-Ogelthorpe meeting of the board of directors. Kara marched through the door alone. She had no backup here. Except for her brother, Doug. He and her father were the only family members on the board. The Wexler-Ogelthorpe board of directors consisted of twelve members, most of the seats holdovers from the old Ogelthorpe Advertising Agency. It was her grandparents who had first earned their place then forged a partnership when wartime propaganda specialist Arthur Ogelthorpe had retired.

Each of the original board members was influential and successful and had earned their place. And like the Wexlers, most of their seats had been passed down to family members. Unlike the Wexlers, few had come up in the advertising business although most held advance business or law degrees except for Liam Brennen and Tom Longboat. They were the bean counters in the group, with Tom currently holding the post of Secretary and Liam the Treasurer. While it was a more diverse group than most boards, many of the names were recognizable as the old guard of Toronto's elite like Shaw, Shuter, Gardener, and Lombard.

Kara nodded her greeting to the ten men and two women of the board, including her father. This certainly wouldn't be her first visit to a board meeting, but this time she was determined: she would win the vote or walk away forever. After days of reflection and soul-searching, not to mention long conversations she'd enjoyed with Madeleine, she knew what she wanted. If Wexler-Ogelthorpe intended to survive, they needed someone fresh to take the firm in a whole new and innovative direction. It didn't have to be her, but it would have to be someone strong, creative, and ready to play hardball, and that was her offer. If the board wasn't interested, so be it. She had a firm plan in her mind. On Monday morning she would either return to the office as president and CEO, or she would empty her desk, return home and begin the initial planning to start her own firm.

Judging by the somber faces quietly taking their seats, Kara knew they had already been briefed on her week's activities including the family fistfight in front of the account executives. Even if no one said a word, her swollen and bruised knuckles, and her father's taped nose and the resulting blackened eyes, were prima facie evidence. Especially with this group. Part of their reluctance to put her forward in the past was a fear of just this sort of thing.

This would be a hard crowd to sell, and for a moment she had to ask if it was worth the effort. She could just take the opportunity to say thanks for the memories, shake a few hands and walk out. That would certainly be a message. But she knew now it wasn't what she wanted. Starting from scratch wouldn't be a problem. She knew exactly who she would hijack from Wexler-Ogelthorpe for her new firm and exactly which old-school hacks she would leave behind. That would be a clean start, but it was still starting over. Taking over meant she would have to find a way to deal with the people in the company, including the deadwood who had long overstayed their welcome.

Surprising her, long standing board member Corine Rusk stood, offering her hand. "It's so lovely to see you, Kara. I can't wait to hear your proposal for the leadership going forward."

It wasn't subtle. Still, Kara smiled. Corine Rusk had been in the advertising business for longer than Kara had been alive. And if she wasn't mistaken, old Corine had just swung her weight behind Kara and done so for the entire board to hear.

That's one vote. Before she could offer her greeting to any of the other board members, her father pounded his hand on the table, calling them to attention like a caveman.

She took a seat in the auxiliary chairs placed along the wall. This was where guests of the board were forced to sit if they weren't members. You didn't get to sit at the big kids' table if you didn't belong. Dougie, from his place at the table across the room, gave her a smile and a subtle wink, wanting her to know he was on her side. He had said so repeatedly, but in these last few days had certainly proven his support. He might not have the backbone to stand up to their father, but he definitely knew what was best for the company, and maybe their family too.

"Let's not waste any time calling this meeting to order," her father demanded. "Before we consider any new business, let's ratify the minutes from the last board meeting."

Kara listened as he rattled on discussing old business and crossing off a long list of items the board was required to attend to, or at least be aware of. Once that was done, the board moved on to new business. The first item on the agenda should have been the vote for CEO. It seemed inappropriate to spend time voting on issues that would die with a change of leadership, at least the change in leadership she was proposing. Still, she didn't officially have a voice in this room. She also knew it was her father's intention to let her sit and stew. He had played this game before. His strategy was to take the board of directors so far down the rabbit hole, any suggestions she made, by the time she took the floor, would seem far-fetched or impossibly off course. He was the type of man who would often say things like, "You can't get there from here." *What a load of horse crap!*

"The next order of business is our prime time network slots—"

"Mr. Chairman, I wish to make a point of order," Victoria Eaton interrupted. Besides Corine Rusk, Victoria was the only other woman on the board and also the youngest. That didn't mean she was without experience. She had grown up watching her grandfather and great uncles piss away the second oldest and largest retail legacy in Canadian history. In its heyday, Eaton's had dwarfed Sears-Roebuck in scope and catalogue sales and its College Street flagship store made Macy's look like a dingy Five and Dime. Even with her long blond hair and her petite figure, she was the embodiment of all the business sense old Timothy possessed. If she had been born the eldest of her grandfather's generation, there was every chance the chain would still exist. Instead she had taken her business savvy and made a practice of turning around legacy companies just like theirs. "I don't believe it's appropriate to set a budget on network advertising much less plunk down a whole load of cash to hold prime time spots if we're planning to move our media efforts in a new direction."

"Well, I… That's not the point. One of the pillars we built this firm on is a clear promise to our clients that we control the advertising spots and have the clout to give them the prime time exposure they deserve. Going forward, we can't afford to risk our reputation—"

"John, I have to cut in too in support of Miss Eaton's point," Corine Rusk interjected. In contrast to Victoria, Corine was in her eighties, and even though she had inherited her seat from her father, Arthur Ogelthorpe, she had earned it too. Coming up in advertising with old Arthur's tutelage, she was considered one of the best minds in the business. "I've been going over the analytics with my own people and Kara's correct, we lost market share on every prime time campaign we mounted in the last four years. Interestingly enough, the results we achieved in some of our small social media campaigns have more than proven the reach and profitability of these new media outlets."

There were a few grunting approvals from the table, but most of the members remained silent and uncomfortably so. Corine continued, "It's not my intention to get on the bandwagon, but I've been in this game longer than most of you have been on this good green earth. Now, we can talk media buying time, and client returns all day long, but we didn't come here to discuss networks and campaigns. We came here to discuss leadership, and frankly, this meeting has already been too long for my liking. I hereby move that the board vote for the next president and CEO of Wexler-Ogelthorpe. Do I have a second?"

Dougie, uncharacteristically brave, cleared his throat and raised his hand. "I second that motion."

With that done, the board members and the guests in the room turned their attention to John Wexler. Caught completely off guard and looking much like the cornered rat Kara considered him to be, he stood leaning heavily on the table as if about to deliver a battle plan— or worse, a warning to each of them, like they were all children caught misbehaving. The corner of his mouth drooped, looking very much like he had just tasted the worst concoction on earth. Spittle was collecting in that drooping corner as if preparing for him to hiss or spit.

Before he could form a retort, Corine pushed ahead. "As per the corporate charter, all nominations for president and CEO must be received as written endorsements and presented to the secretary of the board before today's date. Mr. Secretary, have you received any written endorsements to nominate candidates for the position of president and chief executive officer of Wexler-Ogelthorpe Canada Corporation?"

Tom Longboat sat tall, answering. "I have, Madam." Like Corine, his white hair, tied back in a neat braid hung down the back of his austere grey suit jacket signaled a long life lived, and hinted at the wisdom of his experience. His Mohawk ancestry was unmistakable much like his business acumen. He had earned his seat after years of establishing educational opportunities for indigenous youth and had a reputation as a tough talker and tougher negotiator. "I have received two sealed nominations. If there are no objections, I will proceed to break the seals and read the nominations."

The room was uncomfortably silent as his arthritic old fingers wrestled with the sealed documents. Finally, managing to peel back the first envelope flap and remove the page inside, he read, "Mr. Chairman, Mr. Treasurer, members of the board, and guests, Douglas Wexler has been nominated to take the seat of president and chair of the board. The nomination was received from board trustee Davis Shaw."

"Do we have a second for the nomination?" Corine requested.

When the room remained silent, John Wexler inserted himself, calling out, "I second the nomination."

It looked like Corine would argue. The chair did not usually intervene in motions, but it wasn't against the rules. Instead she remained silent, waiting for Tom like the rest.

It took a long moment for him to peel open the second envelope. "Mr. Chairman, Mr. Treasurer, members of the board, and guests, Kara Wexler has been nominated to take the seat of president and chair of the board. The nomination was received from board member and trustee…Douglas Wexler?"

From his seat, Kara's father hissed at the board, "Is there anyone wanting to second this?"

"I second the nomination," Corine Rusk said without hesitation.

Victoria Eaton inserted herself again. "Point of order Mr. Chair. As Douglas has signaled his endorsement of Kara Wexler with his written nomination, I believe it prudent we ask him if he accepts his own nomination?"

John sputtered again. "Of course he accepts it!"

It was Tom Longboat who kept them on track, asking, "Mr. Wexler. Douglas, I mean. Are you in agreement with your nomination?"

Looking far braver than Kara imagined he was feeling, he stood, answering, "No, Mr. Secretary. I decline the nomination for the position of President and CEO."

"Very well," Longboat answered, wasting no time in making sure they understood who was left standing. "The vote proposed is therefore between the return of John Wexler to the office in question or for Kara Wexler to succeed the current chair."

"Mr. Chairman," Corine said clearly, "As we are well versed in the capabilities of each candidate, I move to skip any debate." When Douglas was quick to second the motion, she pushed ahead before John Wexler caught up. "If there are no objections from the board, let's have the secretary pass out the voting forms."

While John Wexler stood sputtering, the secretary's niece, sitting in the visitor's chair beside Kara, jumped to her feet handing out the forms. She was traveling with her elderly uncle and clearly saw it her duty to take up where the elder man might struggle. It was also a brilliant move on Corine's part. Voting cards and envelopes were passed out so fast, her father had no time to mount his argument. He slumped back in his chair, clearly displeased and glaring at Dougie before focusing his most venomous look at his eldest daughter.

It didn't matter. It took only moments for each board member to scribble a name on the blank form and stuff it in the supplied envelope. Still standing, the perky niece collected them, laying them carefully in a stack in front of her uncle. Kara knew he was a proud man and wouldn't ask for assistance in tallying votes. The board members, in respect for confidentiality, moved away from the table, taking the opportunity to refill coffee cups or continue conversations that had been interrupted by the start of the meeting. It took a grueling ten minutes for the Secretary to open, sort, and record each vote.

He cleared his throat and announced, "Hmm—hmm. If you'll take your seats." They did so in a leisurely, almost sentimental way. "Mr. Chairman, Mr. Treasurer, and members of the board. By majority vote, the board of directors of Wexler-Ogelthorpe has selected a new president and chief executive officer. Kara Wexler."

There was applause all around the table, and a few of the guests jumped up offering handshakes. The secretary's enthusiastic niece gave Kara a big hug, before performing her uncle's duty and leading Kara to the head of the table. John Wexler stood in place, frozen or unwilling to move, shocked by the outcome, perhaps even confused.

No matter how she felt, Kara knew it was now her job to bridge the chasm between them. It was her first duty of the day. She offered her hand, and when he failed to respond, she simply reached over, grabbing the arm and limp hand hanging at his side. "Thank you," she said in a voice that carried throughout the room. "Thank you for your support and leadership in the past and what I hope will be your continued support and insights in the future."

She directed him back to his chair at the head of the table and, standing in deference beside him, she delivered what she intended was the call to action for her pivot plan.

It was another two hours before they were completely finished. That was one of the challenges that came with having a global board of directors. Getting them all together more than once a year was an extreme challenge, and one she intended to rectify by calling a monthly online board meeting to keep them up-to-date with the industry and the ever-changing delivery vehicles for modern media.

Once the board meeting officially adjourned, there were toasts to hear, drinks to share, and well-intended advice she dutifully accepted. The truth was, glorious as the moment was and as much as she cherished it, she so wished Madeleine could be there to share in her elation. Dougie too seemed to be distracted. It took quite some doing to make it to his side, between well-wishers and advice from the old boys who all just wanted to help. "What's up with you?" she asked quietly, slipping up to his side.

"You did it, Kara. You did it! All I want to do is get my phone back and call Samantha, and Joanne and Zack. Hell, I want to call the prime minister! This changes everything. And I'm so proud of you."

As part of the requirement for confidentiality of the annual board meeting, a casino employee had been placed at the door and charged with holding cell phones, cameras, and any other electronic devices other than the little recorder Tom Longboat used as a memory prompt for writing the minutes of the meeting. That meant, while they'd been celebrating and taking libations with the board, their other family members were still in the dark as to the outcome. And as much as both Doug and Kara would've loved to run down to the pool to join her family to give them the good news, etiquette required them to wait until the outgoing chairman of the board, or at least the senior board members, dismissed themselves from the room.

As much as Kara was enjoying the attention, she was itching to tell Madeleine the good news. That was something new. She had never been interested in sharing with lovers or even girlfriends, but Madeleine was different. She was at a crossroads in her life. She had said so several times. Last night while they lay intertwined and clutching each other, it occurred to her: Madeleine was free. Free to leave Minneapolis, but more than that, free to leave the States. It would be so easy for the company to get her landed immigrant status. Kara knew a million people in both Toronto's tourism and entertainment industries. Over the last twenty years, the Big Smoke had become Canada's go to city for television production. More TV shows were filmed in Toronto than Hollywood and New York combined. And there was no shortage of demand for talent or production professionals. Madeleine had said she was tired of booking talent for conventions. She had experience on both sides of the fence but wasn't sure what she wanted to do next. That didn't matter to Kara. She would introduce her to everyone, from talent agents to television producers. Regardless of the direction of her new career, there were loads of opportunities to be had, if she could just convince her that Toronto had more to offer than Minneapolis.

City to city, they were very similar. Same weather, same hockey nuts, and both were cultural enclaves set in the middle of breathtaking woodlands, lakes, and rivers. But Minneapolis, no matter how far north, was still in the United States. Americans were squirrely about becoming ex-pats. Expatriates! What a title for an American to swallow. Kara made a note to herself, *Do not use the term expatriate, or landed immigrant either.* Perhaps she'd borrow the American term, green card, and talk about how many Americans, from top talent to the best producers, directors, and writers were all comfortable working and living in Toronto. Kara shook her head. She was already designing a sales pitch to convince her but what she really needed to do was just have a heart-to-heart.

* * *

Franco slipped into the bench across from Madeleine. This was her favorite diner and they had done all their business here, from their first meeting ten years ago when he initially signed her till today. "Jesus hon, the Jeep looks like it's loaded down for the camping trip of the century!"

"That," she declared, tipping her head to the new Grand Cherokee parked just outside the window, "I will have you know, is everything I own." After a painful pause, she said, "I told her I was headed home."

"Not heading out tonight, are you?" he asked, clearly surprised and checking his watch. "Jesus hon. Why not grab a room for the night and head out fresh and early in the morning? It's almost four!"

"Thanks for your concern, Franco," she said, giving him that look that said, I don't really believe you, but thanks anyway. "The job's over, and my life in Vegas is over too. It's time for me to go."

"That bad, huh? Listen, kiddo. I'm so sorry I pushed you into taking this job," he said, taking a manila envelope from his jacket pocket. "I really thought it would be a breeze. You could walk away with a little finishing bonus. Hell, Maddie, I hate to see you go. You got talent, kid. I'm so sorry we never found the vehicle to truly launch your career. I really wish you would reconsider heading home."

"You know there's nothing for me here."

He nodded. "I've got contacts in LA, good contacts. Why don't you head west instead of east and let me hook you up with some Hollywood types? If nothing else, I know I can get you a ton of extra work. I know you. Once you get your foot in the door, it's all they'd need to see."

She sighed, taking a moment to look around the diner. The parking lot was littered with old beaters, a homeless man was living in the parking spot beside her truck, and another was picking cans from the trash across the street. This wasn't the Vegas Strip. This was the other end of town; the home of broken dreams. "There was a time I would've jumped at an offer like that, but you and I both know LA is just more of the same."

He slid the bonus envelope across the table. "I don't know what you did, but they doubled the bonus."

She smiled at him. "And how much of the bonus have you already taken?"

He tried to look shocked, but broke into a grin, "Dammit Maddie, I'm going to miss you!" His smile petered out, his gaze wandered outside the window too. "You're my greatest talent and my biggest disappointment. You should have been headlining by now. I never realized how much bull went on for you girls. I should have found a way to shield you from that shit. I know that now. I should have done better for you. I'm so God damned sorry, Maddie." His gaze finally wandered back to meet hers. His regret was undeniable, "Ain't twenty-twenty a bitch."

* * *

Kara was leaning against the poolside bar, waiting patiently while somebody found the proper gin to make her a Labrador Tea. She was celebrating, and celebrating called for premium booze. Although champagne might've been a better choice, she was holding off ordering, waiting for Madeleine to pop the cork. She had left a message on Madeleine's cell and hoped she would join them soon. She couldn't remember what Madeleine said she had on her schedule for today. Actually, she couldn't remember them discussing it at all. Hopefully, she wouldn't have some core corporate gig to attend to all evening.

After the board adjourned, Doug had dragged her to the pool where the family elected to wait out the storm, and she had assumed that included Madeleine. Doug had said he wanted to make the announcement to the whole gang and she followed along, just as excited to share the news. The five-day long conference would officially end tonight with a formal dinner and an awards ceremony.

Joining her at the bar, Joanne's husband Zack wrapped his arm around her shoulders. "Hey Kara, how's it feel to be the big boss, finally?"

"Feels about the same as usual, except now I'm going to have to wrangle you badly behaved account guys to get any work done."

He laughed a little too much. Joanne and Samantha, like Zack, had spent the afternoon in the sun drinking bright summer cocktails and splashing in the VIP pool. To say the three were tight would be an understatement. "I see I have some catching up to do. Hopefully, Madeleine will be here soon. I'm holding off ordering the champagne until she shows."

Zack's laugh escalated, culminating in a hard snort. Pulling her in for a sideways brotherly hug, he smacked his head into hers. "No point waiting for something that'll never happen. The game's over. Order the damn champagne!" With that said and a fresh beer in hand, he marched back over to where Joanne, Samantha, and now Doug were sitting.

What the fuck? Kara watched him. He was drunk, not something he normally was. But what the hell, they all had something to celebrate. So what did he mean when he said the game was over? What the hell game was he talking about? It was not like Zack to be a jerk; well not completely. He was a lot like Joanne; they took things literally and had a difficult time looking below the surface.

Samantha, Doug's wife, was different. She was the company's legal counsel, and, by personality, a detail type. Kara waited patiently while the bartender finally found the specialty gin she wanted and she picked up her drink. By then, Doug had found his swimming trunks and joined Zack in the pool for some sort of drunken water polo match. Even Joanne, tipsy herself, got excited and jumped in. Enjoying the mischief, Kara plunked herself down in the chaise lounge next to Samantha.

"Kara, I am so happy for you," she offered genially. On the outside, she appeared more sober than her companions, but Kara knew the woman could drink the saltiest of sailors under the table.

"Sam, how drunk are you?"

Seeming surprised by the question, Samantha took her time to consider a response. "You know, I can't really tell. Definitely not sober enough to drive. And I certainly wouldn't appear in court in this shape. Why do you ask? I thought we were celebrating?"

"We are celebrating. I think?"

That caught Samantha's attention, and she turned her body on the chaise lounge to fully engage her sister-in-law. Dougie had married a brilliant young barrister who had agreed to join their firm long before she'd ever considered Doug's advances. Wexler-Ogelthorpe had been extremely fortunate to snap her up. Doug too had been lucky. Samantha wasn't just brilliant; she had a sexual magnetism that set off all of Kara's bells. Even now, dressed in the basic black one-piece bathing suit with her hair pinned up precariously, Samantha's attractiveness could mess with Kara's hormones and the woman knew it as she smiled her most alluring smile. "Ah, you're looking for counsel." She was still grinning, knowing exactly her effect on Kara. Still, she sat up, taking on a more businesslike posture. "What can I do for my president and CEO?"

"Tell me what the fuck's going on?"

"Whoa!" Samantha leaned back as if slapped but leaned in again, still smiling. The woman loved a good verbal joust. It wasn't just her law training; it was part of her DNA. "Okay, give me some context. If we're going to debate I need to know what we're talking about."

Kara shook her head. "Zack said something weird at the bar. I told him I was waiting for Madeleine before ordering champagne."

A cloud of pain crossed Samantha's face, but she schooled her emotions quickly. Kara wouldn't have noticed a thing had Sam not been half in the bag. Sam prompted, "And?"

"And, he said it was a waste of time to wait for her. To wait for something that will never happen."

Samantha retrieved her drink from the poolside table, taking her time to swirl the ice in the last of whatever concoction. She was stalling, and the delay troubled Kara. What exactly could the woman be stalling over? "Come on Sam, spit it out. I haven't been able to reach Madeleine, and Zack's making cracks about

'I have to accept it's over.' Did she say something to you, or Joanne for that matter?"

Sam shook her head, sighing. After a longing glance at the family members kibitzing in the pool, she said, "Kara, I'm so sorry, but it wasn't supposed to go down like this."

"Go down like what? What the hell are you talking about?"

"You weren't supposed to fall for the girl. She was just supposed to get you out, get you feeling good, maybe get you laid, and get you back in shape to take on the board."

"Get me laid?" It was the only thing she heard, other than the fact that meeting and being introduced to Madeleine had been no accident. "You?" She looked over at the pool. "You guys did this? You got me a girl, for what? So I would have the chutzpah to fight for the job?" On her feet and pacing the pool deck, she was thankful they were in the quiet and uncrowded VIP area. "So all this… all—*she*… It was all bullshit?"

"Hey look, it wasn't my idea. I told the guys I thought it was stupid but once they convinced Joanne, that was it."

"Joanne? Jo agreed?" It was all Kara could do to keep from screaming. "How the hell did they talk Joanne into the idea of hiring a prostitute to get me in the mood?"

"No!" Samantha was on her feet too and trying to corral her. "We didn't hire a prostitute. Honest to God, Kara, that's not what this was supposed to be! This was supposed to be just some fantasy girlfriend thing. She was supposed to be your date for events and take you out and help you have fun. That was it."

"And jumping in my bed, whose idea was that? Let me guess, you had to pay extra. Fuck me! This is so much bullshit!"

"Kara stop, please," she begged, as Joanne and the boys caught up to them. Joanne grabbed one arm while Samantha held the other. Dougie grabbed her shoulders, begging, "Sis, please don't run. Please…come sit back down, and we'll explain everything. Please, Kar, I'm begging you."

Dougie had always been her backup and her sounding board, she'd always listened when he asked, and now, as mad as she was, she would hear what he had to say. Retrieving her gin and tonic, she downed half of it before she could even look at them.

She took a deep breath, closing her eyes. Whatever happened had happened because these dumbasses cared about her and thought it was a good idea. "What the hell did you guys do?"

Joanne planted herself on the same chaise lounge right beside Kara, Doug and Samantha sat side-by-side across from her. Zack was smart enough to stay out of the range of her mouth—or was it her fist? "Sis, we weren't trying to hurt you. Honest," Joanne said.

Doug chimed in, "Honest as the pure driven snow, Kara. We just wanted you to have some fun."

"Fun?" It was all she could do to squeeze out the word without losing her temper or breaking down in tears. She'd fallen for Madeleine; she'd fallen, hook, line, and sinker.

Doug sucked in a ragged breath, but before he could explain more his wife placed a hand on his bare knee. "Let me," she suggested. "Kara, I'm going to give you the condensed version. You deserve to know everything, but I have a feeling listening is going to be a challenge."

Kara just nodded, holding her tears in check; she'd be damned before she'd cry in front of these guys, certainly not Mr. Big Mouth, Zack.

"Back in May when you made it clear this would be your last conference and you'd be leaving no matter what happened with the board, we all sat down to try to figure out if we could continue in the company without you there. The truth is we all knew change would happen this year. The board was dropping hints they were ready for new leadership. They also made it clear to Doug that if you weren't going to take the reins, they would immediately start a search outside the company. No matter what happened, they made it clear that your dad was out. He'd keep his seat on the board but as a junior member with only the clout of his voting shares.

"Kara, when we realized this was finally the year you could step up and take the company reins and pivot us into the twenty-first century, we were so excited. Then you decided you'd had enough. We didn't believe it at first, and Doug couldn't break confidentiality and tell you the board's position. When you handed him your resignation letter, well, we panicked. It was as if the whole of Wexler-Ogelthorpe had come to the end of the road. We could turn right and follow whoever the board dumped on us without question, or we could turn left and do what we've been aching to do and let you lead from the front."

Dougie hunched forward in his seat. "Kara, really, we just wanted our sister back. We knew you could win the board. Especially if you delivered a knockout pivot-and-sprint presentation. We knew the old Kara could do it, but the way you'd been feeling lately, the way you'd been acting, we weren't sure."

"So you thought let's get her a girl and get her laid?" she said acidly. "That was your plan?"

"No, no, oh goodness, no! That's not what was supposed to happen!" Joanne insisted. "Madeleine made that clear. She isn't like that. What I mean is, she decided she wanted to, but she didn't get paid for that."

"And you believed her?"

"Well, you did too!" Joanne whined as her response.

Kara closed her eyes. It was hard to concentrate in the baking sun. Unlike Dougie, she was still in her business clothes, although she had doffed the jacket and thankfully, her shirt was sleeveless. She had intended to return to her room and change back into pool gear. And she had assumed she would need the time to make sure Madeleine could return too. *Madeleine—what the fuck?* Downing the rest of her drink, she bashed the empty plastic tumbler on the side table and stood. "I'm going back to the suite."

Doug begged her, "Kara don't go. Talk to us. Let us tell you everything else."

"Everything else? What the fuck more is there to tell?" Suddenly the color drained from her face. "Let me guess, you paid off the board members to vote me in?"

"Hey," Doug offered, raising both hands. "You won the board all by yourself. All we did was pay some fantasy company to set up a date for you. Just a date! That's all it was supposed to be. They called it the big fantasy girlfriend experience. They even said there would be no expectation of sex. This was an upfront legal escort situation."

"Legal? This is fucking Vegas, asshole," she snarled, walking away. "Even prostitution is legal here!"

CHAPTER TWELVE

Grand Junction, Colorado was the last place Madeleine expected to find herself on a Saturday night. It certainly didn't fit with the week she had just enjoyed. Enjoyed? Yes, she'd enjoyed it more than she imagined possible. She also hadn't imagined spending the last eight hours driving and thinking about Kara, the whole experience. She was tempted to drive all night and into the next day just to reach Minneapolis, but the thought of another fourteen or fifteen hours behind the wheel with nothing on her mind but Kara Wexler was too much.

It was just after eleven p.m. when she checked into the Holiday Inn Express. She tossed her backpack on one of the beds, kicking off her boots and grabbing the remote. She needed a distraction. She needed to find something, anything, to keep her mind occupied. Except some part of her didn't want to be distracted from her thoughts of Kara. She wanted to be mad at her, hate her, but nothing could override the single emotion tumbling around inside her. Maybe it was better to quantify the emotions than trying to stuff them down. Grabbing pillows from the other bed, she stacked them up against the headboard and settled in to watch some TV. Maybe a little mindless sitcom was exactly what she needed to settle down. She knew she was kidding herself as she clicked from channel to channel, watching a minute or two from shows she'd seen or movies she knew. When she stopped at the latest Jack Ryan adventure, she realized she had been gawking at Keira Knightley. She remembered the first time she'd seen this flick. She and a long forgotten boyfriend had caught the midnight show after one of the lame chorus line performances she'd grown to hate.

"It's natural to want more," she remembered Kara telling her as they discussed her career. Of course, the career they were discussing was the fake cover story that Madeleine was an event planner for a convention operator. She couldn't hold back the sigh of regret. The one person she felt she could open up with was the one person who knew diddly-squat about her real life. *What have I done?*

On the screen, Knightley played her role alongside movie partner Chris Pine. The first time she watched this, she'd had focused on Pine and his performance as Jack Ryan. This time, she couldn't take her eyes off the new Cathy Ryan. Had she noticed her classic beauty the first time she watched this? Had she noticed Knightley in the little black dress? The truth was, before Kara, she never spent much time looking at women. She'd always checked out the other women in the chorus line, but that was a competition thing, who's taller, who's better looking, who's the best dancer? Yet, in all that time, had she ever considered women as other sexual beings? Of course she'd thought about lesbian relationships. What woman hadn't? Like all straight women she thought lesbians had it made. After all, they didn't have to worry about birth control, not even HIV unless you were a drug user or crossing party lines. But that really didn't answer the question; did lesbians have better relationships? She always assumed the answer was yes, only because she didn't consider it an option for her. After all, she was straight. *I was straight. Was I? What am I now?*

Madeleine clicked off the TV and tossed the remote on the other bed. Kara had turned her life upside down. No, that was wrong. She'd opened up her life. It was strange to think that was true. The worst part was her lack of options. The last ten years had been about her career, not making friends. That didn't leave a lot of people to lean on or ask for advice. There was Franco. He was always there for her, but as her manager. His advice was always about what was best for her career, and ultimately for him.

Restless, she got up and grabbed the knapsack, tossing the contents on the other bed. She grabbed her toiletry bag, spotting the cell phone underneath. It would be so easy to pick up that phone. So easy just to call her. *What would I say? Holy hell, how can I tell her the truth?* Maybe the truth wasn't necessary. Yes, she would have to apologize for not being there after the board meeting like she'd promised but she could make something up. Kara had said more than a dozen times how her work demands often wreaked havoc on her personal life. That's what she'd do. She'd just pick up the phone and give her a call. "Sorry I had to rush home for an emergency. A family emergency," she practiced aloud. That's something Kara would understand. Picking up the phone, she wasn't surprised to see several text messages. She clicked on the thread from Kara, her apprehension quickly becoming excitement. She read through the first couple of messages quickly. They were all as expected:

Board meeting wrapped, and I have great news.

Dougie, Joanne, and the gang, all still at the pool. Would you like to join us?

Not sure if you're out of your meeting yet? Missing you. I have great news!

The date stamp on the last message read 5:18 p.m. More than six hours ago. Kara hadn't sent her a text in all that time, not even to question when or where they would meet for dinner. They had talked about meeting for dinner, but she had obfuscated, casually insisting they work out the details after the big board meeting. That had been their discussion early that morning, lying in bed together, intertwined and feeling more connected than Madeleine could admit to ever experiencing. It had been so easy lying there in her arms, feeling the warmth of her body, her smooth skin, and comforting embrace. It didn't feel wrong or strange or anything other than perfect. No, it wasn't perfect; it was sublime. Could it be that easy? Really? Was that how relationships, real loving, long-term relationships, felt? She had no idea. It wasn't like she hadn't had relationships before. She'd had plenty, but the connection, the intimacy, the desire, not so much.

She was pacing, phone in hand, trying to decide if a text message or a phone call would be more appropriate when she stopped dead. Reading through her messages again, she realized they'd all come in within twenty minutes of each other. And then nothing. Not one word in over six hours. Did that mean Kara knew? Did they tell her? *Did she know all along?* She tried to imagine how she would've taken the news. *I would've flipped!* If she learned nothing else, she knew Kara wasn't the type to flip out about just anything. No, she was a plotter, a thinker. Not in a bad way. Maybe describing her as a planner and strategist might make more sense, except that wasn't true either. Kara was a doer. She made things happen. *She made things happen to me.* And that was the truth of it. Her job had been to get Kara back on track. But she was already on an amazing track of her own. Yes, judging by her text messages, she'd won the board vote, but Madeleine had come to understand she had other plans too. She had taken herself to a place in her life where she had choices. She'd given Madeleine choices too, choices she'd never expected. And that wasn't just about being with a woman. They'd talked for hours about her skills, desires, dreams. Even under the guise of her fake job she'd managed to talk about her interest in theatre and the performing arts.

Her interest in production and staging had excited Kara. It was as if they'd found a mutual subject to explore in detail. In between lovemaking. And there it was again. Somehow, she had crossed some invisible line. One moment she was a straight woman, never questioning her sexuality. The next moment she was in the arms of this woman. A woman who had made her feel beautiful and sexy and a million things more. Most of the men in her life had had solutions, changes they wanted her to make. Even Franco had suggested a boob job. He'd even offered to pay for it. Kara though, she just wanted her to be herself. Alone, just the two of them, felt like the most natural thing. To hold her, *love* her, and that was what she had stumbled over, what had driven her into her car and out of Las Vegas. *Impossible.* She shook her head, dumping her phone and heading to the small bathroom. *I can't be in love with her. I hardly know her. She doesn't know me, and after this, she'll never want to.*

* * *

It was almost midnight when Kara finally slid into her airline seat. She had managed to get a ticket on the red-eye to Toronto. This was not what she had planned for the evening, not by a long shot. How the hell could this happen? She'd thought she was smarter than this. She'd listened to Joanne's excuses, then Dougie's stupid ideas and the million apologies from their partners, but in the end, she still grabbed her bags and went to the airport. Of course, she kicked herself when she got here, realizing she'd have to wait five hours for the next flight. Still, it was better than listening to their crap. Yes, she'd been out of sorts. Yes, she hadn't been herself lately. Yes, it may have seemed like she'd given up. "Yes—yes—yes," she grumbled under her breath.

"Uh-oh. It looks like someone's not happy to be going home," the flight attendant offered as she stopped next to Kara's seat.

"No, yes, no. I mean… I have no idea what I mean. Any chance I can get a drink?"

"We're not supposed to serve until we're in the air," she said, taking a surreptitious look around the business class cabin. As it was ahead of the aircraft loading door, they didn't have a long line of economy class passengers tramping past them. "Let me grab you a short one to tide you over," she said with a spectacular grin and a conspiratorial wink, adding, "Let's turn that frown upside down."

Kara groaned. It looked like the flight attendant had a better time here in Vegas than she did. Except she had an amazing time. A phenomenal time. *I can't believe it. I can't believe none of it was real.* She was a little more cordial when the flight attendant returned, accepting her drink with gratitude. It wasn't like she needed to drink. She'd spent the last five hours sitting in the VIP lounge drinking premium booze while she tried to pretend she was working her way through the pile of emails that had accumulated over the last five days. Now, sitting in the aircraft, she pulled out her phone again but, in her heart, she knew there would be no reply to her earlier text, and without it, she had no interest in work or emails. Of the few hundred she'd already sorted through, she couldn't recall a single word. Uninterested, she'd tabbed to the only thing that did matter, her IMs, and text messages. Nothing. No subterfuge, no regrets, not even an apology. There was a slew of texts from Joanne and a few from the others. Even her father had begrudged a few congratulatory words. But nothing from Madeleine. It looked like the game was truly and completely over. Samantha had explained, painfully explained, that the fantasy was scripted to end the moment she entered the board meeting. Even after hearing that detail, really hearing it and thinking about the reality of what that meant, she couldn't believe Madeleine had played her. Maybe at the first meeting, out at the bar with Joanne and the guys. That felt a bit like a bar hookup but it hadn't ended in bed. In truth, they had barely kissed. It was the next day, on their adventure to Lake Mead that things began to change. *I thought they were changing for you too.*

"Let me grab your glass," said the flight attendant, back at her side. She was making her safety-round of the business class cabin pre-takeoff. Kara handed it over without comment, feeling the aircraft start to push back. She turned her phone to airplane mode, then tucked it away. The last thing she wanted was to spend the next four and a half hours fixating on a call or text that she knew wouldn't come.

A few rows up, the flight attendant was joking and fussing with another passenger. It was easy to watch the woman at work. She was attractive—practically the first qualification for the job—but not like Madeleine. Madeleine was one of those rare women who could look amazing in anything. From that astounding black cocktail dress, the business suit, to jeans and boots. And she had talent. She remembered that visit to Lake Mead. To Kara, it had felt excruciatingly stunning to watch her, much like the woman herself. *Maybe that's all this was… an excruciatingly stunning crush. A made-up love for a made-up relationship.* Except it had never felt made up. *How did I miss that?*

She prided herself on knowing people, or at least their motivations. After all, that was her job, and she had a shelf full of Clio Awards to prove it. Or, at least until now she thought she knew people. She'd missed all the signs with Joanne, the extra chattiness, the overt willingness to facilitate her and Madeleine spending time together. And then there was Dougie. He'd backed her up after the altercation with her father. He seemed so happy to see her with Madeleine, even giddy. She had called him on it, but he had promised it was just his joy to see her back to her old self. Was she? Certainly, everyone thought so. And to give credit where credit was due, her attitude and renewed self-worth were due to Madeleine.

So why am I so upset? The woman believed in me, and it's what I needed to get back on track.

That sounded more than fair. As a matter of fact, under those circumstances, it was difficult to be angry with her family. They were just trying to do exactly what had been done. She was back in fighting form. She was in charge, and she had a plan.

Except part of me still wants to believe there's a place in that plan for Madeleine.

CHAPTER THIRTEEN

Kara checked her makeup in the bathroom mirror. It wasn't something she usually bothered with, but after a weekend of emotional turmoil she needed something to cover her blotchy skin. Any minute now, Joanne would barge in to tell her the staff was ready. It wasn't quite eight a.m., and she had called all hands on deck, everyone, full-time, contract, and even the interns. It was about time everyone knew their mission and got to work turning their company around. She sighed, judging herself harshly under the stark fluorescent lighting. "You wanted this," she reminded her reflection in the bathroom mirror. "Time to pay the piper."

Wexler-Ogelthorpe was the primary tenant in the old Simpson-Sears Building. The largest of the meeting rooms was designed to impress, featuring natural light from an array of huge skylights. It occupied the center of the top floor, glassed in on all sides, designed to look like an atrium, but all it ever awakened in her was regret over how much floor space was wasted, going unused most days. Walking into the room, she expected the polite applause she received. It was the cheers and hoots and hollers from some of the younger staffers that caught her by surprise. While her ego did the little "they like me, they like me," dance, she couldn't hide her smile and let the reception bolster her mood. Maybe this would be worth it after all.

She listened passively while her new young vice president of sales and marketing delivered a bang-up introduction of their new CEO. Taking her place at the head of the room, she grinned, offering, "Like the man said, there's a new sheriff in town. And judging by the hoots and hollers of our lesser genteel folks, you're all ready?" She looked around the room carefully, making a mental inventory of those who seemed enthusiastic in their applause and those who were just being polite. She might as well know from the get-go who would be on her side and who she would need to convert. Much easier now than in her previous role of underdog. "Well then, it sounds like everybody is ready to rock 'n' roll. If there are no objections, it's time to divide and conquer because we have a lot of work to do. First things first, for those of you who weren't in Las Vegas and were not privy to my pivot or scale presentation, your first job is to stay after this meeting and watch the video. Next thing you need to know is I'll be dividing the working groups. All legacy programs will stay with their primaries. All the accounts that fit within the pivot program will immediately be handed over to the new working group."

"Oooh yeah!" one of the graphic artists hollered. "Do we finally get to come up with fun names for a working group?"

"Just for that," she teased, "we'll call the new working group Underdogs." She listened and watched as they groaned, commented, and offered the odd arm punch or backslap. It didn't matter what she called the new group. Judging by the reaction all around her, she could call it Shit-on-a-Stick and they'd still want in. "Okay. Settle down. Before I get into details, we're going to split up for an hour. Those of you who need to watch the video will stay here. I need the department heads in my office and as for you account reps...I think you guys have some announcements to make to our clients. We'll meet back here at," she paused to check her watch, "nine-thirty. Okay, get out there and be safe," she said as a parting joke.

Returning to her office, she wasn't surprised to see Joanne was first to join her and immediately ask, "Is there something wrong?"

"Not at all," Kara promised her. "I just want to get a jump on space usage. I want to get this place humming, and I can't do it the way things are organized right now."

"Kara, I know you're in a rush, but can you just hold off on moving into Dad's office, at least for a week or two?"

Slipping behind her old desk, she opened a file folder, laying out several lists and what looked like office layouts. "Relax, I'm not moving into his office. At least not this year." At her sister's incredulous look, she explained, "I know his ego is tied to this place, but it's more than that. People here are tied to him too. I won't take that away from him or the staff."

A little shocked, Joanne slid into her chair at the small meeting table, holding her comments as the remaining senior managers crowded in. Kara knew it wasn't the end of the subject. Joanne would thank her and assume it was some sort of act of respect. Hardly. But it was calculated to ease the transition. People really did like the old man, and he lent an air of continuity. Even if he had been going in the wrong direction all these years, they had stayed loyal, and that was increasingly unheard of in this day and age.

She pushed the thoughts of loyalty from her mind, not wanting them to sour her mood any more than they had all weekend long. It was easy for her logical brain to almost justify the actions her siblings had taken. Almost. She couldn't accuse them of any sort of disloyalty. It would've been easier, almost nice, to consider them against her and plotting, but she knew better. She knew Dougie and Joanne were desperate to find a way to reignite her interest in the company and in taking another run at the top job, but even they wouldn't have thought of this on their own.

She wanted to blame her brother-in-law Zack. This was exactly the kind of shit stunt he would pull without a second thought. He must've been absolutely sure this was the answer when he convinced Dougie and Joanne to buy in. What she couldn't believe was that Doug's wife, Samantha, stable and downright judicious, would have agreed. Of course, listening to Sam and her genuine pleading and desperation to explain, she understood that events had gone down much differently than they expected. If only they had gone down differently for Madeleine. Had it been exactly as she expected? She'd certainly delivered on the promised outcome and to be honest, Kara could not identify a single promise she had made to her that she hadn't kept. Well, all except the dinner invitation and she had racked her brain all weekend trying to decide if Madeleine had misled her or if she had just assumed. Everything about their time together was starting to feel like one big assumption. *Or was it just a fantasy, one I assumed would live past the Las Vegas use-by date?*

The meeting hadn't taken as long as the time allotted. It seemed the entire staff was already on board with all the changes she intended to make. That was reassuring and almost frightening. With the senior managers sorted, and Joanne still on her heels, she returned to the large glassed-in central meeting room, announcing to the junior account executives and the interns gathered, "This afternoon, each account team will select the junior reps and the interns who will work with them. Half of you will remain here in this room. This is your office now, and those of you selected to remain here will be part of the new social media onboarding team."

It required another hour to explain what that meant and who and what would be involved. She didn't mind. Talking to these kids was refreshing and reminded her how much she loved this job. Communicating with people, really getting to express ideas and share insights made this job worth doing. That, and she was damn good at it. Still, educating the kids today was more about keeping her mind on business and away from the emotional roller coaster she had ridden all weekend.

"It went really well," Joanne said unnecessarily.

"What were you expecting, a mutiny?"

Embarrassed, Joanne sputtered. "You know what I mean."

"No Jo, I don't. And frankly, I'm way too tired to try and figure it out." Kara watched as Joanne's look slipped back and forth between contrite and concerned. "No. Don't go there. Not now."

"But you know I'm here if you need to talk?"

"Jo! Stop already. I don't want to talk about it, I don't want to think about it, nothing, nada, got it?"

She nodded, although it was clear she still had something to say and was having a really hard time reining herself in. Finally, she agreed, asking Kara, "Okay. What's next?"

* * *

Madeleine pulled her Jeep into the driveway and parked beside her dad's work truck. Her mom, she knew, would have already left for work. She had planned her arrival, driving all night just to be sure she arrived in plenty of time to talk things through with her dad before her mom got home, took charge, and told her what to do. She hated that about her mother. Hated the fact the woman couldn't and wouldn't just listen, like some Civil War general who would only allow subordinates a few minutes to deliver their reports before imperiously delivering a solution and the orders to make it so.

It took a long minute for Madeleine to drag herself out of the driver's seat. Her father was already standing on the front porch, curiosity on his face, and a coffee mug in his hand. There was no mistaking the Scandinavian heritage in the man. Tall, a good six inches taller than Madeleine, he looked more like a Viking dressed as a workman with his wiry red hair, long limbs and meaty hands. He hoisted his mug in greeting. That was just like him. Good God, the man never changed, and for once she was thankful for that. "Hey, Dad."

"Hey, kiddo. Them's some fancy wheels. Never realized you could make that kind of dough kicking your cancans," he teased. "At least your grandparents'll be relieved you didn't come home drivin' some fancy Bavarian schatzie wagon."

"Like that would ever happen," she scoffed as she wrapped her arms around his core, giving him a big warm bear hug. "I'm still your all-American girl."

"Oh, I do know. Still, ten years is a long time," he replied with a grin.

"Too long to go without your coffee, that's for sure."

"Come on," he said, leading her into the house and back into the kitchen.

She followed him and as was their custom, kept her peace until he poured the coffee and set their fresh cups on the kitchen table. "Dad, I have to ask..."

"Whoa, holy hell, kiddo, you haven't even been in the door thirty seconds. Let's get caught up first, and yes, you're more than welcome here. So stop worrying. Yes, your mother can be a pain in the ass, but that's why we love her. Stop worrying about what your mom thinks. We're both happy to have you home and for however long that might be. Although I still don't allow boys in your room. I don't care how old you are!"

She laughed at his stern look. "Oh, Dad. Trust me. That's not going to be an issue."

He grinned, watching her carefully, all while drumming his fingers on the table. It was reassuring and irritating at the same time. "Well then. I guess it's a good thing I got the whole day off. Once we get your things up to your room and settled in, you can come out to the garage and help me with a new project."

"Let me guess. If I'm going to drop a bomb you want me to earn my keep first?"

"That's harsh but true."

"So what's this big project? More custom cabinets?"

"Naw. I can't compete with those big box stores, but I did figure out how to outsmart them. It's the countertops they can't move on. See, everyone wants granite these days, but it costs a small fortune. So I'm making fancy custom counters with concrete. The materials are dirt cheap. Literally. And I can make them look as good as granite and for half the price. Pretty cool, don't-cha think?"

"Dad, I think it's very cool; I can't wait to get to work."

* * *

It was after nine when Kara finally tossed her keys on the foyer table, kicking her boots off and heading for the kitchen. Too tired to cook or even order, she grabbed a beer from the fridge and a bag of chips, neither of which she usually touched. *What the hell.* She was tired and emotionally exhausted, and they were there. There was always beer in the fridge in case she had guests, but she didn't usually stock junk food. Looking at the bag, she suspected her mother's hand. There was no telling what Joanne had said to her, but clearly she'd been out shopping and decided to stock Kara's kitchen, including today's edition of chips and dip. Over the last few years, she had become even more of a mothering hen, constantly on the hunt for anything to improve the life of her daughter, her love life that is. How she had changed. While Kara hated her constant interference in her love life, she had to admit her mother was a different woman without her father. She imagined her mom had been a lot like Joanne as a young woman. They even looked the same. Petite, soft, and slightly insecure.

Heading for the rooftop patio, Kara stopped long enough to toss her socks in the direction of the bedroom before heading outside. The new condo next door blocked her view of the sunset but she could still enjoy the last remnants of twilight. Planting herself in the lounge chair, she twisted the beer cap off and took a sip. She had never been a beer drinker but on a hot day, the only thing better than an ice cold beer might be iced tea, and she had no patience to make it. For the first time in days, she smiled as she scolded herself. *Why do I always have to make things harder than they need to be?* Like her love of iced tea. She always insisted on brewing her favorite flavor instead of using an instant mix. She preferred her home brew and would do without before accepting whatever was available. Maybe that was her problem, always insisting on the best. *Am I a stuck-up brat, or is it knowing exactly what I want that makes the difference?*

"Finally! I see a smile on your face."

Kara choked on her beer. She grabbed a nearby folded towel to wipe away the dribble as it spilled down her chin and onto her shirt. "Shit, Mother…you scared the crap out of me!"

"And it's so nice to see you too sweetheart. How was your getaway?"

"Really?" Kara untucked her work shirt and blotted out the last of the spit-up beer. "Why are you here? I should have known when I saw the chips, much less the folded towels."

Marsha Wexler, unconcerned by her daughter's attitude, planted herself in the twin chaise lounge. "I understand you are no longer speaking to your brother."

"Mom. Please stay out of it."

"I most certainly will not. When my children are in pain, I'm in pain."

Kara groaned. All she wanted was just to spend an hour enjoying summer in the city and maybe further come to terms with her single status. Her mother had always been against it, often going as far as calling it unnatural despite being single herself for the last dozen years after divorcing Kara's father, and describing it as the best thing ever to happen to her. So it was okay for Mom but not for her. That was pretty much how every one of their conversations went. *Do as I say, not as I do* could be her mother's personal motto. "Mom, why are you here?"

"I'm sorry, Kara. But your brother called me, and your sister, and your sister-in-law. Frankly, I'm useless to understand why a splendid roll in the hay has caused so much turmoil."

"Roll in the… Mom!"

"Oh for goodness sakes, Kara. You're not a teenager anymore. We're grown women, and we can discuss grown women topics. Can't we?"

"Yes, of course, wait, no. Mom!"

"So, let me see if I have the story straight. You met a girl. You had fun. You were intellectually challenged. And you had earth-shattering sex. And now you're home, and it's over and you…" she prompted, much as she would when Kara was a child.

"It wasn't exactly like that, Mother."

"You do know they meant well?"

That admission caught her attention. She took in her mother's auburn waves, so similar to Joanne's, and the summer blouse, Tilley shorts and bare feet and tanned legs. Her mother had been a striking young woman with a classic patrician beauty. Kara often thought her profile would have marveled any Roman empress. Even today, the woman turned heads wherever she went. And even though she had thickened slightly she still moved with grace and spoke with earnest determination. "So you know?"

"Know what, dear? That your siblings arranged an introduction to a compatible young woman with whom you might enjoy yourself?"

"Mom. I don't think getting me a girl is the same as a formal introduction." Her reply was harsh and underlined her embarrassment and discomfort.

"I know what your father said about her. And I know why it hurt—it was disgraceful. But I need you to listen to me, young lady. First, regardless of what your father said, that young woman you were introduced to is a card-carrying member of the second profession. Yes, from all I gathered, that young woman is and always was an entertainment professional. From what I understand she sings and dances, and has even choreographed several shows. She is not now, and from what she told me, has never been a member of the oldest profession. Not that I have a problem with those women who are. Goodness knows, not all women are given the same opportunities as you and your sister."

Kara stood suddenly, tossing the unopened bag of chips on a nearby table. She marched a few paces to the patio railing and stopped to turn and look at her mother. Had she heard right? Had her mother spoken with Madeleine? With the night suddenly too dark to make out her features in any detail, she returned to the entry door to flip on the patio lights. "I'm sorry… Did you say you spoke to Madeleine?"

"Well, of course I did. It's my responsibility as your mother to be sure the girl you love will make a suitable lifetime companion."

Unsure how to explain and overwhelmed by her mother's ridiculous notion, Kara made her way back to the lounge chair, taking a seat on the edge. "Mom, I appreciate your concern, but it wasn't like that."

"What was it like then? Tell me, dear, because if earth-shattering sex, and an intellectual match with an emotional connection is not love, I don't know what is. Do you?"

"I…"

"That's what I thought. Now let's begin with what I do know which, whether you like it or not, is more than you do. First, you need to know your father is an asshole. You know that, I know that, it's why I left him. So the sooner you stop with the hero worship, the better."

"*What*? I don't…"

"Oh please," her mother groaned.

Without looking, she knew her mother was rolling her eyes.

"Listen, kiddo, whether you like it or not, you are your father's daughter. You are just like him. Well," she qualified, "excluding the racism, sexism, homophobia, and elitism, you're just like him."

"Jesus, Mom. If I had to be just like him, why didn't I get the tall part too?" It was a joke. Weak at best.

Never fazed, always rolling with the punches, her mother said, "So you got my height, or lack thereof. Get over it. Even your brother got ripped off on the tall genes. I can't wait for the day your father shrivels up into an old man and Douglas can tower over him. I really think it's all the boy needs to see his father is not a giant but just a man, and not a very good one at that. Douglas told me how your father behaved with Madeleine and what you did. I must say, I have never been prouder of you."

"Prouder? Proud that I punched the old man out? You do know he could have pressed charges?"

"Yes dear," she said as if confirming the most natural thing. "You've always looked up to him. In a way, I worried you wanted to be him, especially when you first came out. Yes, I can feel you rolling your eyes now. I will admit there was a learning curve involved in being a parent to an LGBT person…"

"Where did you learn that?"

"What? I'm up on all the PFLAG blogs."

"I thought you were busy trying to figure out how to get Samantha pregnant and keep Joanne's kids in sports."

"I'm a mother, I can multitask. And don't change the subject. I know you must be terribly hurt by your father's actions."

"I wouldn't call it hurt, Mom. More like one too many disappointments. Between that and this whole thing… It's almost like he knew what was going on before I did. It's humiliating. I'm humiliated."

"Oh my baby girl," she offered, setting her wineglass aside and reaching for Kara's hands. "The only thing that happened with your father is he arrived knowing you were going to win the board vote and his ego was out of control. So, like the bastard he is, he took it out on you. He was trying to hurt you. I know that's hard to hear but it's just who he is sometimes. I'm not asking you to forgive him, Kara. I'm asking you to forget it."

"Yeah. And what happens when he finds out he was right?"

"He most certainly was not. Yes, arranging this fantasy date thing was misguided but to be honest, I can understand where Joanne comes up with these crazy ideas, and why Doug is so easily convinced to follow her lead. Frankly, your brother would follow a jackal down the rabbit hole. I swear that boy has no concept of consequence, much less cause and effect. Thank goodness he married well. I know you're disappointed with Samantha too. We both count on her to keep your brother on the straight and narrow while helping rein in your sister when she gets a little impetuous. Still, she had good reason to follow along with this scheme of Joanne's and frankly, I think it's the best thing that could've happened to you."

"Mom. You're not listening. If Dad finds out…"

"Finds out what, sweetheart? That your lady is an actress and not a sales rep? Yes, that would disappoint him. But it's a type of disappointment you've endured, and frankly, I do enjoy seeing your father irritated."

Kara blew out a hot breath, trying to get her thoughts in order. "You spoke to her? Madeleine, I mean."

"If it's any consolation, she is just as troubled. More so I think."

That made Kara mad. She shook off her mother's hands, standing and marching away like a petulant child. Reaching the rooftop railing, she was forced to stop and consider her words.

Before she realized it, her mother was standing beside her and much as she had when she was a child, she clasped Kara's jaw between perfectly manicured fingers and turned her head so their eyes met. "Of my three children you have been the most resilient, resourceful, and successful, and the biggest pain in my backside. You've never taken the easy road. Goodness me, I don't know how many times I've marveled to see you consistently cut a new path instead of following…anyone. Everything had to be your way. I respect that. But it makes life very difficult, not to mention lonely. I don't want that for you. I know this whole thing may feel…well, I don't know what you feel. I never have. I can see you're upset now and I get that. But that girl is upset too."

"Yeah right. Upset enough that she's probably got another, whatever you call it, in her little Venus flytrap."

Her mother's fingers, still firmly clenched around her jaw, forced her head back around to her. "Stop acting like your father! You're smarter than that. Now listen to me and listen carefully. That young woman is not a prostitute."

Kara pried her mother's fingers from her face, but held onto her hand. "Mom, I'm sure she told you that but—"

"Do you think I was born yesterday? The moment your sister confessed to what was going on, I had the agency run a background check. She *is* an actress, or performer, or whatever you call it these days, singer? Her only foray into personal entertainment was this misguided setup with you. And before you ask, she only took it because she needed the money to leave town and get a fresh start. What woman hasn't been in that situation?"

"Me."

"Kara Delphine Wexler, you spoiled brat!" She softened and shook her head, pleading gently, "Sweetheart, you have an extraordinary career. One I'm sure you would have accomplished without your opportunities and family connections. But, imagine your sister. Without your father's indulgence, she would have been lucky to land a job at Tim Horton's."

There were tears in her eyes when Kara hissed out her shame. "Mother, she was paid to have sex with me."

"I will have you know the contract and script for this whole thing specifically stated she was not obliged to have sex with you." When Kara wouldn't or couldn't look at her, she wrapped a consoling arm around her daughter. "I never imagined you so delicate. What with all the traffic you've had through this place. You do realize I've had to replace your bedroom carpet twice since you moved in. And don't get me started on the rate you wear through linens."

Kara shook her head, offering the weakest of smiles. "Mother you redecorated twice. There was no long line of women waiting to grace my bed and wearing out the carpet."

"Did you actually miss the long line of women desperate to make your acquaintance, be seen on your arm, contending to be your wife? According to *Toronto Magazine*, you're one of the city's top ten most eligible bachelorettes."

"What?"

"Oh, did I not show you the article? They called me a few months back and asked a few questions. You don't mind, do you?"

"Oh Mom, really?"

"Darling, as long as you're single, I will do my motherly duty and make sure you're represented in the best light to all the best women out there."

Kara had allowed her mother to act as her personal publicist because as a socialite and a member of Toronto's elite, she had the connections and interest. Interest was a relative word; her enthusiasm was mind-boggling.

"Frankly, I'd forgotten all about it. I was at the Granite Club having lunch with Mrs. Kelly and she pulled out the article. She actually thought you'd be interested in courting one of her grandchildren."

She groaned at the idea. "Eww! I had the worst crush on Casey when I was a teenager. The thought of dating one of her daughters just feels…wrong."

Her mother laughed. Taking her hand, she retrieved their drinks and led her daughter to the outdoor sofa in front of the fireplace. Kara never bothered with the thing. It'd been a gift from her mother, and she'd come to understand it was something her mother enjoyed, so she flipped on the gas and pressed the starter button, watching as flames jumped from the fake wood and embers. She sat quietly while her mother settled in, fussing with the blanket she kept nearby. Kara said softly, "We can go inside you know."

"What, and miss a moment of our wonderful summer! Frankly, I'm not certain I've dried out from that horrid wet winter we suffered through and no changing the subject. I want to know right now, how do you feel about Madeleine?"

"Mom…" Kara fussed in her seat, trying to find a way to explain the mishmash of feelings, not to mention the tears that had hounded her all weekend. "I… She… Mom," she uttered, and closed her eyes, pushing out a hot breath, "I thought it was real. I thought she…"

Her mother reached over, taking her hand again, giving it a firm shake and hanging on. "It was interesting to hear her version of events. She was honest and admitted it was just a job in the beginning. As a matter fact, it was a job she had no intention or interest in accepting but her manager talked her into it, and as she had already decided she was leaving Las Vegas, not to mention a huge incentive bonus your siblings threw in, she decided to take the job. Well, decided is a strong term. She admitted she more or less just gave into her manager's insistence. The thing is, I'm not sure you can understand what it's like to be a woman with few or no choices and no money.

"I don't know if I ever told you, but your grandparents did not want your father to marry me. They thought a nice trophy wife from some presentable family was much more suitable and advantageous for his career. I do honestly believe his marrying me was his one act of rebellion. Your father's family represents much of the last of Toronto's Victorian elite. Your grandmother once told me I was a nice girl from Leaside, but certainly not suitable wife material. She suggested I go marry some banker and move to Scarborough. Can you imagine?

"The irony is, if she'd left us alone and stopped trying to push us apart, I probably would have clued into what kind of man your father was before we were married."

Kara grumbled, "Maybe you could remind your sister of that the next time she tries to set me up with some perfectly suitable young man."

Her mother snorted her derision. "And what type of young man does your senile old aunt think would be perfectly suitable for you? Don't answer that. I know exactly what she thinks, and I'm going to tell you this, young lady. Every woman deserves a mature, satisfying, respectful, intimate relationship. The days of giving up any of that for appearance's sake are over. And frankly, I'm worried. You've been without those things for far too long. And don't mention that previous idiot girlfriend of yours. That was not a mature, satisfying and respectful, intimate relationship. If you want to be embarrassed, that was more akin to prostitution than anything that happened between you and Madeleine."

Kara wanted to argue, but she was right. Dropping ten grand a month to keep your girlfriend happy was not a relationship. It was a business arrangement. In a way that was what Doug and Joanne's agreement had been with Madeleine. "If it wasn't… If sex wasn't part of the package…"

"Sweetheart, I know you're uncomfortable talking about this, but you really needn't be embarrassed. This company they hired really does this fantasy date thing as a business, and no it wasn't supposed to end in sex. Although of course it can, it wasn't what your sister was trying to do. She and Douglas truly believed getting you out, making sure you had fun would get you ready to face the board. They thought it was a good idea. Besides, having fun, having a date, it's something you haven't done in a long time. They knew there was very little chance they could drag you out twenty-four seven so when they found out about this company, they checked it out. Frankly, so did I. They're legit and so was the contract. Yes, the dates were scripted as in they'd already decided where you would be going and what you would be doing. That would be no different than having me arrange a date for you or something like that. Is this really any different than Harjitt keeping your social calendar or scheduling dinner dates for you?"

"Mom, having my personal assistant schedule a dinner *meeting* is not the same as plotting to get me laid."

"That's not what I'm saying. And that's not what happened. Honestly, you're being pig-headed, constantly returning to the same point. You can damn well take my word for it, neither your siblings or Madeleine had any intention this would become intimate. Human reasoning aside, sometimes these things just, well, must I explain the birds and the bees to you?"

"You think this was the real thing? Come on, Mom! Scripted dates! Costumes! They even played the whole 'I'm straight but I'm attracted to you' thing. Talk about aiming for the heart?"

"I'm surprised you raised this point."

"Why? Why, Mom? You read the PFLAG blogs. Don't they ever talk about the kryptonite effect straight women have on lesbians?"

"Kryptonite? I'll be sure to tell Madeleine that, but first I want you to know something. I didn't know Madeleine was straight until your sister told me. Frankly, that sent up all sorts of warning bells for me too. It was one of the first things I called Madeleine on. Now you need to hear this. She was frank and honest with me. I believe she's telling the truth. You were and are the first woman in her life."

Kara didn't believe her. At least she didn't want to think about it. Doing so would undermine everything she had convinced herself about Madeleine. If she had been honest about being straight, had she been honest about her feelings? What had happened to them, between them felt so real; so deeply perfectly divine in sensation and desire. Could it have been real? "How do I tell where the act stops and the real woman starts? Because frankly, Mom, I can't tell the difference. We did things, we said things, then she was gone. She followed the script from beginning to end, so how do I know the middle wasn't all made up too?"

Her mother gave her hand a squeeze to match the consoling smile. "Sweetheart, all I can say is that woman is just as messed up as you are. Even if you're never interested in hearing another word from her, you should know she's in pain too. She's confused, and very bluntly, admitted she wasn't prepared to meet someone like you."

"Yeah, I'll bet." She didn't mean it as agreement.

Still holding her hand, her mother shook off the blanket and stood. "It's getting chilly, and I have plans tomorrow. The yacht club is hosting a regatta next weekend, and I have tons and tons to do."

Kara followed her mother to the patio entry intent on seeing her next door to her own condo. She might have her own keys and was free to use them whenever she chose, but she never failed to see her out. It was an old-fashioned formality her mother appreciated. Her mother halted so abruptly, Kara almost knocked her over. "Whoa."

"I just thought of something. You said she followed the script at the beginning and the end, but that's not true. The script called for her to give you a good night peck at your door Friday night then leave. Nothing more. You weren't supposed to see her again. She broke from the script then and the next day. What she did follow was the contract. Oh sweetheart…" Her mother's hand was back on her face. "Your sister-in-law drafted that contract. It included a nondisclosure agreement and that NDA stipulated she could not attempt to contact you at any time once the board meeting convened. Kara, she *couldn't* contact you. Not then and not now. If you want to hear Madeleine's side of things or at least let her apologize, you'll need to contact her."

With that said, she turned to leave only to stop once more. "Darling, if you want to sort out your feelings for that girl, you are going to have to pick up the phone and call her."

Kara stood frozen in place, watching as her mother marched down the stairs, disappearing out the loft's front door. So her mother wanted her to call Madeleine. What the hell was wrong with the world? She had just been played. Played like the fool her father constantly warned she was. Was it real? It felt real. But it wasn't. And that was the point. What the hell was her mother thinking? Turning to look back out over the summer city night, she couldn't imagine which prospect was worse. What would her father say and do when he found out—and he always found out—or the fact that her mother seemed to be delighted by the entire prospect. "This is what I get for buying her all those romantic comedies. That's it, Mom, no more *Pretty Woman* binge-watching for you."

* * *

Madeleine woke in her teenage-years bedroom. It was strange how foreign and comforting her bed felt, incongruous yet altogether reassuring. The incongruity came from being alone with no room for anyone else in the single bed. That was new. Not the being alone part, but the wanting to not be alone. Who was she kidding? She rolled on her side, hugging her pillow to her chest. In all the relationships she'd ever had, she had never experienced this level of longing. It was more than that; if she was honest with herself, there was a certain amount of grieving. Could it be possible? Could she be grieving the loss of Kara's company? There was no denying the longing, the constant warning that her heart might at any moment implode and all because a woman she barely knew was gone from her life. Five days. That's all it took. Five days to turn her life upside down.

She swung her feet from under the covers and sat up, still clinging to the pillow pressed against her chest. What was it about the woman? It was so hard to pinpoint. Pinpoint the aspects that made the difference. What was it about this one? That she was a woman, yes, that was different. But it wasn't the deciding factor, and it wasn't like she was gaga from the moment they met. If anything, she'd initially felt like hitting her over the head. She'd seemed stubborn, driven, and one-dimensional even. But sitting in the restaurant overlooking Lake Mead, she'd had her first glimpse of Kara's generosity of spirit. The way she would literally step outside herself to examine every situation from a new perspective. More than that, maybe it was the way she wanted to know, genuinely wanted to know, about her. Not just what she believed in but what she felt.

It was an interesting phenomenon that working in Las Vegas within an industry filled with women but controlled by men, words like "feelings" were taboo. No serious performer wanted to risk having a reputation for being emotional. As if men were never emotional. From her own experience, they were ten times worse than women. She and Kara had debated that too. Discussing how society's perception was influenced by the media, and especially how advertisers influenced people, especially the young. And they discussed her ideas, perceptions, and influences growing up. Sitting here now, she could honestly say she was truly relieved she hadn't made up a lot in the discussions. She always stuck to the script when it came to her background story of being a sales rep for a convention company, but she used her own life and experience when discussing everything else. If anything, speaking the truth provided some relief. She could stand up and say she hadn't been a complete fraud. God knows it hadn't felt fake, talking to her, touching her…

Until that moment she hadn't realized her fingers had migrated to her lips, quietly, sensuously tracing the pout of her bottom lip. Yes, it felt like a pout. She felt pouty and emotional, but mostly she felt alone. That too was new. Being with Kara had opened an unknown part of her. A part she had no idea existed but now that she did, she was beginning to understand how much that secret part wanted out, wanted to live, wanted to celebrate, wanted Kara.

I want her.

CHAPTER FOURTEEN

Kara collapsed in her chair. She had just spent a grueling six hours taking a select group of interns and junior account reps through her social media plan. She had dumped a lot on them but judging by their enthusiasm, not to mention the escalating volume in the room, they agreed. It actually didn't matter if they agreed or not. The important part was to get them working. Their enthusiasm was the bonus that would drive their success. Now all she needed to do was make sure no one got in their way. Of course, she would be sure they received the obligatory endless supply of pizza and pop. She almost laughed to consider how much less that would cost than all the business lunches the senior reps charged to their expense accounts. There was a time when meetings like that garnered new business and you could still schmooze prospective accounts, but it wasn't like the old days. Corporations were much more savvy about getting their products out. Most would accept the five-star dinner, but they still demanded to see the analytics in the morning. This was the type of customer support her father didn't understand. He still believed his personal reputation was all the client needed. Analytics be damned—and, for her father, they were. "The numbers don't lie, Father," she'd told and told him. "You can charm them all you like. But when the campaign fails, and it will because we haven't got the numbers, how will you feel when you're forced to drop the Mr. Charming act and explain why we couldn't deliver as promised?"

"You mean *you* couldn't deliver as promised. My job is to please them. It's your goddamn job to create campaigns that deliver!" And he would stomp out of her office. Looking around the room now she realized not much had changed. Except now she was in charge. Lucille Ball had a sign on her desk when she ran Desilu Studios: "The Buck Stops Here!" Kara would follow that mantra too. No more blaming the old man for overpromising when they didn't deliver. No excuses. It was now all up to her. *Perfect! Leave me in charge. I can't even tell the difference between a setup and… and what the hell did I think was happening? I'm not the golden girl of the family or even Daddy's sunshine. I'm the black sheep and the ugly duckling. Who the hell would ever go for someone like me? You know exactly who. The kind of woman who can look past your ugly mug and short ass and see the money your family has. No one is ever just attracted to me. Why the hell would some straight, hot as hell, stunning green-eyed, redheaded, beautiful, kind, and gorgeous woman be interested in me?*

Yeah, that's what I thought.

* * *

Madeleine cleared the dishes from the dining room table. When she returned her father had already topped up her wineglass, and her mother signaled for her to sit down.

"Your dad says it's time to talk. He also told me I'm not allowed to be bossy and tell you what to do. Goodness gracious, Maddie, when have I ever been bossy with you?"

"Mom…"

While her dad was dressed as always in his perpetual workwear, her mom, just home from the hospital, was still sporting her nurses' scrubs. While the pants were the customary blue, the top featured happy faces with crutches, bandaged brows or cartoon wheelchairs. She was tall like Madeleine but thinner, almost caffeine thin. With her bleached blond hair tied in a loose bun, she seemed older than her early fifties and far more serious. "I can't help it if I just want the best for you kids! I never expected much from your sister but you…" She stopped suddenly, seemingly aware of her tone. "I was wrong about you leaving school. I'll admit it. I didn't understand it until I ran into Marybeth. Her dad was in the hospital for a bypass, she came by on my break and took me for coffee."

Marybeth had grown up three doors down and followed Madeleine through grade school, high school, and to the University of Wisconsin. In truth, Madeleine had long forgotten about her neighbor. Compared to the tall, statuesque Madeleine, Marybeth was a squeaky little mouse. "How is Marybeth? Please tell me she's not like my sister and shacked up with some jackass?"

"Unlike your sister Sonja, Marybeth was born with some common sense. She finished school, got married and they adopted two lovely twin baby girls. Ah, you should see them. They're like perfect little China dolls!"

"Mother! That's racist."

"What is? Why can't I call them Chinese? That's where they came from!"

Clearly confused, her father filled her in, "You remember the Darning girl, the one was always helping her dad at his garage? Well anyway, long story short, she and Marybeth got married a few years back. Drove up to Canada. 'Course, you can do it here now too and adopt. Could have saved them the trip to Thunder Bay."

"Wait, what?" Madeleine stammered. "Marybeth and April Darning? They're married, as in gay marriage, and they have kids?"

Her mother waved her off, impatiently rolling her eyes. "Now you sound like your sister. I can't believe you'd be shocked in this day and age. Goodness knows Marybeth was never going to find a husband and that Darning girl, well let's just say she's a better provider and parent than that thing your sister married."

Madeleine sat silently. Finally, picking up her glass of wine, turning it slowly, she raised it. "Here's to Marybeth's happiness. And to a happy family which I can't believe you're okay with, Mom. What changed?"

"Maddie, every day I watch people die."

Her mother was an oncology nurse and considered one of the best. In a department that suffered more patient losses than most others combined it was considered the most difficult and emotionally taxing of assignments.

"There's something about those last few hours in a person's life. I never really understood it before, but then a few years back we had this young native nurse in the unit. Ojibwe I think. One of those girls from up Duluth way. Anyway, she said something that kind of clicked with me. She said her people don't believe in those death masks that some other kinds of Native Americans like. We were talking about dying, and she said some cultures would mask their dying so you couldn't glimpse their true nature. Her people believe you can't hide your true nature during birth or death. She said we were all kind of acting a role we think we're born to play. I think I kinda realized then the truth of it. I don't know how many times I watched some mean old man die in his bed alone without a single soul from his family caring a fig. I used to hate those cases because it put all the pressure on the staff, but the truth was, they were ugly men. You could see it in their eyes. Well, that and the fear. I guess for some the threat of imminent death forces them to face all their vile behaviors."

Madeleine wanted to ask more, but knew from experience her mother wasn't done. Some significant transformation had happened to her, and she knew the best course was to be silent and patient. Whatever her mother needed to tell her was important.

Finishing her wine, her mother set her glass on the table, nudging it toward her husband to have it topped up. "About a year after you left school and headed to Vegas, we stood by and watched Marybeth go through hell with her parents, coming out and all. Now, I was just right there with her mom. 'It's unnatural. It's an abomination,' and all that bullshit. I was just as bad as that woman. And I was mad as hell when Marybeth's grandparents took in her and young April. I'm ashamed of the vitriol that sprang from my mouth. Anyway, things died down, then we got a new patient in the ward. Stage IV lymphoma, and in rolls the most beautiful little thing you've ever seen and before I can decide if this one's going to break my heart, in marches her entourage: wife, three kids, two brothers, four parents, and the whole pack of grandparents. I was a jerk to them all until it occurred to me that that young native nurse was right. I never have seen so much love from so many people for just one sick woman. After she was gone I started to accept the goodness I had seen and not just with her family but with her. Her last four hours were probably the most beautiful I've ever witnessed. She was like a little angel. Her only concern was for her children and wife, her brothers, parents, and grandparents and all in that order. The night before she died, I asked her if she was scared. That girl just smiled at me, the kindest, sweetest smile I've ever seen and said to me, 'I've been fearful for my children, my wife, and my family. All I can do is console myself that they're in God's hands and hope I've taught them well.'

"'Aren't you scared for you?' I asked. I was thinking about all those scared mean old men who died alone facing their sins. In my book, I thought this girl was as sinful as you could get, yet here she was. She was dying. She was fearless. And she was surrounded by love. About an hour before she passed, she touched my hand and thanked me. Thanked me!"

Her mother was choking up, an unexpected sight. So unexpected Madeleine almost choked on her wine, but settled herself, allowing her mother the time to regain her composure. "Then she says, 'Let the love in. That's where God lives. Not in the lies and hate but in love.' I was caught without a damn thing to say. It wasn't her words so much as the truth of her. Next day I went up to our church and asked the Reverend to show me in the book where it says God wants us to hate queers."

"Mom…"

"Oh, I know that's wrong now, but I knew nothin' then. The worst part was when he couldn't find the proof for me, that place that spelled out all the hateful things I'd been thinking and saying. The next day I had it out with Marybeth's mom, and I had your dad go over to the garage and ask young April for her phone number. She's been a good friend to me, Maddie. Talkin' to me about life and people the church never let us even think about. Now your dad says you met a girl and you're worried I'll hate you or disown you the way Marybeth's parents disowned her. Well, I'm here to tell you, Maddie, it happened. I watched your sister with that idiot she married and I can't help but wonder, what was she thinking? I raised you girls better than that. I could sit here like Marybeth's mom and content myself with the fact that your sister's given me grandchildren, but I can't do that. Besides, there's the fifty-fifty chance your niece and nephew will turn out to be just as big dumbasses as your brother-in-law…"

"Now hon," Madeleine's dad said, interrupting gently. "Let's just remember, each to his own gifts."

Madeleine smiled while her mother giggled at her father's gentle way of trying to keep everyone included. "So you're not shocked?"

"Oh, I'm shocked as all get out. Unlike Marybeth, you were boy crazy from the day you were born. I'm having a hell of a time figuring out how you got turned around, and I've got two theories. On the one hand," she offered, holding up her wineglass, "I think this girl you met is something really special. I figure she'd have to be to turn your head. Otherwise," she held up the other hand, this one grasping a cigarette, "and this would make me mad as all hell, I'm worrying some man has done my little girl so wrong, she can't even look at another man. If that's the case, Maddie, I promise you we'll get you all the help and counseling you need."

It was fascinating to watch the dilemma going on within her mother. Also a relief that her scenarios of cause went beyond the typical "women only became lesbians because they've suffered at the hands of sexually and physically abusive males." Her mother was willing to consider that might not be the case. That was something.

What about me? Am I willing to accept my mother's interpretation? Is Kara that one extraordinary woman who could turn my head?

"Nothing happened to me, Mom. Trust me, even in Las Vegas, there are some decent guys. It wasn't like that. It was… Well, it was a sort of accident."

Her father cleared his throat dramatically but kept his mouth shut.

"Okay, I'll admit she is, well, she is extraordinary."

"She must be one hell of a beauty."

"She is, Mom. Not in the usual sense. It's not her looks that did me in. It's, it's a sort of kindness she has."

"Lots of folks are kind, Maddie. I meet kind folks at the hospital every single day, but you don't see me fallin' in love with them. Yes, your father told me it's love you feel for her. If that's the truth I want to hear what it is about this girl that turned your head, especially under the circumstances. Don't give me that look, young lady. Your father told me everything. Now I want to hear it from you."

For the first time since returning home, Madeleine felt the same panic that had overwhelmed her as a teenager whenever her mother would confront her. Back then it was usually about her getting caught with a bad boy doing bad things. Only this time she hadn't been doing bad things. She could honestly say they were all very, very good.

"Maddie I'm not mad at you. I just want to understand."

"Mom, it's just, it's just I screwed everything up. I guess Dad told you I took the role thinking it would be some fast cash. I didn't want to do it but Franco talked me into it and to be blunt I haven't been getting much work these last few years. Not since turning thirty."

"My goodness," her father said, shaking his head. "What's the world come to when people think a beautiful woman is old at thirty? Hell, I think your mother is more beautiful every day."

She smiled at his honesty. For as long as she could remember he had adored her mother and never missed an occasion or opportunity to demonstrate his feelings. He was one of those few smart men that believed a happy wife made for a happy life. "It seems it's thirty for Vegas, forty for LA, and fifty for the theatre. Only TV seems to be free of the stale date for women these days."

"Oh Maddie, just tell me what happened?"

"Mom, I… I hurt her. I guess I convinced myself that somehow it was okay because it wasn't real. Then when I started feeling…I kept thinking this is just some game she likes to play, but she didn't know. She… I hurt her and now that it's over I feel like I've lost part of me. It's like if I don't fix this thing I'll never forgive myself. I guess I don't know what to do."

Her mother emptied the ashtray in the can below the sink and grabbed a fresh bottle of wine, handing it and the corkscrew to her husband. "Come on, kiddo, let's go sit on the new back deck your dad put in. Looks like this is a good evening for lots of wine and forthright conversation."

CHAPTER FIFTEEN

Kara pulled her Land Rover into her usual parking spot in the domed basement of the building she had long ago converted to lofts. When she'd bought the building, she kept the two-story façade as it was, but inside was a completely modern structure with one exception. She had insisted, and the city engineer agreed, to keep the deep vaulted basement intact. The basement of the one-time Dominion Printers to Queen Victoria required no changes or shoring. The builders had dropped steel beams in behind the façade walls of the first two floors, adding four new floors above. The upper four stories had the look of a glassed-in cube perched ever so carefully on the parapets of the Gothic brick base. During construction, and with an exceedingly tight budget, she worried she might need to raise additional cash, and decided to divide the top floor into four condominium apartments. When the real estate agent leased all the rental units during the open house, she held off on finishing the condos. Instead, she took the two south facing units for herself and added the rooftop terrace. A year after the building opened, her mother approached her and quietly negotiated the purchase of the other two units for herself. She confessed to her daughter that her marriage to Kara's father was over. His infidelities were frequent but usually discreet. When his discretion waned so had Marsha Wexler's patience for her husband and the father of her children.

Kara huffed out a breath. The one day her mother wouldn't be home was the one day she wasn't sure she could make it from the car to the penthouse. Deciding to forgo trying to haul in her gear, she opened the door of the SUV and slipped out slowly, bracing her legs and locking her knees to hold her weight. She stood, with one hand clamped hard to the door, the other still hanging on to the holy-shit bar as she tried her weight. The yelp of pain that followed was quickly squashed as she forced herself to suck it up. Yes, her back hurt. Yes, she had overdone the rowing. Yes, it was going to be a challenge to get upstairs. Closing the door, she pushed herself off her vehicle, letting momentum carry her to the old freight door, thankful she had kept the building's original Otis elevator in good working order.

The original and massive cage was the oldest working elevator in the city. When she'd contacted Otis for advice, they were quick to let her know it was also Toronto's first elevator. It was massive, so big it was used to deliver truckloads of paper and huge Victorian printing machines from the street level down to the two-story deep basement with its vaulted brick and stone ceiling. When she designed the new building, she had planned to replace the oversized and ancient thing with two normal-sized cars. Respecting the history, not to mention the pride and service the Otis Company offered, she instead included shaft space on all the new floors, adding new cables and pulleys to have the big car reach the top floor. She was often teased and even bullied for the expense. Today she thanked her foresight and the Otis Company for begging to keep the historic machine operating. Reality was, there was no way she was getting herself up six flights of stairs after the day she'd had.

All week she'd been on the go, moving, working, making things happen. As long as she was doing, she had no time for thinking. Friday night, alone on the rooftop terrace, the city's evening twilight dwindling, she could no longer pretend she wasn't hurting. She missed Madeleine. Longed for her.

Unable to sleep, she'd given up at half past two. Dressing in her workout gear, she grabbed her backpack deciding to head out to the Argonaut Rowing Club, grab a solo boat and be first on the water.

Fourteen hours later, she was nauseated from having forgotten to eat.

She'd given herself a workout of a lifetime. By the end of the day, she knew she'd overdone it. On the drive home, she chastised herself for exceeding the design limits of her short-ass, out of shape body, forgetting completely that she was on her own at home.

Kara made it as far as her own kitchen. Leaning over the sink, chilled and shaking like a leaf, she could feel sweat dripping down and soaking her already damp T-shirt. Grabbing the Tylenol out of the cabinet and the bottle of pink goop that would settle her stomach, she tried to control the shaking. It was easy to keep her mind off the nausea. All she had to do was try and move, causing her back and thighs to scream from the pain. She was at a loss to know whether she should try and crawl to her bed, head for a hot bath, or just collapse right there on the kitchen floor. The marble floor did look nice and cool.

The sound of her cell phone interrupted her debate. She was surprised to realize it was still in her back pocket and not lost somewhere in her car or in her knapsack, which of course was still in the car too. "Wexler," she growled, hitting the speaker button and dumping the phone on the counter.

There was a long pause, then she finally heard a questioning voice, "Kara?"

With pain impinging on her thought processes, it took a moment for her to recognize the voice. "Madeleine?"

"Yes, yes it's me. I'm so sorry. I… I hope it's okay that I'm calling. I just… I needed, I wanted…" A long silence hung between them. "I want you to know…I mean, I want to say I'm sorry and, and, and I wanted to hear your voice."

As Kara battled to balance her physical pain with her longing and confusion, the digital silence between them began to build in to a crisp icy wall.

"It's okay if you're not ready to talk. I...I just want you to know, what happened between us. It wasn't...it wasn't supposed to happen it, it just did. I guess you don't want to talk. I understand. I just want you to know that I don't do that kind of thing. I mean I never have before. And what happened, it happened because...clearly, you don't want to hear this, but I just wanted you to know that I actually feel something for you and I'm sorry and I just wish we could talk. I'll let you go. Just so you know, if you ever want to call or..."

"Madeleine." She took a few quick breaths. "I'm not mad. Sorry." She sucked in more air, trying not to hyperventilate. It was all she could do to stay standing, much less talk. "I am mad but," huff, huff, huff, huff, "I'm hurt."

"I understand and, and it's the absolute last thing—"

"Madeleine!" Huff, huff, "I hurt myself."

"I understand I... wait... Oh my God, honey. What have you done?"

There was panic in her voice, and something else, something Kara couldn't push past her periphery. Was it concern? Was it real? "No!" Huff, huff, huff, huff, huff. "At rowing." Huff, huff, huff. "Pulled my back and—"

"Oh my God, where are you? Are you still at the rowing club? Is there someone who can help you?"

"No," huff, huff, "home, got to lie down but..."

Sitting on her parents' front porch, Madeleine was on her feet and pacing. Did she just hear all the telltale signs of Kara falling? In her mind, she played scenarios from every movie she'd ever seen where someone falls and hits their head and dies from a head injury that goes unattended. With her phone pressed tight to one ear and her hand covering the other, she begged for Kara to let her know she was alive. She suffered through a few minutes of digital silence before she picked up on the faint sound of soft moans. Whipping through the front door past her dad watching a baseball game, she grabbed the kitchen phone and dialed Joanne's number. She had the woman on speed dial on her own phone but wouldn't risk severing her connection with the injured Kara.

"Hey Madeleine, what a surprise to—"

"Jo, I've got her on the line. Something's wrong. Something's really wrong."

"Whoa, whoa, whoa, what are you talking about?"

"Your sister. I called her. She's hurt herself. She said it was at rowing. I think she passed out while she was talking to me. Joanne, you've gotta go over there. Go do something. Please."

"Holy cow you called her? That's so cool Madeleine. I'm so proud of you."

"Joanne! Eyes on the prize, girl. Something happened to your sister. I think she's passed out."

"You sure she's not just messing with you? It's rowing, not hockey. How could—"

"Joanne, please! Can you just go over and check on her? I'm listening to her right now. Something is terribly wrong."

"What did she say?"

"She said she was hurt. She hurt her back at rowing, then I heard her fall. She said she was at home. Can you go over there? If you don't do it, I'm calling 9-1-1."

"Whoa there, girl. No worries. I'm on my way. Are you?"

Madeleine could hear the sounds of Joanne scurrying around her home, her door slamming. "Joanne, I'm still in Minneapolis. I can't get there from here."

"Really?"

In the background, it was easy to hear the sound of Joanne's car's unfastened seat belt warning blare. "Last time I checked, they have airplanes that go from here to there and back again. I'm surprised you don't know about it." The car engine started. "Way I hear it, the whole thing's some sort of American invention. I'll call you when I get to Kara's…can't drive and talk at the same time." And with that, she was gone.

Madeleine placed the handset back in the cradle of the old wall-mounted harvest gold phone that had hung in the kitchen for as long as she could remember. She was still listening intently on her own cell phone for any sign of Kara's return to consciousness when her father stuck his head in the kitchen.

"Everything go okay?"

"She's hurt!"

"To be expected," he agreed with kindness in his eyes.

She simply shook her head. "No, Dad. Physically. Something happened when she was at rowing practice today. I…I think I have to go to Toronto."

Silently he backtracked to the living room, returning with his laptop and setting it open in front of her. "Okay then. Let's get you a ticket."

CHAPTER SIXTEEN

Madeleine was last to board the United flight to Chicago. She'd haphazardly thrown things into her suitcase and let her dad drive, racing her out to the airport in his beater of a pickup truck. After delivering a warm-hearted bear hug to him, she hauled her suitcase out of the truck box and leaned in the window. "By the way, I like the Jessepp and Daughter Construction," she said, tipping her head toward the vinyl graphics wrapped along the sides of his work truck.

"Any day you want to step in and take over you just tell me. And sweetheart, you take care."

She smiled but didn't trust herself to answer. Nodding her thanks, she turned for the terminal unwilling to watch him leave.

The flight to Chicago was short. With her connection details in hand, she made it to the next gate in record time, only to find the flight to Toronto delayed. At least she was in an airport where she could get a decent cup of joe. When the airline announced they would board in twenty minutes, she was touring Barbara's Books but hadn't found anything to capture her imagination. Grazing through the selection of techno-thrillers, romances, and business start-up books she did wonder what she was looking for. Maybe what she wanted was advice. Someone to explain what she was feeling, this longing. Surely someone had experienced this sort of wonder before. She couldn't be the first woman whose head and life had been completely turned around by another woman.

Walking back to the gate she lined up with her boarding pass and thoughts so deep she felt alone in the throng. *What am I trying to understand? Is it my feelings for her? Is it her as a woman?* She smiled at the thought, remembering the feel of Kara in her arms. Yes, she had held Kara just as much as Kara had held her. Entwined together, there had been a balance between them, a symmetry she'd never experienced. And it wasn't just about Kara being a woman. It was more about Kara being who she was. She could be intense and focused, but even when she seemed hardest, she seemed…What was the word to describe it? "Kind" didn't cover it. Not even close. To a certain degree, you could say "intuitive" and "inherently kind," but even these were poor descriptions.

Pinned in the aisle, she was looking for enough room in a nearby overhead bin when a pudgy little man offered to be her knight in shining armor. As if she needed some guy to lift her suitcase up. "I'm okay, thanks."

"Hey beautiful, don't kill the messenger. It's not my fault you women don't know if you want us to be gentlemen or not."

With her back turned to the man, she rolled her eyes before taking her seat, and turning to answer him, said, "Thank you for your good manners, but I'm fine." Seated, she pulled the emergency procedures card from the seatback and pretended to be interested in the pictorial instructions for a water egress. It was easy to hear him mouthing off with his buddy as they took seats in the row behind her.

"What's with these fucking bitches? ~ Yeah man ~ They're all like, act like a gentleman, and then they shoot you down. ~ Yeah man. She's probably a fucking dyke. ~ No fuckin' way is that one… ~ she's got no tits man and look how tall she is!

What's with you and tall bitches? ~ You think that's a dyke? ~ Fuck yeah."

Normally this kind of crap from guys made her want to punch the living daylights out of them. Tonight though, she buckled her seatbelt and shared a look with the flight attendant. Maybe she was switching teams simply because it was time. Her women friends were always saying there were no good guys out there. Lots of guys, so very few good ones. Suddenly it was clear. It wasn't a lack of confidence that drove a woman into another woman's arms, but the heightened level of personal value more prevalent among women every day. Her mother had raised her in the belief that she needed a man to be complete, but more than that, to be safe. The husband, she had been told many times, was a woman's safety net. Without it, she should expect to be preyed upon by men, physically, mentally, emotionally and even financially. But her mother's worldview had changed. Had hers too? She smiled again as the commuter jet rumbled down the runway, seeming to jump in the air, angling itself almost straight up like a rocket. It suited her mood and her mission. Yes, it felt like a mission, a mission to state her case, demonstrate her care, and if nothing more, create a dialogue between her and the one person she truly connected with. *Who am I kidding? For me, she's the new world and I'm ready to burn my ships to demonstrate my commitment!*

The flight was pleasant although rough. Standing in the aisle with the other passengers waiting to deplane, Madeleine switched her phone out of airplane mode. She was relieved to see a text message from Joanne that Kara was okay. She had waited until she was in the boarding lineup in Chicago before texting her that she was on her way.

Entering the Toronto customs hall she was temporarily confused. With signs in English and most everyone speaking English, she had completely forgotten she was entering a foreign country.

When the customs officer asked her reason for entering Canada she stammered. "I... Um... Someone I care for, my friend I mean, has been injured." The officer was a big man with a barrel chest and the looks of grizzled old Scotsman. He stared down from his raised booth, peering over the reading glasses perched on the tip of his nose. By contrast, his deep French accent and jolly tone softened his message. "Ah, it is for the love you come. Who is this boy you come to see?"

"I… Um… It's, it's a girl," she stammered again before forcing herself to stand proud and admit, "She's a girl, I mean woman."

Peering over his glasses again, he seemed to be looking for some telltale signs she couldn't comprehend. He smiled then. Stamping her passport and handing it back, he said simply, "Love is love. *Bienvenue au Canada*. Next!"

With adrenaline still pumping she made a beeline for the exit. Passing through the opaque doors, she was surprised to find herself in the open arrival hall just steps from the exit. So there were two things she could say were different about this country already. First, she had expected the customs officer to react to her admission, demand her name, rank, serial number. His admission that it was all the same to him was both a relief and curiosity. Were all people like that here? Of course there were always bigots. She knew that. So what made this experience different?

Stopping just outside the exit doors she checked her phone again. The directions Joanne had sent said she was to meet their car and driver next to pier four. She didn't know what constituted a pier at an airport, but she put her money on the large numbers posted around the top of each of the giant pillars and began her trek in descending order from nine. This end of the terminal was surprisingly quiet while the high-numbered piers were overrun with people, limos, taxis, and private passenger cars. In her direction, there were only two cars near pillar four. An SUV swarming with teenagers and a black town car. Beside the sedan, the driver stood holding a sign and looking very formal in his black suit and mauve turban.

The moment he spotted her, he jogged in her direction. "Ms. Jessepp, I presume?"

With his smooth complexion and baby beard, she was momentarily confused by his accent. It was more South Jersey than South Asian. She chastised herself, remembering this was the capital of multiculturalism. "Yes, how did you know? Wait, never mind. Do you know where we're going?"

He took charge of her suitcase and led her back toward the town car. "Joanne said they were at Toronto General. Now that you're here, I'll send her a quick text just to be sure they're still there."

Slipping into the back seat she thanked him for closing the door for her. When Joanne texted she was sending *the* car, she had half expected it to be a limousine, not this nondescript Lincoln. Then she remembered a comment Kara had made the night they joined the West Coast guys to go dancing, when they had rented a limo so they wouldn't have to drive or wait for a taxi that could accommodate five passengers. Kara had commented that she thought it ostentatious. Fun for such an outrageous holiday but immodest from a business sense. *An immodest car... hmm.*

Climbing in the front, the driver looked back at her. "Joanne said she's being released to home care."

Before she could ask the young man behind the wheel anything else, her phone tinged its notification. In long texts Joanne was trying to explain the diagnosis in layman's terms. Madeleine quickly tabbed back, *"Mom is a nurse. I'm up on the verbiage. How is she?"*

"Herniated disc. It's 'bulging.' Not sure what that means."

Madeleine enjoyed her conversations with Joanne, even their text conversation. In a way, it was like having her own baby sister back. She tabbed quickly, *Imagine standing inside a shoulder-high stack of donuts. They sit nice and level, tight around you. But if you were pregnant, your belly would bulge out between two of the donuts, unbalancing the stack. Only with Kara, it's not a baby bump protruding but an inflamed portion of the spinal cord."*

"Why didn't the stupid Dr just say that?"

"Not all doctors learn to explain things. That job usually falls to the nurses and my mom's particularly good at it."

"Cool."

"So what's next? Your driver says you're taking her home?"

"Harjitt. He's Kara's assistant, and he's taking you to her place. We should be there before you. If not, just have Harjitt take you upstairs. He has keys and knows where everything is."

Madeleine looked up to the driver, at his reflection in the rear-view mirror. He seemed so young for this job. "Excuse me. Umm, I just got a text from Joanne. She's suggesting you take me to Kara's apartment."

"That makes sense," he answered amiably.

"Can I ask you a really rude question?"

"If it's about my turban, I wear this color because I like it and it looks rad with this suit, and it's the favorite color of the Starfish."

She flushed at his response, relieved to know her face wouldn't be visible in the dark sedan. "I like the color. Actually, I was wondering about your accent. I mean," she stumbled again, "you sound like you're from here but your accent is different from Kara's."

She met his eyes in the rearview mirror. He grinned. "That's 'cause I'm from Brampton," he said, pointing over his shoulder as they flew down the highway and obviously sure she knew where he meant. "Kara and Joanne are Rosedale kids," he added. "Although they don't act like it. They're pretty cool. Especially Kara. She gave me this job. Well actually, she made the job for me."

"How's that," she asked, absently reading through Jo's latest text at the same time. She only clicked back into his rambling story when he began describing his first meeting with Kara.

"...I was so relieved Kara wanted to go downtown. My uncle sent me to cover the airport just because it's such a crapshoot. Everyone takes Uber now or the new train. I'd been sitting in the line for four hours when she jumps in. When she said 'downtown' I wanted to cry, I was so happy, I told her I could love her! She laughed and said she was 'too old and too gay! And speaking of old,' she says, 'there's no way you are old enough to be driving a commercial vehicle!' That's it, I thought, I'm busted! You see, I was using my uncle's license. I had a driver's license but I was only sixteen so not the right kind, but you know what? She was so cool. She just asked if I liked it or did I have plans for college? I love cars and being on the road. I love everything about it. Hey, have you seen the *Fast and Furious* movies? I'm kind of car crazy like that but without the crazy stunts or breaking the law. Anyway. Kara said I should call her when I finished high school and talk about what I wanted to do. My uncle said she was just being nice, but I saved her number and sent her a text to tell her when I graduated and you know what she said? She told me, have fun. Enjoy your day to the fullest. And be in my office Monday at eight a.m.! How cool is that?"

"I take it you went?"

"Oh you bet, and she was so nice. Well, of course, you know that, you're her girlfriend, so you know how amazing she is. Anyway, we talked cars for the whole hour then she asks if I want to have my own car and drive or come be an intern at her office. The office is so cool. You'll love it. Anyway, I looked around, and she asked lots of guys to talk to me about what they did. It was interesting but, well…"

"Well, they weren't cars, right?"

"Yeah!" he said, as if she had just made some difficult connection. "She sits me down at a computer and says to research how much it would cost to operate a car for the company. You know, take people to the airport, pick up clients, run errands, take Kara or Joanne to meetings and stuff. And she warned I might have to work nights and weekends and keep her calendar too. I did, and the next day we went out and looked at cars! You should have seen my uncle's face when I pulled up at home in a new Lincoln just two days later!"

"Wow."

"Yeah, I know. Oh, here we are," he said, flicking on the blinkers for their exit.

"Yonge Street? Is this a major artery through town? Kara told me her place isn't exactly downtown."

"She's crazy. She's in the core. Technically, it was like a different village a million years ago, but it's pretty much all downtown now. Geez, she's all of two blocks from the Eaton Centre. You can't get more downtown than that. Well…" He paused long enough to check for traffic before turning right on the red.

Madeleine used the time to enjoy the new surroundings. The car was comfortable and quiet, gliding by swarms of pedestrians. "I can't believe the number of people out on the street at this hour."

He nodded, slowing for jaywalkers on Front Street. "This is Saint Lawrence Market. It's pretty touristy. A lot like the Distillery District. Still, they're both cool places to party, you know, when they're not filming a movie or something."

Before she could comment or ask questions, they turned up another street. She listened as he pointed out buildings, describing their backgrounds. "Is that the Armoury? Jo told me Kara served there."

"Yeah but not here. This one's Moss Park. Here we are." He turned onto Shuter Street then down an alley and stopped at a tall loading door and clicked the built-in garage door opener. He was finally quiet, tabbing through text messages on the car's entertainment system. "They're here. Joanne wants me to show you upstairs." He put the car back in drive and eased into what looked like a long narrow garage. Pulling up right at the end, he powered down the window and pressed a large green button.

She expected the door in front of them to open and was momentarily confused as the car began to move. It took a moment to understand what was happening. "This is an elevator?"

"Yeah. I guess there was no room for a ramp when they built this place, so they put in the elevator. Pretty cool." They settled and watched as the doors opened into a vaulted garage. There were only a handful of cars in the space. Several shipping crates were bunched in a corner, all marked Promotional. "I'm sorry to bring you through the garage. Kara wouldn't like it, but Joanne said it would be faster."

The car parked and her suitcase in hand, he said cheerfully, "Please follow me, Ms. Jessepp."

Joanne met them at the threshold to Kara's living room. She welcomed them by hugging Madeleine and thanking her profusely for coming as if the emergency were life-threatening. She ordered Harjitt to deliver Madeleine's suitcase to the guest room. She then informed him he wasn't to leave until he'd helped himself to the stores of food she had ordered for them all. It was easy to imagine her dealing with her children in much the same way.

Trailing Jo into the kitchen, she was surprised again, both by its size and the look of rare use. The second shock was just how much food Joanne had ordered. Takeout bowls stood on the counter, only half open. Before she could ask, two little rug rats and their father wandered in. "Zack. Please feed the kids while I help Madeleine get settled."

He nodded, more interested in the food while offering absently, "I never expected to see *you* here."

"Zack!" Joanne shook her head at him before turning back to her kids.

"Mommy, can we sit here?" the oldest asked, eyeing the barstools facing the island counter. The younger girl had wrapped an arm around Madeleine's thigh, staring up with big blue eyes.

"Yes you can, now get your plate and Daddy can help you get your pasta." Madeleine recalled Joanne mentioning her son was a precocious seven-year-old, while the doe-eyed little blonde wrapped around her leg had just turned three.

"Poutine!" Zack sang out opening the last of the trays. Madeleine's eyebrows rose at the sight of a dish consisting of French fries, cheese curds, and gravy.

"I want pizza! I want pizza!" the boy chanted while his mother all but slung daggers at their father.

Collecting her daughter from around Madeleine's thigh, she hauled the small child up on her hip, adopting the typical supermom pose and exhaling her frustration. She planted the child on a bar stool beside her brother then placed one small slice of pizza on her plate and added a spoonful of macaroni and cheese from one of the open takeout containers. As the kids began to chow down, the elder child was on his knees on the stool, eyes fixated on Madeleine. Around the half masticated and the overly large amount of pepperoni pizza, he asked, "Are you Aunt Kara's girlfriend?"

Zack seemed to snort under his breath as he continued to inhale poutine. For that, he was rewarded with a smack to the back of the head from his wife. "Come..." Joanne said in resignation, trying to lead Madeleine from the kitchen and her hungry clan.

They were halted by the arrival of Harjitt. Joanne's son, so excited to see him that he took to his feet on the high stool and started jumping up and down, balancing a slice of pizza in his hands, calling out, "Jeeter, Jeeter, Jeeter."

Clearly a member of the family, Harjitt joined them without hesitation, saying, "Hey, did you get this from Poutinery?" While Zack filled him in on the sources of their impromptu feast, he scooped up Jo's daughter, who'd been holding her arms up for him. She now understood she was the Starfish he'd mentioned. He held her as if he'd done it a million times, chatting away while the three-year-old lay sleepily in his arms.

Taking the opportunity to escape, Joanne hooked Madeleine's arm, dragging her along.

"Your kids are so cute," Madeleine offered, trying to ease Jo's frustration and her own trepidation over seeing Kara.

"They should have been in bed hours ago," she said, in a mommy tone of disapproval. She led Madeleine to the far end of the large condo where two older women stood with heads together in serious conversation. One was dressed in scrubs, the other wore an evening gown. Even with the disheveled hair and the ravages of makeup that had been ruined by tears, it was easy to recognize Kara's mother. She could hear the words of comfort from the nurse. It reminded her of how many times her own mother had been called on to manage the expectations and often unbridled emotions of family members concerned for their loved ones. She wondered if it occurred to anyone in the healthcare system, other than the nurses, that in times of emergency, family members often required as much care as those injured or ill.

"There you are," Kara's mother said to Joanne. "The nurse has just been telling me she should be up and back on her feet within a few days."

"I know, Mom. That's what the doctor said. It's what the nurse at the hospital said too. Now, will you please relax. Besides, I have someone I want to introduce—"

"Madeleine, sweetheart, forgive me. I've been a terrible hostess," Kara's mother lamented with sincerity. "I should have fetched you from the airport myself, but oh, I've just been so worried. You must be too?"

She nodded. "I was so relieved when Harjitt brought me up to speed on the drive here. How is she feeling?"

"Sedated," the nurse explained. As Madeleine's eyebrows lifted, she offered the standard reassuring smile while explaining, "Before she can heal, the body needs rest. The affected muscles and of course the bulging hernia are acutely inflamed. Were the nature and severity of her injuries explained?"

"My mom's a nurse," she answered as an explanation.

The nurse nodded, adding, "We see these kinds of injuries more often with athletes trying to push to a higher level of competition. The type sustained by those less able to maintain an Olympic workout schedule and trying to catch up all at once."

"Oh my dear," Marsha Wexler interjected, "Kara's no Olympian. Her coach told me years ago she was too short to make the team. No, she just goes out to the club and paddles around."

Madeleine knew the story of Kara being axed from the junior Olympic rowing team. It was Joanne who'd shared the story, not Kara. It was Jo who'd grumbled about the experience. It was a strange sort of story, one where Joanne boasted about her sister's accomplishments while complaining about the situation. Kara had taken the demotion in stride, explaining to everyone that she'd been replaced by a better rower who she was sure would bring home plenty of medals to make them all proud. It was Joanne who whined and complained. And it was easy for Madeleine to imagine why the seven-year-old Joanne had felt the sting of the axe.

Kara's baby sister worshiped her. As a child, she'd followed her or joined in all her activities. When Kara went to rowing practice, little Joanne would tag along with whistle and timepiece in hand. She was a natural organizer and the kind of kid everyone loved to have around. Some days at practice she would even be called upon to play the role of coxswain. It was easy for Madeleine to imagine little Joanne bristling with pride and taking the stern seat to pace the team.

"Mother," Joanne interrupted. "Kara does not just paddle around. She's on her own team, and solos as well."

"Joni, please, stop baying at the moon. We all know what happened." Turning to look directly at Madeleine, Mrs. Wexler explained, "Kara's done what Kara always does. She's worse than her father. She swallows up her emotions and focuses all her energy on work or her sports. Joanne, back me up here. Tell Madeleine about your father dislocating his shoulder and breaking his arm playing rugby the day after he lost the Peterson account."

"Mother really, I don't think this is the time…"

"Of course it's the time, dear. Madeleine needs to know what she's getting into."

"And what am I getting into?"

While Joanne and Marsha Wexler looked shocked by the question, the nurse, smart enough to see this as her opportunity to escape, interrupted. "Well, I'm off. If anything changes just call home care. The number's on her care instructions, and I'll be back tomorrow to check on her."

Joanne showed the nurse out. Leaving Madeleine alone facing the still disquieted Marsha Wexler. Before she could think of what to say, Marsha challenged her. "Why are you here?"

"I… She asked me."

"Did she?" Marsha asked pointedly.

Suddenly unsure, Madeleine didn't know what to say. Had Kara asked her to come to Toronto? Or had she simply been asking for help, a request she may have made to anyone who just happened to call at that precise moment?

"You girls..." Shaking her head in resignation, Marsha Wexler reached out, and taking Madeleine's hand led her to the sofa and indicated that she should sit. With Marsha in her expensive gown and elegant jewelry, it felt a bit like a cast production. Was she about to be lectured by the headliner? "I should have expected this."

"Expected what?"

"Expected you to be just as reticent as my daughter in conveying your emotions. That child exhausts me! To this day I cannot comprehend how my three children could be so different. Douglas with his two left feet, Joanne with her heart on her sleeve, and then there's Kara—as if she were a bottle of pop someone's been shaking up all day long. Open at your own risk." She shook her head.

"Mrs. Wexler, in my own defense..."

"Please call me Marsha. Mrs. Wexler is that cotton-headed Barbie Doll married to the father of my children. Now, let's not waste time. Kara is rolled up in a ball in bed and heavily sedated because she thought spending the entire day rowing as a sub on an Olympic-level team was a good idea. I know my child. That level of determination only raises its ornery head when she's suffering terribly and determined to find a profitable distraction. You should know profitable does not always mean money with that girl."

"I do know that."

"Good thing. Let's start there. I understand you're an actress? Do you wish to stay in that profession or have you other dreams?"

"Dreams?" That caught her off guard. Who asked a woman over thirty if she had dreams?

"Yes dear. Dreams! Kara—well, the whole family, is in a position to help you with your vocational endeavors. If you desire such undertakings that is. What I won't have this family do, and certainly not my daughter, is waste time on someone unwilling to help herself. You've joined a family of hard workers, Madeleine. Well, Dougie tries hard. Still, each in their own way, are achievers. Are you?"

Madeleine, sitting tall and proud, had been straining not to take offense. Did this woman think she was some guttersnipe or gold digger looking to use her as a step up or out? Reminding herself that Marsha Wexler didn't know her, she reined in her attitude, explaining, "I studied theatre at school. Well, theatre and literature. I originally went to Vegas for an opportunity to choreograph a dinner theatre act. I only started dancing and singing, well, because those were the only jobs my manager could get me." She hoped honesty would earn her points or at least a softening of this inquisition. What she said seemed to resonate deeply.

"Men!" Marsha huffed. "So quick to judge the outside packaging, so willing to consider the interior inferior to their own world. Sorry..." she apologized. "Sometimes I can be a little maudlin when it comes to the subject of the mutant sex."

"Mutant?" Madeleine grinned at her description.

"Of course, dear. Your mother's in the medical profession. Has she explained how the Y chromosome came to be? According to Kara's biology one-oh-one professor, the male sex came into existence when the bottom leg of one of the XX chromosomes fell off."

"I never heard that before. It certainly throws a kink in the Bible-thumper theory that God created Adam first."

For the first time, Marsha smiled. Standing, she tugged on Madeleine's hand. "Let's have a quick peek at our girl. Make sure she's okay then we'll find the ice and make a nightcap. I'm sure we could both use a drink at this point."

CHAPTER SEVENTEEN

Kara woke with a stabbing pain in her back. Forgetting how she'd ended up like this, she tried reaching around to feel for whatever was pressing into her. The resulting escalation of pain halted her arm movement and pushed her mind back into gear. *Fuck, what did I do this time?* Now she remembered Dougie and Samantha bringing her home from the hospital with Joanne and her entire crew in pursuit. *I should've called a cab. All this fuss for a few sprained muscles.* She needed to pee. *Why did the hospital do that all the time?* Okay, she had arrived dehydrated. Okay, she'd been out on the water and in the sun all day. But they had poured enough IV fluids into her to fill a ship's ballast tank.

Realizing she was in too much pain to get up, she did the next best thing, rolling over on her side, and falling down onto her hands and knees. The jolt of pain that followed was blinding, but she kept her balance on all fours, determined to make it to the bathroom, even if she had to crawl the whole way.

The sound of her falling from bed must've drawn the attention of whoever was still home. Suddenly hands were under her arms, lifting her and she found herself unceremoniously plopped down on the toilet. She could hear her mother jabbering, or maybe it was Joanne. While she relieved her bladder, someone handed her a glass of water and pills of some sort. At her mother's urging, she swallowed them without argument. She allowed them to lead her back to the bed. For a moment she wondered how she got there in the first place, then that thought, like everything else, disappeared.

The next time Kara woke she was more aware. More aware of her back pain, and more aware her injuries exceeded a simple sprain. She also saw she was not alone. She recognized Madeleine immediately, asleep in the chair beside the bed, half wrapped in a blanket. Her feet were bare, a slender hand was outside the blanket, fingers intertwined with Kara's. *Huh… interesting. Madeleine's here… Holding my hand…* It was hard to figure out how that happened or when. *Still, it's nice,* she thought as she fell into a deep sedation-induced slumber.

After enduring a long heart-to-heart with Marsha Wexler, Madeleine had been allowed to retire to the guest room. Kara's mom, along with her sister and crew, then departed en masse to Marsha's condo across the hall. Alone and wide-awake, Madeleine paced back to the master bedroom wanting to make one more check on Kara.

Even with the sedatives, her sleep was restless. She watched her hands flex and move as if she were in some deep conversation or sharing some special technique a card dealer might use. Maybe she was explaining some advanced rowing maneuver. She was starting to understand that Kara was capable of anything. Beyond that, she could see there were times when common sense had taken a back seat to her emotions. It was childish. It also made Madeleine warm inside to know Kara had been so deeply affected by her. Not the betrayal. That tore her apart, down deep in her gut.

Coming here had been more than a knee-jerk reaction. It was a risk. Not only did she risk rejection, but she was also risking her entire future. A real relationship with Kara meant so many changes. Moving to a new country would be the first. Could she do it? Leave the States and come here? Was it even feasible? Putting aside her concerns for meaningful work, she didn't know how she would feel about emigrating from her home. Would people, family, and friends think her less American or less a patriot? And what about this country? Could she get a green card or whatever they called it? She knew it was almost impossible for Canadians to move to the States. They could get temporary visas for school, and some of the Canadian entertainers she worked with had years of experience and some big names backing their visas. Then there were the real hard questions, such as the social and career implications of coming out. Could she do it? She knew Kara would never tolerate having a partner who wasn't out. Kara was an all or nothing type of woman. Which she adored and respected.

Kara, grumbling in her sleep, tried to roll. The resulting shock of pain woke her again.

"Kara, you're okay, you're okay..."

"What..."

"Oh, honey you're okay. You put your back out, so you need to try and sleep on your side."

Kara made some indiscernible noise that could have passed for agreement and then she was asleep again. Watching her, Madeleine made up her mind. Quietly retreating to the guest room, she gathered pillows and the blanket folded across the foot of the bed and carried them back down the hall.

She pushed the upholstered chair from the corner of Kara's room right up beside the bed. Kicking off her shoes and socks, she loosened up her clothing then wrapped herself in the blanket, making herself comfortable in the chair. If Kara woke up and told her to get the hell out, so be it. She would. Until then, she was here, and she would help take care of her. Kara may not care for her, but God knows she cared for Kara. The whole seduction fantasy number and how it was scripted to encourage romance had worked just as well on her as it had Kara. But it was more than that. Could it be that she needed what Kara was offering just as much as she needed her? Was need even involved? She couldn't imagine what Kara would ever need. The woman seemed so completely self-sufficient. She herself could admit her need, but it was hard to define. It was new, for sure, this deep abiding desire for Kara Wexler.

It wasn't just companionship or friendship either. Although both those pieces were integral, her desire ran deeper. It burned inside her, like some ferocious beast newly awakened. She more than craved her. She ached for her.

Sitting curled up in the chair and watching her sleep by the dim light seeping in from the hall, she understood there was more involved than need or desire. Kara would know that and Kara would question her. She would need to be ready for that conversation and she needed to be honest. That meant being honest with herself right now and right here. Did she need her? From the common perspective, no. She could return to the airport tomorrow, fly home, and forget the whole thing. She was quite capable of restarting her life in Minneapolis or anywhere for that matter. So, from a practical sense, she was proud to say she wouldn't need Kara like that. Certainly not the way other women looked at her and thought of her. And that gave her the courage to look deeper.

Did she love her? Yes. There was no question about it. The real worry came in facing her desires. Personal privacy didn't exist in this day and age. Both she and Kara worked in industries where social functions were a regular part of the job. Could she get used to the entertainment ranks reporting on her attending events with Kara Wexler on her arm? By conventional standards, Kara was no beauty. That thought actually made her smile. She loved the way she looked. She'd probably put on a few pounds since her days as a high school rowing champion but nothing ungainly or unnatural for a woman. Grey strands were easy to spot in her thick dark hair. And as she didn't bother with makeup or even concealer, the crow's feet around her eyes and the laugh lines around her mouth were visible. In Madeleine's eyes, they made her seem more genuine, more real, more down-to-earth. She was just who she was, and Madeleine loved her for it. Yes, yes, she would be proud to be seen on any red carpet with Kara Wexler on her arm.

"But what about Kara?" she asked herself unkindly. What about her circumstances? How would she feel about having Madeleine on *her* arm? Would it make her feel proud? Would she know how proud Madeleine was to be with her? She sighed and thought quietly for a long while. The real question was not how Kara would feel to have her on her arm. She knew very well Kara found her attractive. Most people did. But what about Kara's true feelings? Could she forgive her and welcome her into her world, into her life? Judging by Jo's enthusiasm, her family seemed to think so. She knew she would've been on shaky ground if Marsha too did not hold strongly to the belief that Kara would forgive her and wanted her here. Coming here had been a risky bet, but with the stakes this high, she was all in.

* * *

Marsha Wexler had followed the doctor's orders, getting Kara up and moving first thing the next day. She'd taken her breakfast at the dining room table, only choosing that spot when she couldn't actually get herself on the stool in the kitchen. After polishing off a plate of Mom's famous French toast, she promptly threw it back up. Humiliated, she was close to tears as her mother fussed to clean her up. Samantha appeared from nowhere, offering her help and reassurances. They managed to get her to the bathroom where she was able to wash her face and rinse her mouth. Kara had every intention of returning to bed but her mother and Samantha had other ideas.

Marsha, blocking her escape, explained bluntly, "I'm sorry, my dear, but you stink to high heaven. No worries; Samantha and I are here to help. We'll get you in and out of the shower as quickly as we can, then right back to bed. I'm sure by then the pain pills will have kicked in, and you'll sleep."

Leaning heavily on the bathroom vanity, Kara looked back and forth between the two women. No way in hell was she getting in the shower and letting her mother and Samantha, of all people, clean her up. If this day hadn't been humiliating enough, the thought of having her sexy sister-in-law see her naked, much less in the company of her mom… "No! I mean…I can manage on my own."

"Like hell, you can," Samantha said in a peeved tone. She stood with her arms crossed.

Kara couldn't help but wonder if she used this demeanor in court. It was certainly intimidating. "Can we wait for the nurse?"

"No," her mother stated clearly. "We most certainly cannot and neither can you. Now stop being so ridiculous. We're all women here."

"No, please?" She was begging even though she had no idea how she could shift her weight far enough to move from the counter to the shower without falling down.

Her legs were visibly shaking when a third person moved up behind her, wrapping a reassuring arm around her waist. "I can help her. Let me do this," she suggested, adding, "I'm wondering if we should change her sheets too? She did sweat up a storm last night."

Kara stood frozen and confused. *Could it be?* She had been expecting Joanne to make her presence known at any moment, but this wasn't Joanne. Still a little woozy, forcing her eyes open, she concentrated on the arm and hand ever so gently pressed against her abdomen. She recognized the bracelet on her wrist. It was the petite Amulette de Cartier she had given Madeleine. Lifting her head, she took in the scene around her. Staring at her own reflection in the mirror, she caught the tableau of the three other women. The mother, the sister, and the lover. Were they lovers? She locked eyes with Madeleine's reflection and held the connection while she sensed more than heard her mother and her sister-in-law leave to attend to the suggested duties.

It was hard to keep her balance, even with Madeleine's sturdy hold. The shaking continued as waves of nausea rolled through her. "I… You…" She struggled to form a coherent thought. Resigning, she focused her concentration on staying on her feet and not throwing up again. It was the last thing she wanted Madeleine to see. She had no idea when Madeleine had arrived. For all she knew, she had already witnessed her morning performance.

"I know you're confused and you probably want to talk," Madeleine said reassuringly.

Kara listened to the soft voice drifting into her ears. The result was so reassuring she couldn't recall what it was she wanted to talk about. Somewhere in the back of her mind, she remembered she might want to be mad at Madeleine. There was some nagging thing, but right now she could hardly care. If she had to shower, she would certainly rather do it with Madeleine. Still, she was embarrassed and shy. Embarrassed thinking, *We hardly know each other. Yes, we've slept together. Connected. And so much more*. But this was hardly a thing she would ask a new lover to do just weeks after meeting.

"Hey, you. I see your face. You don't need to be like that, Kara. It's just me. Besides, I think you'll recall, we've already done the shower thing together?"

Kara managed a small grin.

"Good. That's what I thought." Still, her tone was gentle and light. She stripped out of her own clothes, folding them neatly and piling them on the toilet seat before starting the shower and adjusting the water temperature. Kara listened while she moved about the bathroom. Now she was back behind her, slowly removing the sweat-soaked T-shirt and shorts she'd been wearing as pajamas. Stripped bare, Kara shuddered at the sensation of Madeleine's arm slowly wrapping around her middle. Even though her touch was gentle, she braced to be pulled into the shower. Instead, Madeleine moved slowly, deliberately wrapping both arms around her and embracing her from behind. In the mirror, she could see their reflection as Madeleine began kissing her shoulder and neck.

Then she halted her progress, telling her plainly, "You're all I've been thinking about. God, I miss the feel of you in my arms."

Still supporting her weight with her arms, Kara began the difficult task of turning around. When she finally rested her bottom against the counter, she was able to remove one hand then the other, allowing the vanity and Madeleine to support her weight. She wanted to look up into her eyes, to stare at that face, to see what she needed to see, but tilting her head instantly increased her nausea. Instead, she rested her head on Madeleine's shoulder. The connection gave her comfort and strength.

Finally breaking the hug, Madeleine moved her carefully into the shower. She was cautious and tender but wasted no time getting her cleaned up, dried off, and into the dry sleepwear someone had set out. When they emerged from the bathroom. Kara was relieved to find the nurse had arrived. The sooner she got her poking and probing done, the sooner she would leave, and she could get some rest.

Back in her own bed, she drifted off while the nurse and the other women discussed her medication and other concerns. It didn't matter to her. They could decide whatever they liked today. Tomorrow she'd be back on her feet. Then, she would decide what was best for her and her injuries. All this care was a little much. Closing her eyes, she could admit she didn't understand the fuss. It wasn't like she'd suffered a near-death experience or even life threatening injuries. Still, she would discuss it with Madeleine. Yes, Madeleine would know what to do. *She's a dancer and dancers are athletes, extreme athletes of a sort. She'll know what to do.* When the pain pills finally knocked her out, she slept peacefully knowing Madeleine was there.

CHAPTER EIGHTEEN

Madeleine had allowed Joanne to drag her out for the afternoon. She hadn't wanted to leave Kara's side, but with a surplus of caregivers, she had no good excuse to demur. Besides, Kara was asleep and still deeply sedated. In a way, it was a blessing. While she slept, she would heal. Madeleine's only hope was that when she woke, she would want to talk or at least listen.

The afternoon had been otherwise interesting. She and Joanne had joined Marsha Wexler for the festivities at the yacht club. Madeleine had been nervous, even a little intimidated when they boarded the water taxi for the private club across the harbor. She needn't have been. If anything, the last ten years in Vegas had taught her more about people than a bucketful of degrees would have done. She easily divided the club's patrons into three groups, putting Marsha Wexler and her cronies in the authentics box. There were a few she would classify as has-beens, and the rest were wannabes. All pretty normal in her book. The interesting aspect was watching Marsha and her friends. They were authentic as in authentically wealthy and generous individuals. They were the kind of men and women most interested in providing a hand up, not a handout. They believed in people and wanted to see the best in them. To rise to the height of their God-given talents. To them, desire, skill, and work ethic meant more than birth and position. The wannabes on the other hand, were quick to judge, and fast to dismiss. Fast, as in faster than light speed. Some of these less than authentic individuals, she was sad to notice, were friends of Joanne's. Jo would introduce her with great enthusiasm. Madeleine, however, wasn't fooled. She would see the chill in their eyes, the way they would give her a look over, taking in her clothing and asking her questions about her investment strategies and the clubs of which she was a member as if that would measure her actual worth.

As soon as the awards had been given out, Marsha linked arms with her, whispering quietly, "Let's get out of here. I'm in no mood for the phony baloneys today." That was heartwarming. That, and the kind of conversation she enjoyed on the ferry trip back across the harbor. Marsha refused to take the water taxi, which infuriated Joanne. "There is no need to be so bourgeois," Marsha explained. "Look, the ferry is almost at the dock. By the time we walk over there, they'll be boarding. We'll be across the harbor faster than the water taxi can get here. Besides, taking the ferry always makes me nostalgic."

And it had. Marsha had hooked her arm, strolling with her to the upper deck and taking a place at the forward rail. "I love this city," she said. Pointing to the skyline, she reminisced, "When I was a child, none of these condos were here. As a matter fact, the harbor pushed in at least a few hundred yards further toward Front Street. Every year they fill in a little more to build more and every year we lose a little more of the harbor."

"It actually reminds me of Seattle," Madeleine offered. "The same sort of ferry boats, lots of traffic in the harbor, even the airplanes flying in and the CN Tower above it all. Except it also has the feel of New York. You know, with the buildings sitting right on the edge of the water. What did it look like when you were a kid?"

"Nothing like this. Just between those tall condos over there is the grand old lady of the lake, the Royal York Hotel. When we were children, it dominated the skyline. In the West End over there by the airport," she pointed, "the Tip Top Tailors Building and the Victory Soy Towers marked the west entrance of the harbor. The grain towers are long gone. And the historic buildings just seem to be swallowed up between condos and office towers. At least they haven't been able to tear them all down. I'm proud of Kara for her little bit of maintaining history."

"Her building you mean?"

"Yes, what do you think of it?"

"I… It's very impressive. I have to admit the upper building, the look of the glass cube perched on top of the old red brick building is like nothing I've ever seen. Did she really design it herself?"

"She did. She is a remarkable girl. Headstrong too," Marsha warned, finally making eye contact. "Are you ready for that?"

"Honestly?" she asked, before taking a long moment to consider the question. "I'm scared shitless. I don't want her to feel like she's stuck with me because I'm here but I don't want to give up either. I just don't know; what's the best thing to do?"

"My advice, for what it's worth," Marsha said, wrapping a motherly arm around her, "do what's best for you, first. Kara will respect that. I think you two have a lot to talk about and you will have to be patient. Emotions, feelings, these are things Kara does not do well. You may find you'll need to give her time. Can you do that?"

Madeleine wanted to shout her affirmative, yes, whatever it takes, but she knew Marsha wanted her to think the situation through. Before she could answer, Marsha launched into a story, and Madeleine immediately knew it was just her way of conveying an important message.

"When Douglas and Kara were children, their father insisted they be enrolled in the summer riding academy. Of course, like everything, that lasted right up until Kara proved to be a better horseman than her brother would ever be. The interesting part of the story is not Kara's skill on horseback but her comprehension of horses. Those summers, dragging the kids out to Sunnybrook Stables, I learned a tremendous amount about my two eldest children. Kara was much like the sole stallion they kept on hand. Regardless of what the humans thought, he truly believed himself responsible for the whole herd. Now Douglas on the other hand, he was so clearly one of the young geldings. Happy just goofing around in the paddock area and running around with the other boys like a crazy man.

"One afternoon I sat watching the various horses in the separate paddocks. The children, of course, were on the school horses and performing those ridiculous hours of trotting in circles. Well, on this particular day, I lost interest. Forgive me for not being a better mother."

Madeleine giggled and gave her a little shoulder bump to acknowledge her understanding of the joke.

"Anyhow, bad me. I was watching the geldings, the fixed boy horses instead of my darlings. To be honest, I didn't know they were boys much less boys sans their family jewels." This she said with a wicked grin. "It was interesting. This young constable came over to talk." She elaborated, "The police keep their horses at Sunnybrook too. Anyway, this young cop wanders over to where I'm standing at the rails and sort of translates what's going on. In the corral next to the geldings were the pregnant and nursing females. Two were blind. He explained how that happened, but I've long forgotten. The important takeaway was how the geldings would behave. They were so much like teenage boys. They would wait until these poor mothers and their babies were quiet then sneak up and scare them half to death. They'd then run around like a pack of idiots while these poor beasts cowered around their little ones to protect them. 'Let's hope they don't try that again,' the officer said, and I thought he was thinking about how hard it was on the mares and the foals. Then he points to the far paddock. The big stallion was watching everything. Sure enough, the geldings start up again. I think it may have been the horse version of calling names in the playground, but that stallion wasn't going to put up with it. He came right over his fence and then the next and the next until he was in with the geldings. He chased them around that pen finally herding them all into a corner and delivering some serious bites to several rumps.

"It was at that exact moment I realized they were just like Kara and Douglas. Kara was the leader and protector. Nothing would change that. Of course, back then I imagined her the heroine of her own nuclear family. Douglas is still all teenage gelding, incapable of more than charging playfully about. Don't get me wrong. There is absolutely nothing wrong with that," she added, but the sadness was there in her voice for the world to hear. "What I learned about horses that day was their selflessness and their need to belong. I'm proud to know all my children fit that description. The difference I've come to accept, and what I think you need to understand, is that Kara is more the stallion than we can comprehend. And don't take that from the male perspective of breeding and sex. It's about her thinking it's her job to keep the peace and protect everyone in her herd from everyone outside of it."

Madeleine knew the woman was waiting for her to make some connection. "And I take it I'm the outside risk?"

She shook her head but remarked, "It's so hard to tell with that girl. What I can say is she's hurt and her pride has taken a hard cross-check. The important thing now is to let her know you care and that you can be patient. You can be patient with her, can't you?"

"To be honest, I don't know how we move on from here. It isn't like I live a few blocks down the street. On the other hand, I won't push her. I won't be one of those instant partners. I think she's going to need some time, but I want her to know I'll be here whenever she needs me. I wasn't sure I could live here," she said, looking out over the harbor and watching as the ferry maneuvered into the city docks, "but this is a beautiful place. I was mucking around on my phone earlier. I can't believe the number of TV and movie production companies shooting here, and that doesn't even touch the amount of theatre you have."

"Do you know what you want to do? I mean, Joanne tells me you have experience and talent, on both the production side and performance."

"Hey," Joanne interrupted. "Did I hear my name?"

"I expected you to be standing first in line at the gangway gate," Marsha teased her daughter. She explained to Madeleine, "Jo always prefers getting off the ferry more than getting on. Always in a hurry, this one."

Turning to include Jo in the conversation, Madeleine answered the question from Marsha as best as she could. "I'll be honest. I really want to choreograph and maybe in time direct, but I'd take just about any job to get my foot in the door. I am worried about getting a visa or green card, whatever it's called here. And I won't put this on Kara."

"You mustn't worry about such things but if it makes you feel better, becoming, as we say, 'landed' is quite simple for entertainment professionals. I'm sure it will be a straightforward matter with your existing portfolio." Madeleine felt doubtful, and her face must have given away her skepticism. "Joanne, what is the name of that outrageously funny American actress I so adore? You know, the one who got her start up here with *Second City*?"

"Andrea Martin?"

"Yes, of course. Andrea Martin. You know her from *Saturday Night Live*, correct?"

"Actually I do. I didn't realize she worked up here."

She nodded, hooking arms with both Madeleine and her daughter. The ferry had completed the docking sequence, and they followed other passengers making their way down the wide staircase and off the extra wide gangway. "I can't possibly do the story justice, but she has a whole standup routine about coming to Canada. It starts at the airport. That's where you used to make your application to be landed. Anyway, she jokes about the difficulty of the process. According to her, the entirety of the intake review involves proving you can handle yourself in a canoe. Once she passed that test, at the airport no less, they stamped her application and that was it. She was landed. I wish I had her gift. You should Google it or however you find all those funny videos on the computer."

Exiting the terminal gate, Madeleine was pleased to see she recognized where they were. Harjitt had dropped them off just a few hundred feet away at the water taxi stand. Now he was waiting, stopped on Queen's Quay, and holding the door open for them. She was a little disappointed. It was a beautiful day, and the lake and lakefront were gorgeous. The wide boulevard was bustling with tourists and invited a leisurely stroll. She could see her and Kara taking that turn. Walking hand in hand, past the galleries, marinas, and open spaces. Oblivious to the people, and only aware of each other and the perfect summer day.

"Madeleine, dear, please don't fret. No matter how you manage things going forward, you can always lean on Joanne and me. Samantha too. She's just as taken with you as our Kara. Now we just need to make sure that child of mine doesn't do anything stupid. I do love her, but she can be as stubborn as her father."

Madeleine got in the car first, sliding across the back seat so Marsha wouldn't have to. It was interesting. She knew the woman was trying to encourage her, but there were warnings too. Maybe they were worth heeding. After all, just how much did she actually know about one Kara Wexler?

* * *

Kara was sprawled on the rooftop daybed half reclined and on her side. She'd been trying to read, sporadically, but it was hard to concentrate. Between the heat of the day, her discomfort, and her visiting niece, she couldn't get interested in the stack of reading materials she had requested. Beside her, and slightly resembling a starfish, her three-year-old niece was sprawled. The little tyke had managed to get herself rolled around to rest one foot in Kara's ribs and the other on her thigh. Her arms were spread wide, her head hung half off the daybed, her mouth open, baby snores emanating. In a way, it soothed Kara. Watching her little niece snooze reminded her of everything right in the world.

She heard Madeleine before she saw her. That was not actually correct. Samantha, who'd been sitting in a nearby lounge chair and reading from some heavy legal tome, snapped her book closed and set it aside. That was all the warning she got before her mother and her sister intruded on their serenity. She watched as they emerged from the stairwell. This time she wasn't surprised by Madeleine's appearance. If anything, she was thrilled to see her here. Before she could decide what that meant, the little starfish beside her began to cry. Awakened by the storm of noise heading toward her, her sobs were a natural result of her confusion.

"Abigail. Don't cry. Mommy's here," Joanne said, before continuing her verbal assault on the actions of their male family members. "Can you believe those guys? Men! I swear, any excuse to plant themselves in front of the TV and drink beer. Even Harjitt couldn't wait to join them. And to watch a stupid soccer game? Can you believe that?" she asked again, clutching the sniveling toddler to her chest.

"Are they watching the women's game?" Kara asked, looking very much like she was ready to jump up and join them.

"Oh no you don't, young lady," her mother warned while giving her the stink eye, a look all children recognized.

Madeleine, who had been silent until this moment began to laugh. "Oh my God. My mother still pulls that one on me too."

Busted for the mother-daughter showdown, Kara laughed too. "How do you like that, Mom? Sounds like we're typical."

Marsha Wexler placed herself on the edge of the daybed, assuming the spot warmed by the starfish. "You, my child, may be called many things, but typical is not one." She took both of Kara's hands in one of hers, her other hand she placed on Kara's forehead as if she were a sick child.

Kara shook it off, "Mom! Cut it out. I'm not sick already."

Marsha ruffled her hair, then stood, "All right, children, let's leave the girls alone. Joanne, you can help me get dinner on," she ordered. As they disappeared, they could hear Marsha quizzing Samantha on her and Doug's schedule for the week.

Kara, still sprawled on the daybed, was having trouble sitting up; when Madeleine offered her hand, she stalled, remembering. She'd noticed that hand before. Long slender fingers connected to a soft, welcoming palm. She followed the line of Madeleine's elegant slender arm to her square shoulders. Her collarbone, inviting, just poking from the neckline of her loose T. If that hadn't done Kara in, certainly that long elegant neck and Madeleine's moss green eyes did. Her skin was so like porcelain, lightly freckled all around the frame of her brassy red hair. Finally, accepting the hand, Kara allowed Madeleine to pull her into a sitting position. It was a relief. "The physio says I can get up and even walk a bit, but I can't spend much time on my feet. At least not until the swelling goes down."

It seemed a stupid announcement to make; after all, Madeleine had been present for everything. But she was nervous and a little concerned by her mother's need to give them privacy.

Madeleine took a seat beside her but remained quiet, almost withdrawn.

As they sat, the silence between them began to build, and she worried. Initially, she'd been confused by Madeleine's presence, even wondering if she'd simply dreamed her into form. She'd been stubborn about her fears and her feelings. "I thought I imagined you. At least I did until the shower."

"Please tell me you're okay…about everything. I mean, me coming here and helping you…and the shower?"

"Why are you here?" Kara asked, her tone harsher than she intended. The question seemed to land like a ton of bricks. She hadn't intended to hurt her. She felt terrible and relieved at the same time. Wanting to soften her stance but needing Madeleine to hear the truth, she asked, "Did I ask you to come here?"

Madeleine's head was down. She looked to be examining her hands. Finally, she said, "You asked for help. I called Joanne. It was the only number I could remember. She challenged me to prove I care."

Kara contemplated what that conversation would have sounded like. She knew her baby sister could be persuasive. "Did she ask or tell?"

"Kara, she challenged me. She didn't ask me to come, she just asked if I cared. And in case you don't believe me, I do care very much…" As tears looked to threaten, she said, "I know you don't want me here. That's okay. I get it, but since I'm here all I can ask is that you listen and ask questions too. I don't want to leave thinking you don't know everything or…how I feel."

"What's to know? My misguided siblings contracted a fantasy company to craft a mood for me and get my motor running. Congratulations. You did it. Brava!"

"Kara, please. I never meant to hurt you."

"Hurt me? You broke my heart!"

"Broke your heart? You stole mine then flew away!"

That statement stopped her dead. She hadn't meant to get upset much less confrontational. Now Madeleine had the nerve to compare *her* feelings to Kara's distress? "Stole your heart? Oh yeah? You broke my heart into a million pieces!"

"I did. I know. What about you? You stole my heart and dragged it to a foreign nation and forced me to come after you!"

"Forced you!" Kara was trying to stand, but when Madeleine refused to assist her, she fell back. "Ow! You, you… I didn't steal your heart. I…I thought I found it."

That revelation forced her and Madeleine into a strange silence. Finally, she admitted, "I'm having a hard time believing you would want to be here. Why did you come?"

Madeleine sighed. She looked to be expecting this question. "The same reason I called on Saturday even though the contract your sister-in-law had me sign specifically assigned great threats if I ever did. Technically, you could sue me just for calling you. Who knows what your legal system could do to me for showing up?"

Kara harrumphed her reply before retorting, "This is Canada. We don't sue. And as far as our justice system goes, they'd probably sentence you to hard years finishing university or some such shit. Either way, I lose."

"How so?"

Kara was quiet for so long Madeleine reached out, taking her hand. "How so, honey? Would you miss me?"

"I miss you now," she roared, jerking her hand away. "How the fuck do you expect me to cope with you popping in and out of my life? For all I know this is some sort of courtesy call. Some contingency in the contract with those stupid twerps I'm related to!"

"Kara Wexler! You're behaving like a spoiled brat. How the hell do you expect me to have an actual conversation with you?"

"You forgot the Delphine," she grumbled sarcastically.

"The what?" Madeleine was so steamed she was on her feet.

"Delphine! I know! It's my stupid middle name and if you're going to yell at me you're supposed to include it too." She crossed her arms and assumed a pout. Only the spark in her eye gave away her amusement.

"Oh, so that's how it is?" Madeleine too was grinning as she sat back down. She caught on fast. "So I'm supposed to pronounce 'Kara Delphine Wexler,' before I bawl you out? Good to know. What else should I know about arguing with you? Are you supposed to win all the time? That doesn't sound like very much fun."

"It is for me." Finally Madeleine smiled, and Kara asked without rancor, "Why did it take you a week to call? I mean, if you cared..."

"Honey, I do care, more than I can possibly understand but I did sign a contract, and I was sure you'd never forgive me. Can you forgive me?"

The question sat between them for so long it looked like Madeleine might cry. Offering her hand, Kara allowed, "I'm not sure there's anything to forgive. Technically, you did your job, followed the script and obeyed the contract. Well, for a week you did. The only question is whether you're feeling...did you feel..."

"Yes! Yes, I felt it all. I felt the rush of dancing with you, the joy of talking with you and making love was...was never like that. Never like you."

Kara closed her eyes and sighed with relief, brought Madeleine's hand her to lips, kissing her knuckles. When she realized what she was doing, her eyes popped open in surprise—just in time to catch a look of relief crossing Madeleine's face. "I... Should we... This is so weird. I want to say we need to get to know each other, but we do, kinda', don't you think?"

"We've made love twice. I can't think of two more honest conversations. But you're right, intimacy does not mean we know what we're doing or what each of us wants. I see your worry, Kara, and I do understand how dubious you are about me. Not all the things we shared were honest, but almost everything was. I think if I were you, I would need to know the difference or I couldn't trust my feelings—or much of anything for that matter."

She nodded. What else was there to do? Madeleine was right. She couldn't be sure what was the truth and what had been pure fiction. "Tell me?"

Madeleine smiled, seemingly reassured. She moved in closer, getting comfortable while never withdrawing her hand from Kara's. "Let me tell you a story I think you'll like. It's about a humble girl from Minnesota who finds herself falling for her costar in a Vegas adaptation. What would be a good movie simile? And please, it's not going to be a *Pretty Woman* remake."

"Naw, I was thinking more *American Gigolo*."

"Oh touché! Except I've never seen that one so I'll just wing it."

"Will there be singing? I like singing."

Madeleine leaned in even closer, offering a sweet peck before promising, "For you, there will always be singing, and if you're really nice, I'll throw in a dance or two. That is, after you're back on your feet."

Kara smiled, really smiled for the first time in days, the first time since winning the board vote. "Okay, I'm listening."

CHAPTER NINETEEN

Kara had endured a full morning in the office. Once she was sure the new teams were progressing and the office humming, Harjitt had driven her home and helped her, along with Madeleine, up to the rooftop terrace and the comfy daybed. The nurse had made her last home visit and left instructions on her care and a warning to get herself to her doctor if she didn't improve on schedule. The physio would still come daily but lucky for them that wasn't scheduled until late afternoon. Right now they had time to enjoy lunch and talk a little more.

Franco had called Madeleine that morning with a hot lead. Technically, he wasn't her manager anymore but if he hooked her up, it would earn him a nice finder's fee and the gig he was offering was definitely worth considering. Except it wasn't in Toronto. It wasn't even in Minneapolis. He had a line on a production almost ready for rehearsals. The show, called *Fever*, was scheduled to open on the Thanksgiving Day weekend. The best part was the role. He had kept his promise. The producers had been in Vegas looking for the quintessential

Vegas choreographer. They wanted someone fresh but with years of experience in the Las Vegas entertainment scene, and they wanted her.

Kara sat quietly, listening to her explain the opportunity. They had talked all Sunday night. Talking, really talking, but it wasn't until this precise moment that Kara could admit she wanted Madeleine, wanted her to stay and understood that what she felt, what she had berated herself for, was exactly what she had in common with this woman. "So you're leaving?"

"Yes, no, wait. How…"

"This isn't New York, but there are opportunities here too. Surely my mom and Jo promised to share their connections. Wait. They aren't—"

Madeleine placed a hand on her knee. "Everything is fine. Your mother—well, your whole family—have been warm and welcoming."

"But you want to leave?" She tried to keep her voice level and without a hint of strain but the thought of Madeleine leaving without giving them a chance…

"Kara, please listen," Madeleine begged. "Franco just called me. He has a line on a choreography gig. A big musical being staged for New York. This would be a huge break for me."

"New York?"

"Uh-huh. I know. Can we talk about it, about everything?"

Kara nodded. "I'm not mad. Not anymore, but I am confused and, well…can we dispense with the beating around the bush?"

"I… Okay."

Taking a deep breath, Kara confessed, "I have feelings for you. When I asked myself why I was so mad, so upset, I had to admit I'd fallen for you. I know part of that is a result of how the damned thing was scripted but now you're sitting here and I want to believe it's because you feel something too."

It seemed like they might be on the road to repeating last night's entire conversation when Kara became quiet.

Madeleine told her, "When I finally broke down and called I had all these things I wanted to discuss, all these things I wanted to ask, then I heard your voice. You were in pain. You needed help, and all I could think about was how fast I could get here. Still, I had a lot of concerns. Then you needed help in the shower. I was watching you, watching your face and your panic at the thought of Samantha and Marsha bathing you. You are so proud and so strong, even when you're at your most vulnerable. If that didn't seal it, holding you in my arms… I know I love you desperately."

"You do? I mean…how do you know?"

"Kara, this is the part where you tell me how you feel."

She nodded, finally making eye contact. "I… You. I fell for you the first time we met. I just don't know if what I feel is for the real you, or the character you played."

"The love we shared, that was all me. The real me. I wish I could go back and change it all, tell you everything at the time, but in a way it's what we both needed." At Kara's upraised eyebrows, she challenged, "Be honest. If our introduction hadn't been arranged, would you have asked me out? Holy hell girl, even if you did, there's little chance I would have accepted. It just never would have occurred to me. No matter how misguided your siblings might have been, I will always be indebted to them for bringing us together. I don't know what you want, or if you want to pursue what we've discovered, but I do. And yes, I do love you; the real and stubborn Kara *Delphine* Wexler."

Kara took the hand resting on her knee, holding it in both of hers and kissing the knuckles one at a time. Finally, she admitted. "I haven't had a lot of experience with this whole relationship thing."

Madeleine leaned in, offering a quick peck to her cheek. "Luckily for you, I have a ton of experience with relationships, all bad. I think it's become my superpower, you know, smelling bad relationships at a distance."

"And how does this one smell so far?"

"I'm happy to report the most beautiful scent surrounds me." This she said up close and the words made Kara smile, and she smiled too. "I know taking a job in New York sounds like I'm moving on, but if I take the job, if I get it, it's only for three months. Your mom says it's only an hour flight. You could pop down on weekends, or I could come see you. The good part is that it will give us time to get to know one another. Please don't laugh but I had this vision of us writing letters and sharing our thoughts and hearts on everything. Sort of like characters in a Jane Austen novel. I know it's silly…"

"I like it," Kara allowed. "I'll admit I was sitting here trying to figure things out, how to go slow and at the same time get serious enough to get you Landed. I guess Joanne warned you I can be a bit of a plotter."

"Trotter more like but I get the simile." She smiled. "Your mother did wax on about getting Landed. She didn't think it was an issue, but of course I get she's trying to encourage me."

"I get that too. Just so you know. She isn't like that with everyone. Actually, she's never taken an interest in anyone I've dated. It's nice…kind of weird, but nice. Anyway, Samantha spent an hour today explaining all the ins and outs of the immigration system. It won't be a problem getting you landed so don't worry about it. When the time comes, please let Samantha handle it. The process is quite easy, but it's a one-strike system. Get anything wrong, and they turn you down on the spot and you can't apply again. Maybe that's why we haven't got the kind of immigration backlog you guys have," she postulated, her mind wandering to the vagaries of their differing national policies.

"Kara," Madeleine said quietly, recognizing that Kara was on a tangent and knowing from the example of her family that it was her job to steer her back on track. "I can manage that myself. I don't want to put—"

"Please. Let us do this part. I know it's early and…" She finally admitted what was troubling her. "You may get to the Big Apple and decide the Big Smoke, and me, are just chapters you can relegate to the past." She felt bad even suggesting it, worried that Madeleine might offer to stay in Toronto and forgo the job. "There's something you should know about me. When I make a commitment, I always deliver. Whatever happens between us, you can rest assured Samantha will handle your application professionally if you decide you want to live here. The only thing I can ask is that you do what's best for you and your career.

Madeleine, you are an amazing talent. There isn't a hope in hell I'll let you give up on your dreams."

"This is a huge opportunity for me. Once the curtain opens, my job is done, and I'll be ready to push my resume on producers and directors here. Kara, I want to be able to hold my head up high. I want you to be proud of me, to be able to introduce me as a choreographer or performer with some real credentials. It would kill me to have people think I'm just some showgirl you picked up in Vegas."

"Like my dad will say to everyone who'll listen to him?"

"I don't think you care too much about what he says."

"I care if he's saying trash about you!" She tried to stand and was forced to accept Madeleine's help.

"Easy, honey. Where would you like to go?"

"The boxing club! I want to beat the shit out of something."

"Okay…" Madeleine looked around the roof terrace in a panic. Finally, she led Kara to the garden sofa and helped her sit. Once she was comfortable, she snuggled in beside her. "I think your dad already got your point. And as for beating the shit out of something, you've already done a pretty good job on yourself. Don't you think?"

Kara nodded, then changed the subject, far too stubborn to admit she was right. "Honey, eh? I like that. Never thought I would like endearments like that."

Madeleine wrapped an arm around her shoulders. How is it this woman could have so much love to give and have experienced so little of it herself? "You are a wonder, Kara Wexler. No matter what the future brings, I love you. I never imagined it could be like this. All I can hope is that you feel even just a smidge of what I feel."

Kara turned her head as best she could, delivering a smoldering kiss. Then she said, "You know what they say, still waters run deep. I do love you. I don't know how that happened and… It's just that I love you and I want to know you. I want to learn about you. I want to share things with you. And I want you to flourish. Go to New York and yes I'll write every day. On some days we can text and others I'll go all Jane Austen on you. So now I'm going to have to send Harjitt on a snipe hunt for handmade paper and sealing wax, and I'll need a seal for the envelope. Any suggestions?"

She giggled at Kara's silly attempt at romance. "Can you see the postman's face?"

"I can, but I'd rather focus on yours."

Madeleine snuggled in as close as she dared, laying her head against Kara's. "Me too, honey, me too."

CHAPTER TWENTY

Madeleine was so deep in thought, she almost missed her stop. Following the other passengers, she climbed the stairs from the subway station, heading for the Joyce Theatre. Today she would start work with the primaries. She'd been promised they were better prepared than the dancers had been. They were already a month behind. Most of the dancers who had been pre-hired before she arrived she'd had to let go. They were young and more interested in celebrating their new gig than actually preparing for it. The routines she had designed were complicated, but no more than any Vegas show, and nothing the average showgirl couldn't master in an afternoon. Luckily for her the producers and the director knew that and supported her position. New auditions had taken up weeks and had been a worry she discussed with Kara more than once. But there was no advantage to letting lesser performers make a half-assed attempt. Yes, this was an opportunity worth celebrating…for a day or two. Now was the time to settle down and focus. Her dancers needed to commit, and she smiled as she entered the theatre. They knew this was her first big gig as a choreographer. Now they also knew she was a serious artist and wouldn't put up with second-best or good enough.

* * *

Kara had just finished another virtual board meeting when she received Madeleine's text: "*Primaries arrived fresh and ready to work. You were right. They are ready to listen and work hard. What a difference!*"

Kara replied, "*It's not like millennials can't work hard, they just don't know they need to.*"

"*TY Honey, 4 listening last night. I was worried about today, but these guys are amazing—real pros.*"

"*Pls tell me they're treating you with respect?*"

"*You were right about that 2. And Dame Anderson may be in her 50s but holy cow!!!! That lady can dance!*"

"*;-)*"

"*U!*"

"*Off to wrangle the Interns now. Want to switch jobs?*"

"*NOYL :) Luv U*"

"*I love you too. Talk tonight?*"

"*Y :)*"

Kara slid her phone into her suit jacket and headed for the social media war room. What she had been calling the atrium meeting room was now overflowing with millennials, tech, and pizza. All of which were producing remarkable results. Once she delivered her daily update and inspiration to the crew, she moved on to the creatives, spending most of the morning working out the design and focus of their newest campaign. Her afternoon too was already committed to interviewing for new positions. She needed a Facebook specialist with some real experience and not just for Facebook. She needed to conquer Twitter and half a dozen other social media platforms that would appeal to the target audience of various ad campaigns. It was important she got this right, and fast. She had a board to satisfy and clients to please.

This morning she had briefed the board, but for some reason they seemed a little cold, even disdainful. She assumed the combination of having this online meeting experience foisted on them and the added work of having to attend monthly meetings, even just virtually, felt burdensome when her father had been satisfied to catch them up just once a year. She didn't care. Annual meetings were inefficient and impractical in this day and age. Her job wasn't to make them comfortable. It was to make them money, and that was her plan. After her rowing accident, she'd been limited to working only half days her first week back. She had spent all her spare time then and since reading reports: financial, business planning, even employee pension assessments. With the numbers now engraved in her head, she was sure she could double profits this year and raise the bar even higher for the next.

It was after seven when she finally took the big service elevator to her apartment, walking in to find the kitchen bristling with activity. Finding Joanne, Samantha, and her mom waiting was not a good sign. In the four months since hurting her back, she had recovered well but still felt a little stiff after a long day. The smaller kitchen table was set for dinner and was loaded with food. Joanne, forever the happy hostess, held out her favorite hard drink, a Labrador Tea. Suspicious and a wee bit worried, she accepted the highball. "I have a feeling this is going to be really good or really bad."

"Girls, let's sit and have supper. We can talk once Kara's had a chance to relax a bit. Now sweetheart, why don't you come sit over here with me? You know, I was just telling Samantha I think it's time to update these kitchen furnishings. Perhaps something a little more playful—"

"Mom, what's going on?" Not often, but sometimes she could prattle on as much as Joanne. But she hadn't heard her mom talk like this in years. The last time she was this unreservedly garrulous she was trying to explain that she and their father were divorcing.

Samantha, never as patient as Kara, clarified the news for her. "Zack spilled the beans to your father. We don't know if he'll do anything..."

"Too late," Kara admitted with a sigh, closing her eyes as she recalled and reassessed the attitude of the board that morning. Flopping back in her chair, she finally opened her eyes to see the worry on their faces and something more. "Joanne, stop. This isn't your fault."

"I know, but I feel like it is. I don't know what's wrong with him sometimes. He said he didn't mean to and he's sorry if that means anything."

"It would if it came from him."

Joanne looked prepared to take all the heat, and it was enough to stop Kara from blowtorching her. Trying to remain reasonable, she said, "It was always a matter of time. I knew that coming home. Although to be fair, my worry was with Madeleine first, then Zack. And don't take that personally, Jo. Zack's just young, and he's loyal. Plainly that loyalty is to the old man, but he's loyal."

Moving closer and wrapping her arm around Kara's shoulders, her mother asked, "Should I call the board? Maybe if I explain…"

"No way. Sorry Mom, I know you're just trying to help, but I will not have my mommy on the phone trying to apologize for something I will not apologize for."

"And Madeleine?" her mother asked. "You're not going to…"

"To what? Dump her over this? No Mom. No worries there."

"What will you do?" she asked, her voice thick with concern. "You haven't been this happy since…since I don't know when."

Kara nodded, thinking this through from every angle she could quickly come up with. "Wait. Maybe you should make some calls to the board but not a conference call. Mom, would you mind taking a quick trip to Montreal and then perhaps West Palm Beach?"

Understanding her implied agenda, her mother agreed wholeheartedly. "You know, I haven't seen Richard Sinclair in years. It's about time I drop in for tea, and while I'm in Montreal I should drop in on Tom too. I understand his sweet niece is at his side day and night. I can spot that girl for an afternoon and let her have some down time with her friends. And after that I should fly down to Florida…"

"I think that will do it, Mom."

"But darling, what about Corine Rusk? You know she's the inside leader of the board. I mean, if Corine approves, the rest will too, but if she's bothered…"

"Oh she's bothered all right, but I think this is one I need to sway myself." She crossed her arms defiantly but inside she was smiling. If her father thought he could play dirty he had it all wrong. Madeleine wasn't a weak point he could exploit. She was the very thing that gave Kara the strength to lead and she would defend her at all costs. "Jo, can you book me a flight to New York? I think it's time I introduce Madeleine to the real power behind Wexler-Ogelthorpe."

CHAPTER TWENTY-ONE

Kara cursed United Airlines as she ran the length of the terminal to catch her flight. The terminal had to be more than a mile long and while they kept announcing her name and urging her to board immediately, she couldn't run any faster. By the time she was down the jetway, the other passengers were on board and seated. They gave her the collective stink eye to let her know they'd been inconvenienced for all of thirty seconds. Rolling her eyes and still trying to catch her breath, she dropped into her business class seat and let the flight attendant figure out where to stow her bag.

While the aircraft pushed back, she found her belt and listened to the emergency procedures briefing. She did enjoy the quick flight on the regional jet. It was fast and quiet, and unlike the Airbus or Boeing 737 sometimes used on this route, the smaller load made getting off and through customs much faster.

When they reached cruise altitude, she ordered a drink. Harjitt was picking her up, so drinking and driving weren't an issue. The flight was short. Maybe she should order two drinks? Two, three, ten. No amount of alcohol would help. Madeleine wasn't coming home. She had found her place in New York and more, she had found the kind of personal attention more suited to a straight woman: a handsome leading man. Madeleine had assured her it wasn't like it looked. They were friends and enjoyed hanging out, not that they had a lot of time with their rehearsal schedule. Kara, sitting in on the full rehearsal, caught the obvious and almost choked. When the leading lady faltered, Madeleine had stepped in, demonstrating the sultry main number, in the arms of the show's leading man. They meshed so perfectly, their movements more than practiced. They were intimate.

Refusing to double over from the shock and biting back acrid tears, she was the picture of stoicism when the cast took a break and Madeleine dragged her leading man, Briar James, over to be introduced. He was charming and attentive, and that made it even harder for Kara to figure out what was going on. The show's opening had been pushed back until Christmas, after Madeleine had promised she would be home right after the American Thanksgiving. Well, that was last weekend. When she asked Madeleine if she still wanted to move to Toronto, the "Not yet" was all the reason she needed to pull away.

She understood that Madeleine still had work to do and she was proud of her work. From what she had witnessed from the rehearsal, *Fever* was shaping up to be a big hit. The logical side of her mind was in complete agreement with Madeleine's determination to see this through to the opening curtain. Technically, her contract had been up weeks ago, but she was a pro, resolved to get her show to the opening. Still, the emotional part, her heart, didn't understand and no amount of logic was going to make that better. Instead, from now on she had to focus every ounce of energy on work. Madeleine had sworn it was just about publicity. Whether there was anything going on or not, there was nothing she could do from Toronto. That is, even if she wanted to do something. If Madeleine was telling the truth, the future would play out in her favor. If not, if not, she had a lot of soul searching ahead of her. Why was it so hard to know what to do and why the hell did it hurt so much?

* * *

Sitting in the ninth row just next to the aisle, Madeleine watched the first dress rehearsal. It was a disaster. The actors and dancers had their numbers down pat, even her leading lady was performing well, but the production people and the costumes were out of control. The chorus line had been fitted with hats designed as replicas of every hotel on the Vegas Strip, big, heavy, and unruly. They had trouble getting them on, keeping them on, and passing through curtained parts of the elaborate stage set. She had voiced her concern weeks ago to the producers, only to receive a scolding that it was her job to wrangle the dancers. Now the executive producer was sitting beside her and begging her to find a fix, and quickly. Every day they weren't open and selling tickets was a day they lost money.

"I don't understand. We measured everything! Why the hell are they having such a hard time?"

Madeleine wanted to hit him over the head with one of the stupid hotel hats. "Measuring the height of a dancer standing still doesn't work. Some of these moves can add two or three feet. And I'm sorry, but that headgear isn't going to work. It's just too heavy and unruly."

"Have you any idea how much those fucking things cost us?"

"Anything was too much. Really. You have to decide if our chorus line is supposed to dance or act as moving billboards for your Vegas buddies."

Her executive producer shot her a venomous look, then settled into a half-assed grin. "Franco told me you could be a bitch on wheels when it came to getting things right. Okay, how would you do it?"

"Go with the glitzy look. This is supposed to be Vegas of the sixties, so drop the hats—they don't even match what the Strip looked like back then. Go with a simple hairpiece with the peacock feathers. Then use pageant-style sashes with the hotel names on them, you know, a la Miss Desert Inn, Miss Flamingo, Miss Riviera, Miss Stardust, etcetera, etcetera."

He stood, pulling his phone from his jacket while calling a halt to the rehearsal. "Get those stupid fucking hats off!" he shouted, sending the cast on break. "We need to make some changes."

Madeleine smiled to herself. They'd get this right she was sure, and the sooner they did the sooner she could have a sit down with Kara and find out just what was going on with her. Ever since her last visit she had been acting strangely.

Briar James, the star of the show, chose that exact moment to dump himself in the seat beside her. "How we looking, Guv?"

"Better," she said, and grinned. "Now that we can dump those stupid hats we should be on our way."

"'Bout time," he groaned. "Now if you could just teach young Miss to stop stepping on my feet."

It was their standing joke. The female lead, Hollywood's latest princess, was twenty years Briar's junior and not a professional dancer. That she could sing and act was a given but dancing at the same time was turning out to be a greater challenge. "Admit it. She's getting it. Except for that one misstep today. And really Briar, most of it is star envy. I swear that girl practically breaks into hives when she gets near you. You could work on making her feel less of an off-stage gawker and more of a cast member and costar."

"I could," he admitted, then grinned his trademark grin. "But where would the fun be in that?"

"You know you're incorrigible?" she accused.

"I know. Listen, why don't we discuss it tonight. I've got tickets for the new Clive Owen show. We can grab a quick sup at Daniel or would you prefer Gabriel Kreuther? Either is fine with me. I just need to know by four, so my publicist can handle it."

"Leak it, you mean?"

"Hey now. It's all good for the show. Besides, even your friend said we looked good together. Might as well keep the media abuzz. What did that *Entertainment Today* piece call you? This season's surprise catch, a sensational young choreographer from *Fever*! Huh? Huh?" he coaxed as if she should be pleased with the attention.

She wasn't naive enough to think his attention wouldn't help her career but the constant reminders were wearing thin. Besides, the magazine had called her Briar's sensational new thing and only added the fact that she was the show's choreographer in the last paragraph. She wanted to believe Kara's withdrawal stemmed from Briar's insinuations that he could help her career more than she could. She knew Kara could help too, and she kept her promises. Her application to become landed had already been approved, not as Kara's lover but on her own merits under the category of "Talent." There was just something about Kara knowing and understanding the importance of earning her keep and she fully supported her need to prove herself capable. In comparison, Briar wanted to be the center of everything, even her career advancement. That didn't mean he couldn't serve up some awesome opportunities, but she did wonder what the catch would be if she lowered herself to accept.

What a difference. Kara and Briar were polar opposites. While Briar flourished in the spotlight, Kara shied away. She wasn't shy, just more interested in making sure all those who had earned time in the spotlight got it. Then there were the promises. Briar was always holding out all sorts of potential connections and opportunities but rarely came through. She'd asked him to stop with the name-dropping and was sure it was one of the reasons they had become friends; she wasn't interested in using him the way others were. She never had to worry about that from Kara, who could name-drop with the best of them, even though Madeleine didn't always know who she was talking about in Canada. The other difference was how Kara shared her contacts and information based on her desire to learn what and who Madeleine wanted to meet first. She'd had more calls and emails from TV and theatre execs up in Toronto than Briar would mention during one of their "see and be seen" evenings. That too was starting to wear.

While it was easy to think of Briar James as a friend, she was tired of most of New York thinking she was his latest conquest. She hadn't thought much of all the media attention until her mother called, asking if she'd switched back to the home team. Just last night they had spent an hour on the phone discussing everything. She wasn't sure which was more of a surprise, her mother's renewed and sincere interest in her or the fact that it took her mom to explain why Kara would be pulling away. "Now Maddie, I can't pretend to know everything, but if my girlfriend's face was on the cover of every tabloid, smiling for all the world to see, happy on the arm of Hollywood's most eligible bachelor, I might be thinking twice about what it is my girl wants."

"Damn it, Mom! Kara knows better."

"Does she? All I'm saying is you girls didn't exactly have a lot of time to get the basics worked out, and now you're running around with the sexiest man alive...even I would be having a hard time."

Off the phone, she'd sat quietly trying to look at the situation from Kara's perspective. For one thing, if she was worried or even just jealous, she hadn't said a word, and Madeleine had taken that to mean she had no concerns. Yeah right. Here she was, sitting in New York, putting in six-day weeks trying to stage a new show, and all she could think about were those yacht club wannabes and A-listers who did take an interest in Kara. And Kara wasn't seen each night on the arm of the competition. Briar wasn't the competition—or was he? Not in her mind, but would Kara see it that way? In a way her mom was right; they'd hardly had time to work on themselves and their relationship before she was off to the Big Apple. They had been writing, and that helped. Or at least it had. Now Kara's emails were sporadic, and her romanticisms had dried up. That didn't mean she was anything but sweet when Madeleine called her, but a distance was building between them.

Madeleine removed a folded piece of parchment from her bag. Staring at the broken wax seal, she carefully unfolded it. It was a work of art. Handwritten text spoke eloquently of

Kara's feelings for her. What that woman wouldn't vocalize she mastered on paper. Maybe it was the skill that made a difference in her work, but it had made a difference with her too. How could so few words say so much?

Pulling out her phone, she sent a text to Kara, *"I'm missing you something fierce, and I'm worried too!"*

"Worried? Why?"

"I'm worried about you. I know I was supposed to be home by now and I'm concerned that you might be thinking I've changed my mind..."

"Have you?"

That reply pissed her off, but she reeled it in remembering her mother's warning that Kara really didn't know what was going on.

"It's strange. I like it here. NYC is a vibrant place. I don't know if I'll feel that way when it comes to moving to Toronto."

There was a long delay before Kara's reply came. *"Do what you need to do. I support you."*

Madeleine read the text again, *"Do what you need to do. I support you."* She wasn't sure if that was support or some passive-aggressive bullshit. Was she mad? She had to know the delays in production had nothing to do with her? "I support you," she muttered under her breath. Not I love you, or I miss you, just I support you. What the hell did that even mean?

Her phone beeped with another text. This one was from Briar. *"Reservations for Daniel at 9. Wear something sexy!"*

She snorted at the message. "At least Briar knows what he wants. Why the hell can't Kara just tell me what she needs?"

CHAPTER TWENTY-TWO

Kara waved Harjitt back into the car. Uncharacteristically, she slipped into the front seat of the Lincoln, grumbling as she wrestled with her seat belt.

"I take it the meeting did not go well?"

"I don't know what I hate more, that bullshit racist, sexist, elitist asshole or this place."

Harjitt seemed to be focusing on navigating the sedan through the pothole-littered and unpaved parking lot. "It's pretty down here. I'm surprised this part of the lake isn't covered with condos and marinas. Of course, they could pave the parking lot."

"They could do a lot of things but the Boulevard Club is old money, and old money is cheap money. Fuck!" she uttered, letting out her frustration. "The outside smells like piss and the inside's filled with pissy old men!" Pointing to the entry gate as they slipped by and out onto Lakeshore Boulevard, she complained, "They're even too cheap to pay for real security! I swear half the homeless people in this city head on down here nightly to piss on the privileged and arrogant membership."

"So lunch with Dad—not much fun?"

"You know, I'm ashamed to even walk in that fucking place and here he is, planted in his big wingback chair and acting like the king of the world."

"Did you eat?" he asked, as much a mother hen as the rest of the Wexlers.

"Did you?" she retorted, suspecting the kitchen staff was less than accommodating for her non white driver. But Harjitt didn't just drive her car. In addition to chauffeuring her mother and sister around, he acted as a proxy to all of Kara's social media accounts, and he kept her extremely fluid schedule current.

"Are you kidding? Those jerks wouldn't even pour me a coffee."

She looked at him, her mind in several places at once. "I don't know how you put up with it. Fuck, it pisses me off. Fuck!" She was quiet for a long time, seeming to drift away. Finally, she pointed ahead of them. "Don't turn. Stay on Lakeshore. Let's head over to the Docklands and get a burger and a beer. Are our golf clubs in the trunk?"

"Does my Nani like to tell people she was born a great Ranee?"

She laughed, finally releasing the tension she was carrying. "Good. We can hit a bucket of balls, and I can get this monkey off my back. Then we'll grab a burger and beer."

"Sounds like a plan," he said, turning right on to Cherry Street and heading for Poulson Pier. "I love coming down here. It's like, I don't know…kind of special since it's so undeveloped. You know, compared to the rest of the lakefront."

She agreed as they bounced their way across the Cherry Street lift bridge. "Now that the city's approved plans to develop the Docklands, I kind of worry no one will ever see this place the way we do."

"I kinda wish they hadn't put the dome up over the driving range yet. Like I know it's the first week of December, but it doesn't feel like it. I'm going to miss that view of the lake."

Sitting in the pub just feet from the Cherry Street Lift bridge and the Keating Channel, Kara pushed her plate away.

She had polished off exactly half her burger and was playing with her fries. She wasn't hungry anymore. The truth was she hadn't been hungry for some time now. She ate out of necessity and nothing more.

Pointing to her plate, Harjitt asked, "Do you think they should be called chips or fries? I mean, if they're not made with regular potatoes…"

"Sweet potatoes are still potatoes, wise guy, and I guess we're in a quasi-English pub, so my vote is for chips."

He nodded as if he were really contemplating her choice of verbiage. "By the way, my grandmother finally watched that Katherine Hepburn movie, you know, *His Girl Friday*. She wants to know if I'm half as smart as Katherine Hepburn's character."

"How is Nani? I do miss that woman. Did she like the bolt of Italian red silk I sent her?"

"Of course! I swear she loves you more than me. So thanks for that."

"Ah, you'll always be her number one baby boy. So, did she really like it?"

He smiled, giving her the point in their endless debate on who his grandmother loved best. "She says she's too old to wear it. She hoped you wouldn't be too offended, but she wants to save it to make a wedding dress for my sister."

Kara laughed for the first time in days. "I'm not saying it couldn't happen, but when it does, my money is still on her walking down the aisle on the arm of her blushing bride. How do you think Nani will handle that?"

"Oh, she'll kick and fuss for a bit then she'll see how happy Priya is, and that'll be it. I know if you were walking my sister up the aisle, she would already be over it. Nani thinks you're the best catch in town."

"I hate it when your grandmother and my mother agree on something. Scary," she mouthed, making a face. Not wanting to get too deep, she asked, "How is Priya doing with her residency?"

"She just finished her family care rotation. She wants you to know you were right. She said if she had to wipe one more snot nose her head would explode!"

"Your sister is too smart to waste her life in family practice."

He nodded. "She's applied for a surgical fellowship. Which you predicted she would. So, now I have to ask...how come you can figure out complete strangers like me the day we met and Priya from one cup of tea, yet this thing with Madeleine is killing you? Is it really all the grief from your dad or...?" He tilted his head. "I don't know. I don't think love is making you very happy."

She was quiet for a long time. Most people would be too scared to confront their boss on her feelings for another woman but Harjitt was as much family as Samantha or even Joanne. "You know, the night I got into your cab, I took one look at you with your baby fuzz beard and your man bun and still wearing that doily thing like a tween boy, and I knew you weren't old enough to be driving a cab. Hell, I didn't think you were old enough to be behind the wheel, but the first thing that popped into my head was, get him talking—find out if he's in trouble—then propose a solution. It never occurred to me to get out of your cab or question whether you could drive much less if you should. Maybe my brain doesn't work right. I mean, that's what most people would have been thinking, but there I was all worried that someone had made you into a little limo slave."

"Well, I for one am very glad you don't think like other people. If you did, I'd still be sitting at the airport praying for a decent fare or any fare at all."

Kara harrumphed. It was never easy for her to take credit. In a way she was the textbook leader, accepting fault for mistakes and losses while passing all the accolades of her successes onto her team. "You know, I used to hate my old man whenever it came time to accept awards for the company's hard work. Everyone used to think it was jealousy or envy but it was more about him not sharing the glory with the people who made the wins possible. This year is the first year the company will attend the Clios without him hogging all the glory. I decided I want to take all the principals for the campaigns who are finalists for awards. I imagined standing at our table, standing to applaud our winners, and sending them up to accept the awards. I also imagined it would be the first year I would attend with a guest. I really thought Madeleine would be at my side. Now…"

He was quiet. Finally, he asked, "Did she say she wouldn't be there?"

She shook her head. "Frankly, at this point, I didn't even ask."

"Kara…dude! You have to talk to her. She's not a mind reader; not like me," he offered with a wide irreverent grin.

She threw her cloth serviette at him. "Am I talking to my friend or my mother?"

"I'll take that as a compliment. Marsha is a straightforward woman, and she's got a wicked sense of humor." When his quip didn't seem to elevate her mood, he grabbed her cell phone. At first she didn't react; after all, daily social media posts to her accounts were part of his job; that and keeping her schedule, running her errands, and keeping her car, which he claimed as his, at the ready.

"Don't tell them which restaurant. If you're doing a check-in, just say we're at Poulson Pier. I don't want to share this place with the world." When he didn't immediately respond, she asked what exactly he was posting. Instead of answering, he placed the phone on the table, suggesting, "We should get you a new outfit for the awards."

"What?" she asked before shaking her head, "I'm not going."

"You have to." He held up her phone. "Madeleine said yes. She's excited and looking forward to it, and she wants to know if you'll be her guest for the opening night of *Fever*. It looks like next weekend is shaping up to be something special."

She grabbed the phone, reading the text message he sent and Madeleine's immediate and positive response. "Huh… Where the hell am I going to get something formal this late?"

"Since you asked, my uncle has been pestering me to take you to his shop. He says he's found a perfect ladies' tux pattern for you. Come on," he said, getting to his feet. "If he fits you today I know he can have it ready for Friday."

Still staring at her phone screen, she looked up to him. "Are you sure about this?"

He smiled, offering, "A wise woman once told me we can never be one hundred percent sure of anything. We can prepare, and we can aim higher. That's the one hundred percent we put our faith in, not what we're sure of, but what we prepare for."

She shook her head. "I'm never speaking to you again," she warned, following him to the car.

"I can quote you all day," he said with glee.

* * *

Madeleine set her phone aside. How interesting, and not to mention a relief. She had been so worried about Kara, about her feelings and her wishes, that she had put off inviting her to the opening. At first it was about not being confident they would open on time, then it was about Kara being so withdrawn from her. She knew the Clios were coming up, but when Kara failed to mention them, she had assumed she wasn't invited and worried that Kara would be there and just didn't want her along. Now it would be a very busy weekend. *Fever* would open on Friday night, then the Clios were Saturday night and at Lincoln Center no less.

Almost panicking, she grabbed her phone and searched the web for images of previous awards nights. "Shit, shit, shit!" *Where the hell am I going to find something this formal...* She grinned like a mad woman. *This is New York, and Briar is always saying it's the world in microcosm.* Briar might know all the hot spots in town, but that wasn't the expertise she needed.

She made her way from her workspace, a folding table she shared with the stage manager, to the dressing rooms. She knocked hesitantly and waited for the royal proclamation to enter. Dame Anderson wasn't really like that but all the kids—oops, young people in the cast—had gotten to calling her the queen just because of her title.

"Enter."

Madeleine pushed the door open to find Dame Anderson's expectant face looking up from her book.

"Madeleine, how lovely to see you. I was half expecting Briar to stomp his big feet in here and demand another rehearsal. That man does fret."

She smiled, closing the door behind her and taking a seat in the straight-back chair. Letting out an exasperated breath, she asked, "I'm afraid I need your help."

Swinging her feet off the love seat crammed into the modest space, she set her book aside with a conspiring grin. "You want to know what it's like living in Canada in the winter?"

Madeleine held back a sigh. "I'm from Minnesota. My momma raised me ready for that. But…"

"You know Vancouver is very different from Toronto. Don't get me wrong, I adored Vancouver, but the rain does rival English weather. At least Toronto has its brilliant summer, but you pay for it in the winter. Of course, a Minnesotan would understand that, but that's not what concerns you."

"No, yes, I mean, how?"

"You're smart, you're beautiful, and extremely talented. Which I can attest to. No one has ever gotten my two left feet as well harnessed as you. I must say I actually feel like a dancer these days. That's your doing. You took a cast of rambunctious man-children, chorus girls, and aging actors and turned them into something wondrous. Now you must ask yourself, can I do it again, and should I continue here or head to the 'Great White North.' Yes, they do call it that, and unlike Americans, when they say white they mean snow, not people. That is one difference I would suggest you put in the plus column."

"I wanted to ask you about buying a formal dress, but you're right, I'm worried about moving to Toronto."

She nodded her understanding. "Everyone is different, but for me, moving to Vancouver both made and broke my career. Yes, I say made because the show launched me. It also broke it. That wasn't about filming in Canada but Hollywood looking down on the genre. I did a few films but never A-list material."

"I like the one you did with Angelina Jolie," she contended.

Smiling, Dame Anderson hauled her rather large purse open, digging out a mini folio of pictures. "She sends me updates of the children each year." Handing over the folio, she explained, "In many ways moving to London saved my career. Perhaps I should say it gave legitimacy to it. Instead of being that TV actress clawing her way into movies, a la little fish in a big pond, I was a Yank actress with a hit show under my belt and the roles, real roles, began pouring in and suddenly I was queen of the costume drama. But you didn't come for career advice, did you?"

"No, well yes, I appreciate it and…I just want you to know I hear what you're saying. It never occurred to me, but you're right. It may be easier to kick things into a higher gear as a big fish in a small pond."

"Toronto is not such a small pond as many would imagine. For the stage, it ranks just third after New York and London. As for film and television, it truly is Hollywood North. Now, what can I actually help you with?"

Madeleine smiled, handing over her phone. "Kara's been nominated for an award, several actually. It's Saturday night, and I don't know where to get a dress, a real dress."

Dame Anderson swiped through the Google images associated with last year's Clio Awards. "Have you a thought for what Kara may be wearing?"

She admitted she didn't, then added, "I can ask, but I kind of want to surprise her." At the look she received, she explained haltingly, "It's just that—well, I've been so busy—I mean, things have run so long…"

"And every gossip rag in the world has pics of you on the arm of Briar James and assumes you're also gracing his bed." Madeleine had real panic in her eyes when the woman explained, "This is a nasty business and Briar's a bastard for using you as his beard or whatever the appropriate slang is. Now tell me. This thing with you and Kara, who, by the way, I deeply respect, is it…is she, as they say, the one?"

Sucking in a deep breath she nodded, almost afraid to risk her voice and cause the tears to start up. "I've fought with it, especially these last few weeks. The thing is, no matter what I want to do, what I think may be best for me, I just can't give up on the idea of her and me. Is that foolish?"

"What does she suggest?"

"When we talk, and it's been strained, all she ever says is, 'Do what's best for you and I'll support your decision.'"

Dame Anderson smiled. "I knew there was a reason I liked her so much." Handing back Madeleine's phone, she said, "I know just where to take you. Madeleine, are you up for facing the media? I mean, if Briar can use them for his own agenda why can't we?"

Not sure what she had in mind, but more than thankful for her help, she nodded. "I'll go put my face on while you make your calls."

CHAPTER TWENTY-THREE

There was an envelope waiting at the front desk when Kara checked into her hotel. She waited until she was in her room and the bellman was gone before opening it. She was so sure that Madeleine had changed her mind and sent a Dear Jane letter, she held her breath. But inside was a note from Madeleine along with a theatre ticket and backstage pass. Taking a seat on the side of the king size bed, she opened the note and read it carefully.

Madeleine missed her.

Madeleine was excited to see her.

Madeleine loved her.

It said lots more, but that was all that mattered to Kara. Checking her watch and then double-checking the curtain time for *Fever*, she planned the next few hours carefully. She didn't know if Madeleine would be joining her in the audience or looking on from the side curtain, but she intended to be the one true thing she was looking for.

* * *

Madeleine delivered her ultimatum, hands on hips, steely determination in her eyes.

Wexler-Ogelthorpe's most influential board member Corine Rusk stared at her. Finally, she motioned to the chair. "Sit down. For heaven's sakes you're more stubborn than Kara, and that child…"

"She isn't a child, and I'm none of the things he said. Frankly, I don't care if you and the rest of the world think I'm a whore, as long as it doesn't hurt Kara, and you know this was done to hurt her, to hobble her career. Surely you can see the threat for what it is?"

Corine nodded, her deeply lined face troubled. "You want to speak plainly, then I will. You girls have put me in an untenable position. If I vote with John, he will take all of thirty seconds to undo everything Kara's started. If I vote for the plan to bring in new blood immediately and let her go, we risk her taking the best of the best with her. At least John has the advantage of being a known commodity. Better the devil you know."

"You can't seriously believe those are your only options. Goodness, Corine, if you're so worried, why don't you just demote her and then come back and run the place yourself. You could see with your own eyes this thing isn't holding her back and the staff could care less. If you don't believe me, ask Joanne. For God's sake, she works there too!"

"I'll not have you take the Lord's name in vain," she huffed. "Frankly, you girls have made this impossible. It was one thing to overlook Kara's peculiarities while she was single but now, with you two so public and flaunting it, and right on the cover of the paper!" Her toe nudged a section of the newspaper she had dumped on the floor.

Madeleine scooped it up, surprised to realize her outing with Dame Anderson and their joint remarks had found their way into a business newspaper. She read on, realizing the story centered on the changing face of consumers. "It says here Kara's a genius at intuitively knowing how to find and reach new and untapped markets. They expect her to walk away with several awards for last year's Super S'hero hair color campaign. I don't know what that is," she commented, more to herself, before turning back to the curmudgeonly woman stewing beside her. "Corine, I get you're not comfortable with her sexuality, our sexuality," she corrected. "That's your right and I respect it, but you can't really be thinking that letting her go is the best thing for Wexler-Ogelthorpe. Can you?"

"I just don't understand! You girls have it so good today. You can have a career and family. You can have anything you want! But instead you act like a pair of wartime bomb girls, shacking up until the boys come home. Well, the boys are home and—"

"Really! If you feel that way, why did you nominate her for the top job? Come on Corine, even you must have known she would eventually meet someone?"

"I expected her to turn things around, not upside down!" With that, she crossed her arms like a dismissive teen.

Madeleine was utterly frustrated. This was worse than trying to talk Grandma Jessepp into afternoon walks. Then it hit her like a bolt from the sun.

Setting the business paper down she asked gently, "I hope you know you can speak openly with me. What you say here I will keep to myself. I know you don't know me from…" She decided a Biblical reference would not be wise. "Corine, I can hear your pain. The regret in your voice betrays you, but I won't. I can't imagine what it was like to live through a world war much less the pressure put on women to welcome home the boys and resume jobs society once relegated to women." She let out a sigh, both pained and worried for what she was about to say. "I think you did what the world expected and you did well. You maintained a career. You worked at your husband's side for years. And from what I understand you raised two wonderful sons who have each gone on to create their own legacies."

Corine's head was up high. She was proud and had every right to be.

"But it cost you, didn't it?" When Corine didn't reply or even respond nonverbally, Madeleine knew she had to chance it. *Looks like I'm all in again.* Gently she asked, "What was her name?"

She wasn't sure what to expect. Corine Rusk had been described to her as being like molten lava on a hot bed of coals, and that was on a good day.

The tears streaming down her leathery cheeks were the last thing she expected. Reaching over, Madeleine took her hand, squeezing it in hers.

"It wasn't, we weren't like that," she finally said.

"But you loved her that way." The silence she heard in return explained everything. Corine was smart and hardworking, and she had done what was expected of her, marrying after the war and dedicating her business savvy to aiding her husband's career while raising a family. She was a hell of a woman, and Madeleine didn't want to say anything that would take away from her successes or sacrifice. Still, she couldn't leave it there. "I'm so sorry, Corine. I wish it had been different for you. I wish you could have had the kind of love you deserved. I do. I can't imagine keeping those feelings locked away all these years, how it must have hurt you. Tell me, is there a possibility your experience, your heartache, is influencing your reaction? Please be honest with me. She deserves that, and so do you."

She watched as the elder matron of the Ogelthorpe clan struggled with how to react. The light finally sparked from her sad eyes as she said, "I was all right with it, with you and Kara, right up until John called and started his vile rumors circulating."

"So you accept that what Kara's father is peddling is not what happened?"

She grimaced. It was hard to read her. The lines of life and experience played across her face. She sighed. "You girls… Fine, tell me what happened, the real story and I want all of it. No leaving any bits out no matter how you expect I might take things."

"Corine. I've told you everything except this: I escalated things with Kara. It wasn't part of my contractual obligations, and you have copies of those contracts now," she reminded her, tipping her head toward the courier envelope Samantha had forwarded. "Some may think my actions were unethical. I don't care. I was falling for her, and I wanted her. It was that simple.

All I can hope is that you accept Kara isn't to blame for any of this mess. She hasn't done anything unethical or illegal, even by your more stringent standards. I love her. I think you do too," she said. "Please. Just think about it, please?"

Finally, Corine nodded. She was a tough old bird and a little bit on the righteous side, but she had a heart, and she was right. If they torpedoed Kara, either by restoring her father to president and CEO or demoting her and bringing in new blood, Kara would leave, and she would take the best of the company people with her.

If the board of Wexler-Ogelthorpe was unwilling to keep an open and proud lesbian in the top job, they deserved the projected losses and more. Even and maybe especially in the current political climate, LGBT communities and LGBT friendly companies were working hard to out and to shame those businesses unwilling to stand by the rights and privileges of LGBT people, long legally established basic human rights. Even more troubling about their position, Wexler-Ogelthorpe was a Canadian company and as such was required to adhere to the Charter of Rights and Freedoms. Unlike Americans, Canadians still believed in universal rights and got downright mean when treatment of any group appeared unfair. Pushing Kara out was more than a lose–lose situation. They would end up defending their position in court.

Corine had read through the documents Samantha had sent. She had listened to Madeleine's explanation. And, she knew Kara; had known her since she was born. Reaching to the side table, she picked up a small bell, ringing for her nurse. "Leave the details with my assistant."

Madeleine stood. "Can I count on you?"

Corine offered her dainty hand with a dissatisfied grumble. Her tone said *don't mess with me* but the spark was back in her dulling eyes. "I'll be there."

CHAPTER TWENTY-FOUR

Kara was shown to her seat. It was one of six-seat setup in a private box. She couldn't remember being in a theatre with box seats much less ever sitting in one. She wasn't sure which seat to take and was caught staring at the stage and watching the other patrons find their floor seats when Doug and Samantha were shown in. "Hey, look who's here!"

They shared generous hugs, typical for this bunch. Doug was giving his sister a big bear hug when Samantha announced, "We may have some good news for you."

Kara smiled. "How about telling me how these seats work? Any idea which seats are ours?"

The curtain behind them moved, and suddenly Madeleine was there. "They're all ours, honey. Sit where you like, but I would keep the best seat for our guest."

Smiling, Kara waited behind her brother and sister-in-law for her chance to welcome Madeleine. The house lights flickered signaling the show was about to start. She had just pulled Madeleine into her arms and was delivering a sincere, I missed you kiss when the curtain pushed aside again, and Corine Rusk gasped at the sight of her.

"Kara Delphine Wexler!"

Madeleine jumped, while Samantha also gasped in surprise. Kara, more confused than anything else by her presence, offered her hand to help her to her seat. "I knew our guest had to be someone important with Dougie waiting to claim the second-best seat in the house."

Corine harrumphed her approval, taking her seat at the rail. "This is Madeleine's night. I'm here to support her. You and I will have a discussion later, but," she said, acknowledging the hushing crowd as the house lights dimmed, "time for the show. Madeleine, you and Samantha come sit with me." To her nurse, she said dismissively, "You can sit with the boy."

Kara grinned. It looked like she had been relegated to the second row. They sat behind their partners and, in the nurse's case, behind her charge.

As the curtain lifted and the opening number kicked off, she could admit she had no idea what was going on. Just days ago she was sure she had lost Madeleine, sure she had found better in the arms of the British heartthrob and America's favorite leading man. She had planned to be here tonight, even if it was just to say goodbye. She had been working from the moment she learned her father was spreading malicious rumors about her and about Madeleine. The two of them might not work out, but Kara was still a gentlewoman. She wouldn't stand by and allow Madeleine's personal reputation or her career be sullied by her father.

After visiting Harjitt's uncle's upscale tailor shop and ordering a very curvy women's custom tux, she had also asked for a more conservative business suit. She wore it now, but with a linen shirt, a color of green that could only be compared to Madeleine's eyes. She caught those eyes looking at her. The warmth of the accompanying smile, and the hand that reached back to find hers, answered every question Kara had been harboring about them.

* * *

Madeleine had finished getting her hair just right, her face on, and was now, after deciding against pantyhose, spreading body lotion on her legs. She was smiling at the sounds of Kara in the bathroom completing her ablutions. Madeleine had elected to spend the weekend with her at the hotel, collecting her bags including tonight's formal wear from her sublet with zero intention of ever returning to the cute Soho apartment. The show was staged, and the reviews were in. *Fever* was an instant hit, already booked solid for the next several months.

Last night they'd celebrated. Having Kara there made her success even sweeter. After the show, they had headed backstage to congratulate the cast and to receive her own well-earned accolades too. Briar James was the man of the hour, and Dame Anderson hailed a titan of the screen and stage alike, but it was Madeleine who everyone cheered. As she walked down the backstage stairs, the cast and crew gave her a standing ovation. It was especially sweet after everything that had been said for and especially against her. As much as she was enjoying her success at having delivered her first big production, it was Kara at her side to celebrate her achievement that felt like the greatest success.

She had been standing backstage with one of the producers when she noticed Corine Rusk and Dame Anderson cozied up in a corner and chatting. The last of her anxieties disappeared. Whatever happened going forward, she knew she and Kara were good. She was about to go looking for her missing partner when Kara stepped up beside her. Beaming with pride, she handed Madeleine her phone. Confused, she was about to slide the device into Kara's jacket when she heard her mother's voice. Looking at the screen, she realized Kara had Facetimed her parents. She didn't even know her parents knew how to use Facetime, much less that Kara was comfortable contacting them herself. Her parents too were so proud. While they only took her away from the celebration for a few minutes, it was wonderfully freeing and heartwarming to have their support and respect, not to mention their acceptance of Kara as her partner. It had been a perfect night. She hadn't thought it could get better but the

Wexlers, along with Briar James and half the cast too, took their celebration out on the town.

When Kara finally opened the door to their hotel room, Madeleine was sure she would pass out in seconds, but Kara had other plans; plans she enthusiastically shared. She hadn't forgotten what it was like to make love with Kara and to have her in her arms. Still, something had changed or more accurately clicked into place. They were together, whether working blocks away or in differing nations, and she knew they were solid. It was a solidity she couldn't quite define, but it was beautiful, much like the heart and mind of her lover.

Looking up from her impromptu leg massage, she was surprised to see Kara standing transfixed. "I never want to leave this room."

She laughed, pulling her in for a hug. "I can't begin to tell you how much I love you. Promise me," she pleaded, holding Kara's face in her hands, "if you ever doubt that, you call, write, or swipe. Whatever you can and I'll be there to tell you just how much."

Kara sighed. "They asked you to stage the away production?"

She nodded, amused. "Yes they did." Kara's face looked like she was preparing for bad news. "I told them I want to choreograph and direct, and they said yes!" A measure of Kara's ardor returned, but she still looked prepared for bad news. "And I said the show should open in Toronto first, and since we would gain an immediate forty percent discount in production cost because of the exchange rate, we would be better off staging the entire road production there too." Now Kara held her breath, her hope unmistakable. "And they said YES!"

Kara wrapped her strong arms around her, pulling her in tight and swinging her around with sheer joy. "You are amazing!" she said, finally putting Madeleine's feet back on the ground. "I am so proud of you!" Checking her watch, she added gently, "I want to celebrate you and your success, but we're going to be late. I'm so sorry. I would blow this off and take you anywhere you like, but with Corine attending and my job in jeopardy, I don't think we should."

It was obvious by the way she said it that Kara would indeed change her plans if Madeleine asked. They needed to support each other and their careers. That wouldn't change for as long as they worked and wished to succeed. The amazing part was Kara intuitively understood that. Yes, she would have been disappointed to have her remain in New York for another six months, but she would have lived with it, as she had explained last night. The separations would always be hard on them, but with love and respect, not to mention their complete support of each other, they had committed with eyes wide open.

She never imagined it could be like this; the intuitive understanding, the heartfelt respect, but more than that, the way it felt to be loved completely. "Zip me up, honey?"

"As much as it's killing me," she joked, taking up the zipper on the long silky bottle green gown. "This is so perfect. It matches your eyes."

Madeleine fingered the buttons on Kara's tux shirt. It was a classic design but cut so low that just a half inch or so of the shirt collar was visible under the softly rounded silk lapels. She fingered the green buttons. "They look like the green stone on my bracelet," she said, holding up her wrist to display her Amulette de Cartier Kara had given her way back in Las Vegas. A lifetime ago but in truth less than six months. "I can't believe you turned my world around so fast. Honey, you are..."

"I'm yours. I love you. All I can do is support your work, support your hopes and aspirations, listen, love, and be yours. I hope that's enough."

"Enough?" she asked as Kara finished closing the zipper of the gown and smoothed her hands down Madeleine's sides. "Honey, you are more than I will ever deserve," she declared, turning and taking Kara in her arms. "I've been trying to put this into words for days now, but I'll just have to give you the analytics and let you sort the numbers. Okay?"

At Kara's grinning affirmative, she counted out as if making a presentation. "One, you showed me respect, even when you had zero reasons to. Two, you forgave my part in the fantasy date thing, even before you forgave your siblings. Next, you stayed true even when you had reason to believe I didn't, but most of all, you gave me love, the kind I never imagined existed. Well, except in movies but then the lovers always die, a la *Romeo and Juliet*. And no way am I letting that happen for at least another sixty or so years, so..."

"Point four," Kara interjected, "the promise of a sixty-year return would certainly sway the board, but it's point three that I like best. Not the dying part but the love. I love you Madeleine, never Maddie. I never imagined I could. And you're right. Not like this. I feel giddy, like a kid and happy all over. Is that silly?"

"Kara Wexler silly? I do believe I've been a very good influence on you."

She felt as much as saw the last of the tension Kara had been carrying ease from her shoulders. "Ready?"

"I am," she said, straightening Kara's Windsor knot, hooking her arm and heading for the Clio Awards ceremony at Lincoln Center. Her company was up for several categories, but she was especially hopeful for one, last year's Super S'hero hair color campaign. Kara had threatened to reveal the shade of her hair as the one color name rejected by the clients: Bad Ass Red Brass. Yes, walking through the hotel and later the Lincoln Center with Kara on her arm did make her feel a superhero.

That's right, look at us. Bad Ass Red Brass and her partner and object of her affection was not Briar James or any other man the gossip sites suggested. It was Kara, her Kara, and for the first time in her life everything fit, everything made sense, but mostly everything just felt right.

She squeezed Kara's arm as they made their way to join the rest of the Wexler party. "Just so you know, I love you too."

Acknowledgments

Nia:wen' ko:wa

What a strange and perfect phrase, *Nia:wen' ko:wa* (pronounced: Nee-ah,wayn. Ko-wah). Loosely translated, it means Thank Them, Greatly. And I am so grateful.

This book, like each before and with the grace of all the universe those that will follow, is not a solo endeavor. Neither is it collective. We each have a part to play. Katherine V. Forrest is my editor. She is an extraordinary author and brings so much wisdom and insight to the process I can't help but learn and grow. My thanks to her are endless. My publisher, Linda Hill, is an astonishing and discerning woman. I am so grateful for her inclusion and to be a part of the Bella Books family. Jessica Hill is another woman who deserves more than my simple thanks and my annual gift of maple syrup. Her enthusiasm for my work makes the long process of getting my thoughts on paper so worth the effort. There are others at Bella that deserve my thanks. Those women who work in the background, proofreading, formatting, designing covers, writing the jacket copy, sending out ARCs and so forth. Thank you each. Your efforts make a difference for me, and I suspect many, many women.

An Elder once told me a story is a gift, one compiled from the words long given to us. My job is to tell the story, allowing others to claim the content, word by word, for themselves. The truth is, we write stories to share both our real and imagined experiences, without which, real or imagined, we are nothing. Diving into lesbian fiction is about finding the women and experiences we crave. When I create a story world, it looks and sounds like the world we live in, but deeply bathed in hope. In these dark times, that hope must come from us no matter how exhausting or frustrating.

It's our job to create the realities we desire.

When I feel the pain of these accelerated times, I look to the women around me for inspiration. You needn't look far. Real change comes in small, almost inconsequential steps. And a positive word, character, or story, offers a far more lasting impact than political postulating could ever do. All change starts with action. All action starts with ideas, and all ideas are born from hope. LesFic is a safe place to look for that hope. We must see, hear, feel, taste, and fully experience the changes we want before they can take root. The women who devote their lives to this version of the literary craft are change makers. If that's you too, read all you can, take these words for your own, and create the story-perfect lives we all deserve. It's not easy, but it's not impossible. Remember, small steps, just one word at a time, and change will happen.

I want to commend the board of the Golden Crown Literary Society. This group, with their laser focus on improving and promoting lesbian literature, host an annual conference where new and experienced, not to mention brave, would-be authors meet to learn and share. This camaraderie, especially among the Bella Books family, doesn't just keep me writing; it keeps me reading. Yes, I still read LesFic every day. Why? These stories are our stories, however realistic, or fantastic. When we write for us, we create a legacy and not just for lesbians, or the LGBTQ2 community as a whole, but for all women who hold out hope for their future and the future of their children.

I want to send a special thanks to fellow author Laina Villeneuve, for agreeing that details matter; and chocolate. Love that Nova! MB Panichi for taking the time to chat with me about growing up in Minneapolis. Michelle Barrett for recognizing my Samson complex. Karin Kallmaker for her tutelage on text messaging, not to mention her kindness. KG MacGregor for letting me wax on about her wife, and Stefani Deoul for her unwavering support and her great laugh. Geneviève Fortin and wife Denice, for their warmth and welcoming hugs. And Mercedes Lewis, Mary Griggs, Ann Roberts, and the board, including all the volunteers at GCLS. Your efforts make a difference: *transmittat; simul*

I can't leave out my biggest fans:

Kerry-Ann Kelly. I still can't believe you can buy beer in cases of 60 bottles in QC or that you got three of them in Dawn's car, even if you two did abandon me at the National

Aviation Museum just to buy beer! Although I can't think of a better place to spend an afternoon alone.

And Norma. I salute you! I deeply respect your service in uniform and on the bench. I can only hope I'll be half as cool as you as a nonagenarian.

Finally, I need to thank my partner, Dawn. How she puts up with me I do not know. As I sit at my desk, actually the dining room table, I can see nothing but stacks and stacks of papers, books, and a million other things. It should be declared a disaster zone. To her credit, tidy and neat Dawn walks by my mess a thousand times a day and never says a word, turning a permanently blind eye to my creative mess. Once this book is finally ready for release, she will sit with me and help me file and catalogue everything I've printed, found and scrounged to write this work. The table will be clean, and I'll be ready to start something new. Let me make you a cup of tea, honey. It's the least I can do until powwow season when I can get you some fry bread and strawberry juice. Always know, you, your patience and your support are what I need to do the work I do. Without you there would never be this book or any other.

Nia:we

A Note on Music

In this book I mentioned three numbers performed by my character Madeleine Jessepp. I'll admit it, I'm not so much an audiophile as an old school rocker. When my editor, Katherine V. Forrest, suggested I name the songs Madeleine performed I was lost. Let's face it, there isn't much in the way of torch songs from Heart, BTO, the Guess Who, or Robbie Robertson. To find songs that expressed the feelings growing between my characters I wasted a day on YouTube with no results. My partner, however, knows her music. It took her all of ten minutes to compile this list. I share it here because it's worth repeating.

Enjoy.

"Mad About You"

Composition by Paula Jean Brown, James Whelan and Mitchel Young Evans. Performed by Belinda Carlisle on her debut album.

"It's All In The Game"

Composition by Carl Sigman and Charles G. Dawes. First performed by Tommy Edwards in 1951. The version my wife played for me was recorded by Carmel in 1987

"The Look Of Love"

Composition by Burt Bacharach, Lyrics by Hal David. It was first performed by Dusty Springfield in 1967, and also released that same year by Bacharach himself. Another interesting version is from Isaac Hayes, but it is the Diana Krall, 2001 release I'm familiar with and the one my wife played for me.

A Note on Creating an Advertising Agency

When I first penned the idea of an exemplary advertising executive, my mind went immediately to David Ogilvy, founder of legendary advertising company Ogilvy and Mather. Known as the man who wrote the rules of advertising, even when credited with saying, "I hate rules," this eclectic Englishman, and pioneer of the craft, got his start just down the street from my home in Whitby, Ontario, at the one-time Allied secret spy school, Camp X. It seems ironic that a man known as the icon of "gentlemanliness," trained alongside characters like OSS Commander, William J. (Wild Bill) Donovan, Col. US Army; James Bond creator, Commander Ian Fleming, RN; Hollywood leading man Stirling Hayden; and even infamous double agent Kim Philby. Where Ogilvy's story diverts from his cohorts was in purpose. He recognized the effect propaganda had on the German public and proposed fighting fire with fire. Legend is he created fake news reels, which the SOE then arranged to have "accidentally" fall into enemy hands. It's alleged one such reel included a visit to the fake Allied pre-D-Day invasion army holding site in Calais, leading the German command to believe the cross channel attack would come from that location.

After the war, the film unit he built was considered too valuable to lose and with the Canadian government not imagining a use for propaganda films, they refocused on using it as the seed of what would become the National Film Board of Canada. Ogilvy left the NFB in good hands and established his advertising agency with offices in Toronto and his HQ in New York. What I respect about Ogilvy most and wanted to instill in my character was his treatise to, "Treat everyone with intelligence and grace." He is quoted as famously reminding his writers, "The consumer isn't a moron; she is your wife!"

When I created Kara Wexler, I wanted her to be the embodiment of everything good David brought to the business, and her father all that was wrong with it. Of course, real life isn't so earnest, but this is fiction and what the hell, it's how I imagine a little on the short side, a little on the awkward side, gentlewoman to be.

A Note to My Readers

I always like to hear what my readers think. I really do. If you enjoyed *Cause and Affection*, please consider returning to your retailer and leaving a review. If you hated it, why not send me a note and let me know why?

Sheryl Wright (info@sherylwright.com)

To learn more about me or read the irreverent and stray thoughts that make it into my blog, please visit https://sherylwright.com

Want to read more of my work, or explore the most complete and exemplary catalogue of lesbian fiction? Then I suggest you visit Bella Books at https://www.bellabooks.com

Bella Books, Inc.

Women. Books. Even Better Together.

P.O. Box 10543
Tallahassee, FL 32302

Phone: 800-729-4992
www.bellabooks.com

CPSIA information can be obtained
at www.ICGtesting.com
Printed in the USA
LVHW031516300519
619609LV00001B/102/P